A Dark and Secret Place

By Margaret Summerton

A Dark and Secret Place

MARGARET SUMMERTON

PUBLISHED FOR THE CRIME CLUB BY

DOUBLEDAY & COMPANY, INC.

GARDEN CITY, NEW YORK

1977

All of the characters in this book
are fictitious, and any resemblance
to actual persons, living or dead,
is purely coincidental.

ISBN: 0-385-12476-7
Library of Congress Catalog Card Number 76–42404
Copyright © 1976, 1977 by Margaret Summerton
All Rights Reserved
Printed in the United States of America
First Edition in the United States of America

A Dark and Secret Place

CHAPTER 1

Exhausted by the long drive, with an obligatory stint of work ahead of me, the letter caught me off-balance, reinfected me with a bitterness I'd counted long dead which now exploded in flames from its ashes. I fumed with what I persuaded myself was justifiable indignation. Typical Olivia! A summons to fly out to her instantly. Not an invitation, not an appeal, but an order that on the first skimming glance appeared to be hedged around with a host of contradictions. Do this; don't do that! With half the writing illegible I had neither the patience nor the mental energy to decipher it.

Olivia positive that, at the tweak of a finger, I'd go running, or rather flying. Assuming that, like hers, my time was my own to fritter how I chose. It wasn't and never had been. Olivia had been married for three years; moreover she was rich and pampered, well equipped to extricate herself from any awkward or embarrassing situation.

I thrust the grubby, creased sheet into its envelope, shoved it into a drawer. I'd unravel it later, sift fact from hysteria. All right, I was tired; I had two hours' work ahead of me before I was free to go to bed, and I had an early start in the morning. Two legitimate excuses, but there was no excuse for my satisfaction in forcing Olivia, for once, to wait upon my pleasure. I deserved the little ink-black devil that squatted menacingly in the farthermost reaches of my consciousness.

My day had been spent examining the contents of a Victorian mansion in a Herefordshire backwater, sifting from the trash a few genuine antiques, odd pieces of tarnished silver which the heirs to the estate had not deigned to claim, plus an assortment of bric-a-brac that had currently risen sufficiently in value to interest Bedale. That's what I was, Bedale's scout. Now over seventy—though he wouldn't have admitted that sum of years, even to himself—I was his front-runner who chased all over the United Kingdom sizing up the contents of houses prior to the sale. If I reported favourably, he might deign to put in an appearance himself; if his interest didn't quicken he would dispatch me. Writing the report amounted to a couple of hours of forced labour. So, Olivia's illegible scribble would have to wait. How many times after that night was I to plead that I wasn't to know?

As a penalty, when I climbed into bed, Olivia flew into my head, locked herself inside it, so there was no evading the clash of images she presented. The first time I'd seen her she'd been in a wheel-chair on a hospital balcony, both legs in plaster, her forehead bandaged, what hair the surgeon had left her no more than a crown of pale fuzz. My mother had briefed me on who she was, the tragedy that had befallen her. She was the daughter of my mother's dearest friend. Both only children, they had been brought up in the same village, been inseparable until Mary-Anne had married what my mother described as a "gentleman in the Foreign Office" who had been dispatched to serve abroad. They had been flying home on extended leave from South America when their plane had crashed in southern England. Olivia's parents had been killed; she, though severely injured, had survived.

It was the third or fourth visit my mother had paid to the London hospital; my first. I dawdled behind as she laid her presents on the table by Olivia's side, bent and kissed her cheek. Then, smiling as though I were an extra gift, she drew me forward. "There, I've kept my promise and brought Elizabeth with me. You remember, I told you about her. She'll be nine in December, and you'll be ten next September. That makes you a little bit older than she is."

Confronted by a wraithlike child, with bandaged arms, white plaster legs, horror froze my wits, numbed my tongue. My mother gave me an encouraging prod and I slid my feet forward. Olivia's eyes, like holes in her face, a funny, off-putting shade of pale blue, with dark lashes that did not match the amber hair, were glued to my face as I clutched the bunch of flowers I'd been ordered to hand her. I saw the triangle of a face, waxlike in colour and texture, as a little death-mask, the hands gripping the wheels of the chair as bird-claws.

When I was within a pace of her, she swung the wheels, and, her back to me, gritted through her teeth, "I don't *have* to like you, not ever. I don't have to like anyone."

My mother soothed in the voice that could tame a couple of fighting tom-cats, or reduce a mutinous child to sweet reasonableness. "Of course, you don't, my darling. All you have to remember is how much we love you."

Memory blanked out at that point. Presumably I sulked in the background while my mother in that soft yet gay voice soothed and beguiled Olivia. The first time you are totally rejected it is as though all your roots have been shaken out of the firm earth of life, and you become terrified they will never settle again.

In the train on the way home, I questioned my mother. "What's going to happen to her?"

She answered with a hope she tried dutifully to suppress. "It's not definitely decided, so we mustn't count on it, but there is a chance she may come and live with us. Her father appointed a Mr. Hayward Carstairs as her guardian, but he and his wife are middle-aged and haven't any children; also his business keeps him travelling abroad. They couldn't provide Olivia with a settled home, and it would be too cruel, quite out of the question, to send the poor wee lamb to boarding school. So it may be that Mr. and Mrs. Carstairs will agree to Olivia living with us." She squeezed my hand. "Wouldn't that be lovely?"

With my whole world tumbling about my head, I grabbed for a life-line. "Daddy might not want her."

She gave me a shocked look, admonished: "Darling, what a dreadful thing to say! You know that Daddy would be overjoyed for us to look after Olivia, love and cherish her as her own parents would have done. He'll be home soon, and meanwhile I've written him all about Olivia. He knew her father and mother." Another squeeze of my hand. "Your Aunt Mary-Anne was as like a sister to me as you and Olivia will become when you get to know one another."

I was smugly content with my life-style as an only child. I didn't want it laid in ruins by a proxy sister who'd rejected me on sight; a hideous little skeleton with eyes unlike any I'd seen in a human face. Doom lapped round me. Even at that age I doubted whether my father would exercise his authority. The decision would be my mother's. He was a dutiful if somewhat abstracted parent who periodically visited his home as opposed to living in it. A field-worker employed by a world charity organisation, his heart and mind were committed to the starving children of the Third World rather than to his own petted and overfed daughter.

He was kind, sometimes fun, with a saintlike patience; even so, I sensed he was never wholly at ease in our comfortable house where three highly nutritional meals were set before us seven days a week. I had once, with a couple of friends in tow, dashed into his study and surprised on his face an expression that suggested he found the sight of our plump limbs, pink cheeks and bounding energy so painful as to be offensive.

She patted my hand. "Darling, your father loves children, all children. He devotes his life to them. There are thousands of them alive in Asia and Africa today who would have starved to death if it hadn't been for him. Remember the pictures he showed you."

Children with sticks for arms and legs, hideously swollen stomachs. I reached for my last shred of hope. "But he might not like Olivia living with us. She might disturb him when he's working."

"Darling, she's not enough strength to smile, let alone make a disturbance!" She patted my hand in mild reproof. "A little girl falling out of an aeroplane, breaking her bones, losing her mother and her father!"

I knew when I was beaten.

Two months later Olivia arrived in a Rolls Royce, sandwiched between Mr. and Mrs. Carstairs. They'd already inspected the house, interviewed the headmistress of the school at which she was to join me. Now they met my father, a man with the minimum of flesh on his bones, blazing eyes beneath a jutting brow, a harmonious voice that charmed everyone within earshot and, what is called for want of a better definition, an air of distinction. He was vetted, passed the test, and when the Carstairs drove away in the chauffeured Rolls Royce, they left Olivia behind, so rocking the axis of my inner world that it was years before it steadied.

The white heat of rejection had burnt itself out; perhaps the skeletal figure had not sufficient physical strength to sustain it. In its place was a blankness, as though at will she conjured up a mist before her eyes to shut us out of sight. We were each so wary of the other that I never spoke directly to her without rehearsing the words in my head. My mother loved, cosseted and fretted about her, tempting her nonexistent appetite with tid-bits. But it was my father who accomplished a miracle by reading to her, telling her stories until she fell asleep on a stool set between his feet, never expecting any acknowledgment let alone thanks for the expenditure of time that had to be recouped by sitting up half the night. It took him three weeks to coax a smile out of her, two months before her laughter rang through the house. He'd taught her to play chess, and she'd won her first game. I worked out that except for her colouring, flat stomach and high school uniform, she must remind him of the stick-armed children who possessed his heart.

By the time he left for India she was walking without a limp, there was a thin layer of flesh on her bones and the fairylike, pale honey-coloured hair that in certain lights had a greenish tinge reached her shoulders. By mutual consent never expressed in words, we had established a routine for existing under the same roof. We chose our friends from different cliques, took care that our out-of-school activities never overlapped. Olivia joined the Pony Club and revealed a talent for acting. The tragedy that had befallen her, and a nature that was by turns biddable and wildly unpredictable, garnished by a natural charm, made her a favourite with the school staff. Also she was physically delicate, subject to bronchial colds and all the childish diseases against which she'd never been inoculated.

I dabbled in art, practised my violin, indulged in a passion for wildlife that took me on long solitary treks. And from my fourteenth birthday, by which time I'd decided on the pattern of my future, I worked all day Saturday for Mrs. Floris, who owned an antique shop in the village that catered not to local trade but hard-faced dealers.

A shrewd, tart-voiced woman, without an ounce of sentiment in her make-up, she became so infuriated by the sight of my face steaming up her window that she dragged me inside and demanded an explanation. Initially I was only allowed to dust the legs of the furniture, threatened with instant dismissal if I as much as laid a finger on the porcelain or glass. But gradually she developed a tolerance for me. I was allowed to sponge the Dresden and Rockingham, lift the ticking chiming clocks from their niches. My reward was not the money she paid me—it was a pittance—but learning to distinguish between Hepplewhite and Chippendale, to recognise hall-marks on silver, but the correct names to Meissen, Dresden and Bow. We parted when I was eighteen and she sold the business, with mutual respect but no liking.

Scholastically Olivia was a flyer; I, a plodder. She was a mixture of energy and lethargy, brilliance and periods when she appeared not to have a brain in her head. Education to my mother was as sacred as a commandment engraved on a tablet of stone, alongside which success, fame, riches were mere dross. Knowledge, a finely tuned mind, that was her ambition for me, and mine for myself. But scholastic success played no part in Olivia's life. She was indifferent whether she came top or bottom of the class. Any suggestion that she should apply her mind she sweetly disregarded.

We rarely quarrelled outright, but when we did we took care never to do so in my mother's hearing. She would have been mortally hurt, and even I admitted that if Olivia loved no one else, she

loved my mother. You might say that with a false smile of acceptance we suffered one another. It was years before I realised that my
mind and heart was so barred and bolted against Olivia that I had
been blind. I'd wanted so little to do with her that I'd never known
her at all. The fault was not entirely mine. There were veins of
deviousness and secrecy in Olivia, facets of her character that she
kept hidden, an inner self she never revealed to anyone.

I was twelve when my father died of cholera in a village in Bengal,
where he had been supervising the digging of a well and the laying
down of a primitive irrigation system. There was a service of thanks-
giving for his life in the village church, and letters paying tribute to
him from all over the world. After my mother had answered them, I
sat by her side and pasted them into a scrap-book. Except that she
was so deeply withdrawn into herself that I had to repeat a question
twice, sometimes three times, she displayed no signs of ravaging
grief. I assumed that she accepted with her usual stoicism the loss of
a husband who, on an average, was home three months out of
twelve, and with whom she would one day be united in heaven.

One afternoon when I came home, through the half-open dining-
room door I saw Olivia with my mother's head cradled against her
chest, her hand lovingly stroking the sleek, greying hair.

When she became aware of me, she relinquished my mother,
kissed her brow. Her head erect, the glacial moonstone eyes stared at
me with the bitter, relentless hate of the hospital child before she
ran out of the room, holding a hand clamped to her mouth as
though she was going to be sick.

I moved snail-like towards the gate-legged oak table at which my
mother had spent hours acknowledging the hundreds of letters of
condolence. The big scrap-book was beside her. Her head was bowed,
and she was gazing at a coloured photograph she was holding in her
hand. Closer to her, I witnessed the unbelievable, a tear slide down
her cheek, fall on to the picture.

I stood appalled by weakness in a woman I'd supposed to possess
none. Without looking up, she slid one hand into mine, held it so
tightly I felt as though all the bones in my fingers were being
crushed to pulp. My eyes found the photograph that was blistered
with tears. A funeral pyre, a massive couch of interwoven branches
piled on giant-sized logs, through which flames spurted upwards
from the scarlet incandescence at its heart to reach and consume the
body of a man. My flesh became rigid, and I could not, however des-

perately I tried, wrench my horror-stricken eyes away. So I screamed, as though the demented sound had the power to massacre terror.

My mother pulled me close. "Darling, I didn't mean you to see it until you were older. But truly he died and was cremated as he would have wished, fulfilling his heart's work." She kissed away my tears. "A body is only a shell, and fire is a clean, a beautiful way to consume it and allow the spirit to fly free. Ali, who had worked with Daddy, and loved him, went to enormous pains to borrow a camera and buy a colour film, which would have cost him a great deal of money, so that he could send me the photograph. To him there is nothing sad in treasuring a picture of the release to God of a great and good man's spirit."

So it was I who sobbed on her shoulder, not she on mine, not only in the aftermath of stunning shock, but because Olivia had seen the picture, and my mother's tears, before me, which I counted a theft of my rights.

My mother's pension was small, so, being a trained teacher, she returned to teaching at the village school. She taught what was known as "the backward class," made up of those pupils who chose not to apply themselves to the arts of reading and arithmetic, those who were unable to learn however hard they strived and a minority of rebels who sat out the school day planning nuisances to inflict on the community at large, which meant they were constantly under the eye of the local police, in peril of being hauled up before a juvenile court. Problem children to everyone except my mother.

To her they were the deprived who had either been cruelly mishandled or misunderstood. Such was her joyous dedication to her work that when, ten years later, arthritis bit so deep into her joints that it crippled her and forced her into retirement, there was not only a civic reception for her in the village, but the right murmurs were made in the right quarters, and I went with her to Buckingham Palace to receive the O.B.E. from the Queen. Her pride was mingled with bewilderment. She could not understand why she had been singled out for an honour. Were we all absolutely sure there had been no mixup in the names? Now that walking and standing for any length of time was a concealed agony, selected problem pupils trekked to her door, and our dining-room had been converted into a schoolroom.

When she lived with us, Olivia periodically visited the Carstairs in Chester Square, collected and returned by the purring Rolls Royce. Once she reached her teens her visits became more frequent, suggesting that Mrs. Carstairs found a semi-adult more congenial than a child. She took pleasure in buying Olivia clothes, and an extra wardrobe was bought for her bedroom. The surplus she threw out bumped up the receipts from the village jumble sales to an all-time record. She invariably tossed off casually before they were bundled up: "Help yourself, if there's anything you fancy." There never was.

It took me a while to differentiate between Mr. Carstairs—full name Hayward Kingston Carstairs—and our own bank manager, Mr. Porteous, a plump little man, with a deferential manner, who lived in a semi-detached house on the other side of the village street. I questioned my mother. It appeared that Mr. Carstairs was a *merchant* banker, forever hobnobbing with others of his trade in Paris, Zurich, Bonn and New York, who maintained four separate establishments in Europe: the house in Chester Square, a villa in Mentone, an apartment in Paris and a skiing lodge at Chamonix. Also an estate near Miami in Florida, which he had inherited from his American mother. By the time she was fifteen Olivia was familiar with the five residences between which the Carstairs flitted as sun and financial crises dictated, forever in migratory flight. She took to travel without fuss or visible excitement and I, never having flown in an aeroplane, secretly envied her.

My mother, I knew, cherished a hope that the Carstairs would include me in one of their flights, but when they failed to do so, I convinced myself I was thankful. I breathed more freely when Olivia was whisked away by the chauffeur-driven Rolls to Heathrow.

With my A levels looming ahead, I was cloistered in a life or death struggle to hammer the abstruse hieroglyphics of mathematics into my brain, while Olivia either set her hair—she shampooed it twice a week—drifted out of the house or sat chatting and laughing with my mother. Infuriated by her airy nonconcern, I demanded next morning as we waited for the school-bus: "I suppose you couldn't care less about your results?"

"There's not much point, is there, since I'm moving on to a finishing school in Montreux in September."

It was the first I'd heard of it, and the news startled me. Good or bad? Well, good, of course. Very! I assumed that the merchant banker was paying her fees, and said as much to my mother. "Oh, no, there's no need for her to be beholden to him." (Being beholden to anyone was my mother's idea of ultimate degradation.) "Olivia has her own money. Of course, Mr. Carstairs looks after it, and will continue to do so until she is twenty-five, but her father left her comfortably off."

"Was he rich like Mr. Carstairs?"

Her face puckered; she found the remark in poor taste. "As I've said, he was comfortably off. His father, who died before Olivia was born, was a most capable businessman, or so Mary-Anne gave me to understand. Olivia shouldn't go short of anything she needs."

From which I deduced that when Olivia reached the age of twenty-five (why not twenty-one, I wondered) she would be rolling in money.

A few days later I was walking home across the common when my eye, caught by a pale gleam, was drawn to a wooden pavilion that had been erected to the memory of a long-dead parish councillor. Olivia and a man were bound so close that you couldn't have inserted a sheet of paper between them, their faces hidden by the spun-silk amber curtain that now reached to her waist. In slow motion the man lifted his head, and for a few seconds I had a clear view of his profile, rapt like a sleepwalker's as he ran his hand in wonderment through her hair, brought strands of it to his lips to kiss. No more conscious of playing the role of peeping tom than if I'd been in a theatre, I stared as though hypnotised. I did not stir until, with his arm encircling her shoulders, he drew her deeper into the shelter where they were hidden from my spying eyes. Not a whisper, not a thread of a laugh. Silence as though they'd both fallen into a depthless sleep.

What we, with exaggeration, termed *"affaires"* with the boys of the grammar school or the brothers of school friends, and which never escalated beyond mild flirtations, were commonplace. Olivia picked them up, flicked them aside. I even had one myself, a near-mute youth who sweated profusely when driven to speech. His sole virtue was that he could dance like an angel.

But the wordless passion, the ecstatic, almost unearthly communion of body to body, as though they were indivisible, belonged to a realm which I had not known existed. Pallis Green was a close-knit village, and the permissive age—apart from a discotheque on a Saturday night which closed sharply at 11 P.M. or the village policeman appeared—was slow in reaching it. Slower still in invading my mother's home. A man, not a boy, with a man's passion. It was a haunting memory. I wondered who he was, where he had come from since he wasn't a local. I would rather have gone to the stake than ask Olivia.

"We'll miss her dreadfully," my mother mourned, as we waved Olivia into the Rolls Royce (new model) for the last time, and she put her arm about my shoulders to comfort me in my loss. And, to my amazement, she was right. In some inexplicable fashion I did miss Olivia; it took me months to adjust to her not being around. The house was duller without her wit, her absurd extravagances, her secrecy, her refusal to involve herself in any activity she found even faintly distasteful—or, worse, boring.

Every month or so she dashed off letters to her darling Mother Clare, rippling with anecdotes concerning people of whom my mother had never heard. There were the extravagant presents which, except for perishables like glacé fruits and sugared almonds, my mother hoarded in a special drawer still wrapped in the glittering silver and gilt paper in which they'd arrived: diaphanous scarves, chiffon negligees, costume jewelry and perfume by the half-pint. Olivia was always promising she was coming to see us, but she never did until that summer afternoon I walked down the front path and through the open windows heard her voice. I stood rooted into the stones thinking, as though I'd never heard it before, what an enchanting voice it was, soft, yet with a high musical lilt. I ran, alight with joy, cleansed of all the murky traumas of childhood: the canker of jealousy at the usurper who had displaced me as the doted-on only child, outlived, forgiven, to be laughed out of sight.

There was a second when the three of them were so engrossed in each other that they did not see me in the doorway. My initial reaction was simply to marvel that the skinny girl had been transformed into—not a raving beauty—an ethereal creature of matchless grace. She was sitting on a stool, wearing a greyish blue cotton dress that matched her opaline eyes, her amber hair piled up in a shimmering mass of curls with wild flying tendrils, a blaze of happiness and light.

She saw me, came running, holding her arms wide. "Liz! Dear, dear Liz, isn't this the most wonderful, most perfect day ever?" She did a half-turn, linked her arm in mine, and together we faced the man who was standing beside my mother. "Liz, this is Leo. And Leo, this is Liz. You know all about her." Her pale glance flew to me, radiant, ecstatic. "We were married a week ago, so you see I had to bring him home to you."

He wasn't the blond lover from the pavilion, though why, after the lapse of time, I should have expected him to be, heaven only knows. He was dark, with ebony hair that was as shining as a raven's wing, waved carelessly about his narrow, taut face, with a neat, svelte figure, not quite as tall as his wife. The eyes that flickered over me were not the deep brown one might have expected, but a curious blackish slate, his skin an ivory shade that emphasised the bold curve of his lips. In those first few seconds I had a sense of a man deliberately presenting only one facet of himself, keeping the rest under wraps. A man who activated no warmth in me.

"Elizabeth, the daughter of Olivia's beloved Mother Clare! I count myself fortunate to meet you." He dipped his head in feigned courtliness, and smiled to ridicule the gesture. It was a sly, calculating smile, and I was baffled that Olivia, with all the world to choose from, had married him. Oh, he was handsome, and he possessed a degree of personal magnetism, but his bearing had a sheen of arrogance and I knew intuitively he was not willingly in my mother's house.

"Of course you had to meet." Olivia slid her hand into his. "I lived in this house for nine years. It was my home. I know every inch of it, even the holes in the wainscotting where the mice dart in and out."

"And I know," my mother countered, hauling herself to her feet and reaching for her stick, "what you are having for tea. Your favourite sultana scones." She shook her head at them. "Why didn't you let me know you were coming?"

"Because you'd have baked half a dozen cakes, been up at the crack of dawn, wearing yourself out when all I wanted was to see you and"—she smiled at him with such yearning love that for a moment she was beautiful—"introduce you to my darling husband."

In the end we all trekked into the kitchen, and Olivia went on a nostalgic journey, touching the china on the dresser, sniffing the plants on the window, stroking each piece of furniture, explaining its history to Leo, while I cut sandwiches and, despite her locked finger joints, my mother made scones and spread them with the season's new strawberry jam.

It wasn't until tea, which we ate in the sitting-room, was half-way through that my mother in a tactful but characteristic forthright manner set about informing herself about the background of the man her adopted daughter had married. "And where do you live, Leo? Have you parents in this country?"

"My father is, unhappily, dead. My mother is a Sicilian. She and my father met while he was on holiday. She married him before they returned to England. I grew up in Manchester. But after my father's death when I was sixteen, Mother and I returned to Sicily to live." In my ears it sounded remarkably like a prepared biography.

"And that's where you and Olivia will make your home now you are married?"

Olivia laughed. "Darling, I warned you, Mother Clare likes to have everything neat, settled. Darling Mother Clare, we haven't decided yet. We haven't had time. But first we intend to have a long honeymoon in the United States. Leo has never been outside Europe. It's high time he saw the New World."

"Mr. and Mrs. Carstairs must have been very happy at your wedding." I recognised it as a question, not a statement.

Olivia gave a pettish shrug. "Oh, I wouldn't say that. Uncle Hayward has become so boringly conventional, so rigid-minded. In this day and age he wanted us to have a long engagement so, as he put it, we could get to know one another. But time's for living, not wasting. Besides, Leo and I knew everything about each other in the first five minutes of meeting. So we had a quiet wedding. Only Leo's mother and Maidie."

I wondered who Maidie was, but before I could ask, she leaned forward, her smile as dreamy as though she were reliving the ceremony, and kissed Leo on the mouth, her lips clinging to his. It was like watching a close-up on film. I remained detached, unembarrassed. A natural declaration of love or what amounted to a piece of exhibitionism? I couldn't decide, for the reason that I lacked experience. My own loving, my first loving, lay nine months ahead. I had yet to experience that transfiguration of body, heart and mind; a world that bursts into shimmering wonder because one man lives and breathes, in which every particle of me was vibrantly alive from the moment of waking until sleep enveloped me at night. When no chore was boring, no job irksome because one was steeped to one's bones in love, blessed with love's supreme gift: being loved one loved not only the beloved but everyone.

Drawing back, Olivia cried in lilting triumph: "I'm the luckiest girl alive." Then, curiously, as though we were likely to contradict her she insisted: "You've got to believe me."

We assured her we did and Leo swore—he could hardly have done otherwise—that he was the luckiest man in the world.

But my mother hadn't reached the end of her fact-finding mission. "You know, Olivia, you haven't told us your married name."

"Johnson," Leo said curtly. "My father's name was Rudyard Johnson."

He sounded less than ecstatic about it, but my mother found it a charming tribute to her favourite poet. Then, as I could have predicted, she wanted to know what profession he followed.

His response was a fluent, high-flown exposition of his present and future, made slightly confusing by digressions, as he swung from peak to peak, so transformed by eloquence that he bore little resemblance to the young man who had greeted me with barely veiled disdain. He was, it appeared, an entrepreneur marketing a new and revolutionary scheme for the promotion of various unnamed products, involved in deals with multi-national corporations. Delivered with enormous panache, it was certainly impressive. My mother, on whom he focussed his whole concentration—you could almost say attack—was enthralled to find herself privy to the problems that beset oil tycoons.

To me the most bizarre aspect of the whole extravagance was the intensity with which he strove to convince her of his close involvement with wealth and power. Dream-world or reality? I decided the likelihood was that Olivia's husband was a P.R. man, which would account for Mr. Carstairs' reservations about the marriage, P.R.s being small fry in the rarefied atmosphere of merchant banking.

Because the work to which anyone dedicated their life was of paramount interest to my mother, when he paused for breath I knew she was likely to plunge deeper, demand facts and maybe—heaven forbid—figures, so I made a diversion by gathering up the crockery, carrying it into the kitchen, piling it into the dish-washer. I was closing it when I heard the door snap behind me. Olivia was braced, palms pressed to the panels, her face shorn of light, as menacing and coldly embittered as the skeletal child in the hospital. The transformation confused me, merging past with present, so that momentarily I could not disentangle one from the other.

Even her voice was different, without its high lilt, hard as stone. "What's being done for Mother Clare?"

"How do you mean?"

"I mean," she whipped back, "that she's much, much worse, a cripple. Hobbling! In pain and you don't do a damned thing about it. You don't even appear to notice."

With the skin of my teeth I held on to my temper. "Knowing her, you surely don't imagine she'd allow herself to be babied, treated like an invalid!"

"So you don't do anything for her!" She left the door, advanced on me like an avenging angel. "There are new treatments . . ."

I broke in. "She's had treatment."

"From whom? The village doctor! That old fool!"

"Dr. Crane sent her to an orthopaedic specialist. And for a month she was under treatment in a London hospital. A great deal has been done."

"But to no good. Why not call in other specialists, instead of accepting the fact that she'll be a cripple for the rest of her life?"

My mother's arthritis had begun to distort her joints before Olivia left us, but I could not remember that she had shown any undue concern. Now she was accusing me of not caring, of neglect. The ancient hate gushed up, nearly choked me. "You're an expert on arthritis!"

"No, but in your place I'd damned well learn to be."

I *had* learnt, the hard way, but I didn't choose to explain the process to her. "She has physiotherapy once a week, injections, tablets, and she's examined by a London consultant every six months."

Her condemnation gave way to a wail of anguish. "But she's a cripple. They've done nothing to cure her." She drew in her breath in a half-sob. "Money would buy her the top specialists, the best in the world. I . . ."

My temper was released in a burst of laughter that made an ugly sound. "Ah, yes, money, the miracle-worker! But I'm afraid money won't buy her a new set of knee-joints, nor a pair of arms. Not even new fingers. Not yet. And she alone has the right to decide because sometimes an operation involves sacrificing power for loss of pain. You seem to have forgotten that Mother has a mind of her own. She's not in her dotage."

Hurt and disbelief stained her face. She moaned: "Crippled, hobbling around in pain, and you leave her all alone during the week! She could fall and lie helpless for days."

"Hardly alone. Emma Humphry is here every day. She has sessions with her pupils. Bill Roberts is around taking care of the garden." Now it was my temper that raced out of control. "And she has more friends in this village, people who love her, than you'll ever have in a lifetime. She doesn't want pity, yours or anyone else's. She lives her life the way she chooses."

She flinched, her mouth quivered, and I remembered suddenly that she was made up of odd pieces, none of which matched. For a moment I was ashamed of myself. Her concern had been genuine . . . or at least I was willing to give her the benefit of the doubt.

I heard my mother's step outside the door, saw it was shut and went to open it for her. In a house in which no door was ever closed tight because for anyone deprived of muscle-power, dependent on a stick, twisting a knob was a laborious business.

My mother smiled serenely at us, and we smiled back: an automatic reversion to our role of never inflicting our differences on her, transformed into two amicable little girls who no longer existed, if they ever had. "Leo tells me that you are dining out in London tonight and he's afraid if you don't start back soon, you'll be late."

Olivia ran to her, wrapped her in her arms. "Oh, I hate to go. I don't want to leave you."

Leo said over my mother's shoulder: "Darling, we promised faithfully to be there by seven, and you know what an age it takes you to dress. This meeting with Fokker is important."

She eased away, and smeared the tears from her cheeks with the back of her hand. Like a child. "I know. I won't make us late." Her meekness was a revelation to me. The Olivia I'd known had never accepted anyone's domination. Yet this svelte, ebony and ivory young man had tamed her. Knowing nothing of love, I marvelled.

This time she drove away from the house not in a Rolls Royce but an Aston Martin, with a handsome young husband at her side who thanked my mother charmingly for her hospitality, shook my hand with grace but no pleasure and swept at such speed down our narrow lane it was obvious the visit had been a chore endured for Olivia's sake.

There was, of course, no reason why he should like us. Yet it wasn't so much covert dislike as the impression that under his suave manner nerves were juddering as though we posed a threat to him.

As I put my hand under her elbow, to help her up the path, I asked: "What did you think of Leo?"

She took so long to answer that I thought perhaps she hadn't heard. Her voice pulsed with yearning. "All I ask is that he loves her. That's the heart of it. Any other fault I'd forgive him. If you lose the people you love when you are a child, for the rest of your life you're forever seeking to recapture the love you lost. Above all else Olivia needs to be loved."

"*You* loved her!"

Her look was wry, deeply knowing. "Yes, I loved her."

The tiny emphasis on the pronoun told me that our thin gloss of friendship had not deceived her. For a split second I felt a stab of regret for an opportunity lost forever. Then I shrugged it off. It was swallowed up in the past. For all Olivia's promises I thought it unlikely we'd see her again.

But letters and panoramic postcards arrived from all over the globe, plus the usual exotic gifts at Christmas, and always, on my mother's birthday, two dozen long-stemmed blood-red roses. The proprietor of the florist shop handled the Interflora order personally and took a pride in delivering it herself. "I have to order them from the London market specially for you, Mrs. Ashley. Not much call for hothouse roses round here, except at weddings, but I know every year I'll have to telephone ahead to have them for you on September the seventh."

It fretted my mother that there was never an address to which she could write back. Olivia and Leo were forever on the point of flying off to some other country. Like a couple of gypsies, my mother swore. It was Leo's business, Olivia explained, that kept them on the move. By next year they would have established a permanent base and then we must both promise to visit them.

On the morning of my mother's sixtieth birthday I overslept. I had intended to take off for Pallis Green at 7:30, be there by 9:00. Instead it was after eight when I began piling the presents into the car. About half-way I remembered I hadn't retrieved Olivia's blotched scrawl out of the drawer. I persuaded myself it was no more than a lapse of memory. The roses! They'd be waiting as proof that the letter was no more than the expression of a sudden impulse. Olivia was ruled by them.

My mother heard the car, and was waiting at the open door as I ran down the path. "Oh, it's such a beautiful day." Tranquil happiness illuminated her face. "Perfect!"

"It wouldn't dare be anything else. Happy birthday, darling, happy, happy day."

Over her shoulder I saw Emma carrying a loaded tray into the sitting-room. I groaned.

"You know very well you left the flat without a bite to eat."

"Your mother," Emma explained, "thinks you should have a bit more fat on your bones. I keep telling her modern young ladies don't fancy fat, but she won't listen to me.

As a benign form of blackmail she refused to open her presents until I'd swallowed every mouthful. The mantelpiece was stacked thick with cards, many of them hand-painted. The table and sofa were loaded with presents: potted plants, chocolates, stockings and gloves. There was a vase of mop-headed chrysanthemums on a side table. No roses. But it was early yet.

Emma joined us for a cup of coffee. "Your mum says you're taking her out for a smart lunch at that new hotel."

"That's right. No cooking today."

She cackled with laughter. "That's what you think. She's beaten you to it; wait till you open the larder door!"

"You promised . . ."

"I know, darling. But Basil is coming this afternoon, and I decided he must have a cake. He had his eighth birthday while he was on holiday and I can't be sure his father would even remember the date; he's such an absent-minded creature. And in any case, Basil wouldn't have had a cake."

"Since when have you been giving lessons at the weekend?"

"Only this once. Basil had a bilious turn on Thursday, so I promised he could come this afternoon. Now his father's old prep school have agreed to give him another chance at the Common Entrance examination he failed in June, it's important he doesn't miss a lesson."

"Do you think he'll get through this time?"

"I'm sure of it. All he's short of is confidence. Latin is his weakest subject, and mine is disgracefully rusty. That's what gave me this brainwave: we'd switch roles. He teaches *me* Latin. And it works. So far as Latin's concerned he's brighter than I am, so he no longer feels a dunce."

Basil was waiting on the doorstep when we returned from lunch, a singularly unattractive small boy, wan-faced, a bit shifty-eyed, his size-too-big pants belted in wads at the waist. His parents were divorced and his father, who had custody of his son, employed a series of housekeepers to feed Basil and make certain he was in bed before his father arrived home. He presented to my mother a splintered hunk of wood, the purpose of which defeated even her ingenuity. He muttered that it was an ink-well.

"Hand-carved, especially for me. That's my initial, isn't it?" she said pointing to a deep gouge. "I shall use it every day." He smiled and suddenly he looked less repulsive.

She ushered him ahead of her into the old dining-room, now a schoolroom, and I did not follow them. The roses weren't likely to be there. I glanced into the sitting-room. Not there either, nor in water on the draining-board in the kitchen where Emma would have left them.

For the first time in the years since she had left us Olivia had failed to lift the telephone and send a message that might have to wing half-way round the world to bring red roses to my mother on her birthday. I refused to allow myself to speculate, to be intimidated by the memory of that crumpled sheet lying in a drawer of my bureau.

Basil had been sent home with the remains of the joint birthday cake packed in a cardboard box, and we were sitting on the terrace when my mother set down her glass of lemon squash—she never touched alcohol. "I can't believe she would forget. She never has, all the years she's been away. I have a feeling that something's wrong. That she might be ill . . ."

With no warning, the image of myself became hateful. "She could be, equally she could be travelling on a plane. Or there's been some hold-up with the order." I added guiltily: "If it will stop you worrying about her, I'll telephone Mrs. Carstairs tomorrow, ask her how Olivia is, where she is."

She shook her head. "When nine months had gone by without a line from her, I telephoned the house in Chester Square. A young woman answered. She said her husband had bought the lease from Mr. Carstairs a year ago. It seemed he'd been in poor health for some time and decided to retire. She didn't know where they were, so I wrote to Mrs. Carstairs at the villa in Mentone. She never answered."

I had a weird feeling, as though I was someone else staring at a picture of myself: ugly, incomprehensible. I could not understand why that self, instead of skimming the letter, had not painstakingly deciphered every word. With deadly force the truth pressed itself on me. I hadn't wanted to read, to know, to have to care.

Retribution, if such it was, called for guile, even outright deceit. "If Mr. Carstairs has retired, there'll still be someone at the bank who knows his address, and Olivia's. I'll telephone in the morning. First thing."

I made the fastest time ever back to the flat. I flew up the stairs and paused only to slam the door before I wrenched open the drawer.

The single sheet of thin paper was as creased as though it had been crumpled into a ball, been roughly smoothed out before being thrust into the envelope. That accounted for some of the smudging but not all. The address at the top, which was hand-printed, laboriously, as though in a child's hand, was "Villa Fossita, San Giorgio, Caromezza, Italy." Beneath, also printed, was "Signora Mariani" and then underlined "Not Johnson."

I read "Dear Liz" and then began the hard task of deciphering Olivia's appalling writing. It was made more laborious in that the ball-point had functioned erratically, sometimes making thick, blurred letters, followed by others that were colourless indentations on the paper. At the end of twenty minutes I had decoded approximately a third of the disjointed sentences.

Please come and see me. Please, please. Don't write you are coming. Arrive. A plane to Milan airport . . . a car to Caromezza. San Giorgio near. Please come soon, or it will be too late. I think I'm . . .

I pored over that word a long time because I refused to believe what my eyes semaphored to my brain. I struggled to make it spell out a different word, but the letters obstinately refused to reshape themselves. What Olivia had written was: "I think I'm dying." At the bottom right-hand corner there was a blotched scrawl that suggested two capital letters. I turned the paper over, read the postscript. "Among other things I lost the baby."

I was waiting in Eustace Bedale's office when he arrived at the gallery on Monday morning. Mrs. Anstruther, his middle-aged secretary, was on guard to ensure that I didn't pry into his mail, disturbing the neatly arranged pyramid.

Eustace removed his homburg hat, divested himself of a mohair coat and eyed us with the cynicism that was his normal facial expression. "What's this? A committee meeting."

Mrs. Anstruther giggled. "There have been three telephone calls for you, Mr. Bedale. I've put a list of them on top of your mail. They're all urgent."

"Naturally! Thank you, Mrs. Anstruther."

When she'd reluctantly left the room, he addressed me. "Well?"

I laid the report on Friday's private viewing on his desk. The ascetic face, so pale-skinned that it appeared to have an undertone of grey, regarded me with cool disinterest. I had to remember—as if I could ever forget—the day when he had revealed a depth of compassion that had saved me from being drowned in a cataclysm of grief.

I had known David for two months; we had been in love one day
short of that time. We met at a party where his awareness of me had
been swifter than mine of him. When I was leaving I found a slight,
tow-headed young man posted by the door. "Elizabeth Ashley?"

"Yes."

He grinned and all that lovely zest, his certainty that the world
was a super place, flooded his being. "I was wondering if by any
happy chance you were free to have dinner with me."

"But you don't know me."

"That was the idea." He slanted his head, and I swear there was
love in his eyes. "That I might get to know you. That is if you fancy
getting to know me."

When I woke in the morning I was in love for the first time. Each
day that week he was waiting outside the gallery to take me to
lunch; in the evening to dinner. To me it spelt a miraculous exten-
sion of all my senses, loving and being loved by a man whose nature
was sweet and gay, quixotic and endlessly inventive. At the end of a
week Eustace eyed me as though I'd become demented. "I take it
that young man who spends half his day leaning against my bow
window is an admirer of yours?"

"You might say so."

"If he's nothing better to do than hang about blocking the window display, you'd better tell him to do his waiting inside. He appears to have an extraordinary amount of free time. How does he
earn his living?"

I laughed. "You're not going to believe this, but I don't know."

"Then my advice to you is to find out immediately."

Over lunch I did. "Aeroplanes. I vet the whizz-kids' blue-prints,
make sure they've put all the nuts and bolts in the right places, don't
get their sums wrong. In Bristol. My five days' leave is up, and I'm
due back on Monday. But most weekends I can drive up to London."

I explained that weekends I went home and why.

"Then we'll re-gig the plan. The purple monster will do the journey
in two hours. So provided I clock off at five-thirty twice a week, I can
be at your flat soon after seven."

Obstacles didn't exist for him. That was the pattern for the next
two months. Once, when Mother was visiting an ageing cousin in
Devonshire, I drove down to Bristol. He lived in half a wing of a
mansion occupied by men who talked and breathed aeroplanes.
They threw a party for me in another flat that belonged to a young

man called Hal Forman. As it was thinning out, he came and ran his eye broodingly over me. "You look as if you might do. Is that your objective?"

"If that's the way David wants it."

"If he does, jump at the chance. He's a very special guy."

"You think you have to tell me that!"

"I guess I don't. And he's crazy about you, besotted. We've all been shaking in our shoes at the prospect of entertaining a combination of Her Majesty and Princess Grace."

"What a let-down!" I sipped the rest of my drink. "What precisely is David's job on the airfield?"

"He didn't tell you! Well, he tends to underplay it. Keeps it under wraps whenever possible. But if you're in his life for keeps, you'll have to know. He's a test pilot, one of the top three in the country. Bloody good."

For a few seconds the room seemed to darken and then David touched my arm. "I've loaned you out for long enough."

It didn't make any difference, except in the middle of the night, or when I sat with my hands clenched waiting through the minutes that he was late.

He never proposed; I never expected him to. We assumed we'd be married, as though it was laid down in the stars. He had ten days' leave coming up. "We could get married then, couldn't we?" I said we could, added: "But I'd want to take you home first."

"Of course. That'll be my treat, to meet your mother. And my treat to you is Willie. My step-father. Used to be in the Navy but he's retired now, living in Stromness, in the Orkneys. My father died when I was five years old, but Willie was so darned marvellous I have to admit I hardly missed him. And when Mother died, a couple of years ago, he was a rock, an absolute rock." His face cleared of memories, shone with pride, with love. "So I can't wait to show you off to Willie. Next weekend for your mother, and the one after for Willie. Okay?"

When I suggested that Stromness was a long trip for a weekend, he look mystified. "We'll take the Cessna, if I book it ahead, it'll be ours. We can fly over the hundreds of islands floating in a sea that's sometimes emerald, sometimes sapphire, and on the odd day grey, take Willie with us. He gets a kick at skimming over the waves. Always makes out he wants me to hover so that he can fish."

I didn't break the news in advance to Mother. Partly because she'd have organised Emma into spring-cleaning the house, laid up supplies to feed an army; partly because I wanted her to know David before we dealt with the future, which might involve uprooting her, resettling her into a house near us.

I was ready, singing under my breath, by six. I stopped singing at seven, sat with the phone on my lap. It was five minutes past nine when it rang. Hal Forman's half-strangled, barely recognisable voice asked: "Is that you, Liz?"

I knew instantly, and it was as though a giant hand was squeezing my heart to a slow death. David was dead, killed in a multiple pile-up on the motorway. David was dead.

When I replaced the phone, I remember being sealed in a deathlike calm, as though I were enclosed in a block of ice. I dialled my mother's number, framed some plausible excuse for not coming home that weekend. I listened to and made suitable responses to items of news she passed on to me. I promised, without fail, to be down the following Friday night.

The rest is a blank. Through Saturday and Sunday I existed in a limbo where normality did not operate. When the phone rang it never occurred to me to answer it. I don't remember eating, only drinking countless glasses of water. I didn't sleep. On Monday morning, like an automaton, I dressed in my working clothes, arrived at the gallery at 9:15. I thought how odd Mrs. Anstruther looked with red eyes, a moist nose, as though she'd a cold, or had been crying. She stuttered: "I just want to tell you how sorry I am. He was a lovely young man . . . a wonderful, wonderful boy." She turned away, head bowed deep with convulsive sobs.

Dutifully I thanked her.

Cedric grasped my hand. "Liz, I hope you know you have all my sympathy. It's an appalling tragedy. If there is anything I can do . . . I can cope here; wipe that side of things from your mind."

"I'm fine," I said, "just fine."

I couldn't think how they knew, then it vaguely percolated through to me that there must have been a picture, a paragraph in a newspaper.

As Eustace passed through to his private office, he held the door open, waved me ahead of him. For a second I saw the room swim, then literally turn upside down. Some time later I found myself lying on his Regency sofa, my wet shoes marking the delicate primrose brocade. I jerked up, tried to swing my feet to the floor, crumpled.

"Lie still," he ordered. "Jenkins will be back with the Daimler at any moment to take you home."

"I can't go home. I don't want to."

"My home, you silly child. Or rather mine and my wife's."

That he owned a house in Wimbledon and possessed a wife was all we knew of Eustace's domestic life. He was a fanatic at keeping his privacy inviolate. Occasionally he'd telephone her, a factual statement without endearments, advising her that he would be early or late. I imagined her as dry and bloodless as her husband. Instead she was dumpy, fresh-skinned, with snow-white hair bound in plaits round her head, a husky voice with a hint of an Austrian accent. Her most beautiful feature was her hands, the fingers creamy and tapered, with pearl-pink buffed nails, and the gentlest touch in the whole world. Her name was Lottie. Dear, dear Lottie.

She was waiting when the car drove up to the door. Without a word she took me in her arms and kissed my forehead. When, for the first time, I was wrenched apart with successive storms of grief, she wound an arm round my waist and, wordlessly, led me upstairs.

I stayed with them for five days. After forty-eight hours the doctor allowed me up and in the summer heat the two of us spent hours on the wide terrace so shrouded by her beloved garden that we might have been in the depths of the country. When I could not read because my brain could make no sense of words, she read to me. There was a Belgian cook who came personally to present to me the delicacies she had prepared especially for me, and whose face was like a smiling sun when I managed to eat one. By Friday I had relearnt the rudiments of existence. I could trust myself to drive home. Though I did my best, there were no adequate thanks I could make to Lottie. She had probably only acted out her nature, to cosset, comfort and befriend. Eustace's gift had been immeasurably greater: he had opened to me a home that was to him an inviolate sanctuary. It did not surprise me that, back at the gallery on Monday morning, he lowered the shutters. It was as though I had never shared his home, met his wife. But I had, and I remembered. There were only a handful of people, none of them close to me, who had been witnesses to that winged period when David and I were in love. One of them was Eustace. Once I'd entered the main showroom to find them laughing together, Eustace's hypercritical faculties dormant, so that he had opened the door, waved us off with expansive good humour foreign to his nature. Next morning, he had said with a sardonic half-smile: "I suppose you could do worse."

That was David's supreme talent: to communicate his happiness to everyone with whom he came in contact. In me he had released wells of tolerance and gaiety that I had not known existed. I'd had to fight stubbornly to keep them flowing, and had not always succeeded.

And so on that Monday morning I made my plea to Eustace. It was simply to change the date of the remainder of my annual leave.

He assumed his most waspish air. "I was under the impression that you were jaunting off to Casablanca in November. If I remember rightly, I advised you to have your injections well ahead of your departure date. They frequently have side effects."

"That was the plan." A holiday with Audrey and Bob Longman, who had been loaned a villa in Marrakesh for three months. Audrey was one of my oldest friends.

"So what changed it?"

As he was impatient with lengthy explanations unconnected with the routine of the gallery, I summarised. A girl, an orphan, who had been adopted by my mother, and who had lived with us during her childhood, now resident in Italy, was ill and I wished to visit her.

"Critically ill?"

"She may well be, but I won't know definitely until I see her."

"You realise this disrupts the holiday schedule?"

The schedule was composed of four people. "Mrs. Anstruther has already taken hers. Cedric is due back on Monday."

"Ah," he said as though he'd produced an ace, "but will he turn up! I recollect that last year he took an extra week."

Cedric spent his annual holiday with his sister and family in Torquay. Last year he'd collapsed with gastric flu the day before he was due to return to London.

"I do remember, but surely by the law of averages he shouldn't catch flu a second time!"

"I wouldn't count on it. You should know by now Cedric is a hypochondriac."

This was marginally true, but I knew better than to argue back. "He usually returns to London on Saturday. I'll telephone him in the evening and confirm he's fit and will be on duty on Monday morning."

"No overlap," he snapped. "That leaves too many margins for disaster." He piled on another objection. "And Halkins is away sick. His doctor refuses to give me even an approximate date when he'll be fit for work. Those boys need supervision. It's inviting chaos not to keep an eye on them."

Halkins, nearing pensionable age, was foreman of the workshop in Fulham, a master-hand at restoration, who could work miracles of delicate reconstruction. One "boy" was in his mid-forties, dedicated to his craft. The other was a responsible workman nearer sixty than fifty.

"I should have thought a telephone call would have served to allay your anxiety."

"I'm sorry but I must see her, and as soon as possible." I made a final appeal. "I wouldn't have asked for the change-over of dates unless it had been urgent."

He informed me acidly he'd consider the matter and give me his answer in the morning. If it went against me, I wondered whether I'd walk out. On balance I thought I would.

However, it turned out that he had, characteristically, arrived at a compromise that afforded him a small bonus. Highly inconvenient though it was, my holiday date might be changed, but only on condition that I overlapped Cedric by one day, so ensuring he had returned to his post and was brought up to date on the diary of events —which he could have read for himself. Also, as I'd be in the region, I could call on two fine art dealers, one in Milan and the other in Padua. It was always useful to renew contacts when a suitable opportunity arose. He'd brief me before I left on the items in which he was interested.

I expressed my gratitude; it was no moment to quibble. Back in my own cubby-hole, I booked a flight to Milan on Tuesday morning, laid on a self-drive Fiat to meet me.

That left me with the problem of Mother. Because she was a woman who dealt in absolute truth, lying to her was a degrading experience. Yet I could not bring myself to hand her Olivia's letter, watch her unscrambling that final sentence, turn over the creased paper and read the postscript. And I'd no answers to the questions she would ask, the same ones that rampaged through my head. What had become of Leo? Was it death or divorce that had parted them? Olivia remarried, but to whom? On the telephone I'd told my mother no more than I had obtained Olivia's address and promised to fill in the details on Saturday.

So I was left to meet the lying head-on. The bank had supplied me with Olivia's address. She was living in Italy, near Caromezza. I plunged on, racing to get the multiplying sequence of half-truths behind me. By a coincidence, Eustace had two dealers in Italy with whom he carried on a two-way traffic in antiques whom he needed to contact. But as he didn't wish to make the journey himself, he'd asked me to deputise for him. So it would be relatively simple for me to make a short detour and look up Olivia.

So long and intently did she scan my face that I became convinced she didn't believe a word of what I'd flattered myself was a credible tissue of fact and fiction. Then she turned her head away, and for a moment her upper lip shook and she pressed it hard with her fingers to subdue it. "You must think I'm making a fuss, that by now I should accept that Olivia is a grown woman, with a husband and independent life of her own, that it is unrealistic and unreasonable to expect her to remember us. Oh, I agree. I've no right to hang on to her coat-tails, as though she owes us a debt. Maybe I'd manage it if it wasn't for the dreams. In them I see her unhappy, terrified of something, though I can never discover what."

Exasperated at her weakness, she scolded herself. "There, you can accuse me of being a maudlin, fanciful old woman." Slowly she raised her head, her eyes mourning something lost forever. "I'd always hoped she'd have children to prove to herself that, at last, she was a real person."

"A real person! Wasn't she one?"

"Never a whole one. Half the time she was playing a part. Even you must have noticed that."

Curiously I hadn't.

CHAPTER 2

A young man by the car-rental desk was waving a piece of cardboard chalked with my name. He seized my hand, shook it vigorously. "Welcome to Italy, Mees Ashley. It is a beautiful day, is it not? *Bellissimo.*" Like a stage Italian he actually kissed his fingertips. After I'd signed the forms, paid the deposit, I enquired if he could supply me with a large-scale map. Indeed he could, and spread one over the desk with as much pride as though he'd drawn it himself. "You instruct me which place you wish to travel to, and I will mark the route for you."

"San Giorgio. About four kilometres from Caromezza."

He pinpointed Caromezza on the map. The distance worked out at approximately 250 kilometres. The car was an electric blue Fiat, grubby inside, with sweet-papers on the seat which he nonchalantly swept on to the floor. He offered to pilot me as far as the exit to the motorway, but I thanked him, said I could manage.

Northern Italy was an hour behind English summer-time, which made it 11:15 when I manoeuvred my way out of the airport into the grey urban streets that wound themselves round the heart of the city. The traffic was thin and I made good time to the motorway. The hire-car man had been right: it was a beautiful day, with limpid blue skies and an all-over spread of sunshine. Once I was clear of the industrial complexes, pink and white oleanders wove a continuous garland behind which a green sea of maize swayed rhythmically in a warm scented breeze.

I allowed myself a brief stop in Como for a snack lunch, ate it in the square by one of the landing-stages from which midget steamers hooted off to weave their criss-cross patterns over the lake. For a while the inked-in route took me along a highway that was walled in between mountains and lake, plunging in and out of cavernous tunnels blasted out of the solid rock. By now Sunday afternoon trippers, too many of them with boats hitched to their cars, slowed me down, and my impatience was mounting when, one kilometre short of Caromezza, I turned off a narrow road sign-posted San Giorgio. It climbed in swinging hair-pin bends, at first through an area scattered with modern villas and blocks of flats, their balconies dripping with geraniums until, gradually, the buildings thinned and the forest took over, hemming me in. By now the road was an unsurfaced track, so split with ruts and strewn with boulders that in heavy rain it must be a rushing torrent.

I scanned the dense green curtains in vain for a house, a driveway, a gate. Then, abruptly, I found myself on the brow of a hill, looking down into a village with tight clusters of terra-cotta and apricot houses crammed round a toy-sized piazza with a church rising from its centre. I eased my way down to the single street, shuttered and slumbering in the afternoon heat, the only visible sign of life a grey cat gnarling a bone in the gutter.

I parked in the cobbled piazza by the church with its cut-down campanile and took my bearings. Farther up the street was a taverna with some green painted tables outside. The Villa Fossita could lie in any direction; to find it needed help. As I approached the taverna I could hear voices, bursts of raucous laughter. I parted the bead curtain, walked through it. Two men and a woman seated on benches at a rough-hewn table swivelled their heads towards me, their faces sullen with affront at my intrusion. She was a bony, ungainly woman with dark frowsy hair outgrowing its red dye. The two men, glasses held suspended in mid-air at my appearance, wore stained work shirts and dungarees. As my eyes adjusted to the dimness, I glimpsed a third man behind the counter. As his back had been turned, he was a second later than his companions in seeing me. His glance was no more welcoming than theirs, but not quite so blatantly resentful. In contrast to their begrimed working clothes, he was wearing a spanking white shirt, a multi-coloured silk scarf knotted about his thick, sinuous neck. He didn't utter a word of greeting, just stared with unblinking curiosity. My Italian was rudimentary, consisting of odd words ungrammatically strung together. "*Per favore . . . do è il* Villa Fossita?" When there was no response, not even a syllable to break the choking silence, I repeated: "Villa Fossita, *per favore.*"

The man behind the bar leaned forward, revealing a heavily fleshed body, a low brow under a mat of dense black hair, thick, coarse features. In comparison with the leatherlike texture of the three faces around the table, his was a pallid suet colour. His lips parted, stretched, and two gold teeth gleamed. His smile, if such it was, afforded him maybe a quarter of a minute to examine me from the top of my head to my sandals.

"An English young lady? That is so, is it not?"

"Yes." My relief was such that I probably smiled back at him. "Could you tell me where the villa is?"

Again there was that suffocating silence, as though the answer to a simple question posed immense problems. The younger man at the table, scarcely more than a boy, with long fawn hair, a lean, aggressive face, lifted his glass and drained it. The second, older, man and the woman continued their nerve-strained scrutiny of me. The man behind the bar spoke. "Not good road. You travel by automobile?"

"Yes."

"Better a truck."

"I'll manage. How far is it from here?"

The woman's head swivelled again towards the man behind the bar, the movement so violent that it distracted my eye from her two companions. Suddenly, unmistakably in the claustrophobic silence, I recognised a scent: the sweat of animal fear. A girl stopping her car, parting a bead curtain, enquiring her way, had set their sweat-glands working overtime. In other circumstances it would have been ludicrous, but in the breath-held atmosphere it was like being plunged into the heart of a small nightmare.

The man behind the bar demanded: "You go on a visit?"

The woman looked back over her shoulder, hanging on my answer.

"Yes, a visit."

"Four kilometres. If you like I drive you. I tell you rough road. Very bad."

"Thank you, but I'll be fine." I plunged through the bead curtain. For a second in the blinding sunlight I panicked because I could not remember where I had parked the car. Then I saw it in the piazza. The silence behind me did not break and would not, I knew, until I was out of earshot.

Driving up the narrow street, I accused myself of over-reacting. The village, crouched deep in a hollow, was an isolated community, off the tourist track, the inhabitants unaccustomed to strangers and suspicious of one who suddenly materialised in their midst. Maybe I had disrupted a family conclave, been suspected of eavesdropping. That was plausible as far as the three round the table were concerned, but not for the man behind the bar. He was no peasant, to be thrown off balance by the appearance of a stranger. He spoke— with an American accent—some English; his clothes were town-bought, expensive for the keeper of a village taverna, and why had he been so anxious to drive me to the villa? Well, even that wasn't a crime, maybe no more than inquisitiveness. Determinedly I tossed the dark furtive scene out of my mind. Olivia's villa was only a few kilometres distant; I was on the threshold of learning the answers to the questions that plagued me. Olivia with a new husband, a lost baby, so terrified of dying that she implored me to come to her. Me from whom she'd never asked a whisper of a favour, who'd once shared a roof with her, but nothing else, certainly not her confidence. My fever of impatience mounted into a mild frenzy.

Gradually the trees thinned, revealing wide spaces reaching into the distance, of clear rising ground where white veins of limestone looked like half-buried bones. The engine was beginning to overheat when I reached a levelled patch of gravel, behind which was a wrought-iron gate, its intricate tracery so delicate that only a Florentine craftsman could have fashioned it. Or rather half a gate; the second panel was missing, wrenched from the support of its massive stone pillar that had been reduced to a heap of rubble. At the far end of the level space stood a grey Jensen, getting on in years, with a G.B. plate. I parked the Fiat, wiped a clear peep-hole in one of its side windows made opaque by dust. A man's tan suede jacket, a pair of binoculars and a sleeping-bag were spread on the back seat. Since Olivia's new husband was Italian, a car with a G.B. plate was unlikely to be his. So who owned it? With no answer in sight, I turned to examine the villa.

I placed it as eighteenth century. Three storeys high, a balcony jutting out from the second floor, above it a blue-faced clock that had stopped at five minutes to twelve. Drowsing in the sun, its grey shutters latched, even at a distance it wore an air of desolation, of abandonment, as though it was slowly crumbling to dust in its sleep. I walked through the half-gate. Beyond was a circular pool where stone cherubs sported with a dolphin, watched over by a couple of Roman gladiators. But moss coated the statues and the pool was a sludge of scum. Two flights of steps, starting from opposite directions, zig-zagged upwards, chipped or broken clean away, littered with shards of urns that had been overturned, half-buried under a decade's growth of rampant trailing and climbing greenery. Climbing, I could see the cracks in the plaster, the splintered shutters, that most of the balustrades were supported only by vines that bound them together with thick, snakelike tendrils. By now it was obvious I'd missed my way. What lay before me was a villa subsiding in its own time into decay that could not conceivably be Olivia's home. If the Jensen had not been parked below, I would have retraced my steps. But its owner was my only hope of being directed to the Villa Fossita.

From my vantage point on the cracked, disintegrating paving of the terrace, from which weeds and grasses sprang as high as my knees, I glanced back over the tops of the trees that formed a slanting green table down to the valley I could no longer see. Sky and trees and silence. Viewed in solitude the villa evoked a sense of desolation, the heart-ache of someone's loss that was both eerie and forbidding.

The bell beside the studded door could not function because the clapper had fallen out and been buried somewhere in the debris. With no expectation that the door would open, I gave it an experimental push. It swung back, the wood screeching on its hinges. I stepped inside and found myself standing beneath a cupola, the plaster veins between the curving panels of glass inset with Wedgwood placques. On the right a marble staircase with delicately traced rails seemed literally to take flight to a gallery circled by Corinthian columns, a marvel of architectural composition that by the irresistible stream of time was being reduced to a ruin. Plaster dripped from the pillars, the gold-leaf flaked from the capitols and there was a three-foot gap in the balustrade curving round the gallery where a temporary guard-rail had been contrived out of a filthy knotted rope. The walls lining the staircase were pitted with what appeared to be bullet holes. Every horizontal surface was coated with dust and grit, and the air itself carried a stench of must and rot to my nostrils.

For minutes I stood with my back against the door, tracing the soaring splendour of the staircase, what had been and would soon be no more. It was with an effort that I jerked myself back to the present: how to locate the owner of the Jensen with the G.B. plate. I called out, but my voice cracked in my throat and failed to carry for more than a few yards. I made a flying visual survey of the hall: it contained no piece of furniture, not even an outer garment someone might have discarded on entering the villa, no evidence that feet had trodden its marble floor for decades.

I opened a door on the left, peered into a twilit room. When I'd unbarred a shutter, opened it a couple of inches, I saw not one room but two, a perfect-double-cube, stripped to its bones, the damask wallpaper mildewed and hanging in shreds on the walls, the painted ceiling reduced to shadow scenes of disporting gods and goddesses. The single undespoiled treasure was the milk-white marble fireplace.

In the far room, I unbarred the window and two shutters, opened them wide. In the distance were the white tents of the snow mountains, and below me a lemon tree in fruit throwing a shadow over a sheet of bougainvillaea that blazed out of a wall like a fire and spread itself over the stone-paved terrace. On the far edge was a girl —or a child—lying on a magenta towel, her face masked by outsize dark glasses, ebony hair spread fanlike behind her head, motionless, naked. A child, I decided, or at most a girl of twelve or fourteen. Too young to be the driver of the Jensen. A sun-worshipping child in a semi-trance and living proof that some portion of the villa was occupied. Or was she, like me, an intruder?

Back in the hall my eye came to rest on the double-door on the right. The inlaid wood at the base was kicked and splintered, but the exquisite hand-painted finger-plates were unchipped. Curiosity won; one more act of trespass seemed neither here nor there.

On the far side a shutter hung awry on its hinges, admitting a narrow band of sunlight that revealed a finely proportioned salon, its floor a mosaic in ochre, cinnamon and grey, the delicate cornices of the ceiling gilded. In the centre was an oblong table of Carrara marble, one of its massive claw feet smashed and propped up by a wedge of bricks. Suspended above it was a Venetian chandelier—about a third of its crystals missing. The walls had been so thinly and inexpertly whitewashed that ghostlike shadows of the pattern on the silk paper beneath were visible. At the head of the table was a French Empire chair, its original disintegrating tapestry neatly patched with what looked like sail-cloth. Along one side of the table were three scarlet plastic chairs facing four others—the type made to stack. The table was littered with an empty Chianti bottle, tumblers, cutlery, a basket containing some hunks of bread baked brick-hard by the heat and a brewer's ash-tray in which the butts of two cigars and one cigarette had been stubbed out.

I stared at the juxtapositioning of chain-store plastic, a battered tin ash-tray with the crystal chandelier and the marble table. Only one thought sprang to mind: squatters who had commandeered the villa as a temporary camp. I wondered if the sun-worshipper was one of them.

I returned to the entrance hall, conscious not only of trespassing, but that I was frittering away time I could not afford to waste, more aware now of the bullet holes in the walls, a stain that might have been a splatter of blood, grace, beauty not only abandoned but pillaged.

My hand was on the door when I heard a barely audible sound from the gallery, so faint it was impossible to identify—a husky cough, a low exclamation, a moan. But a sound that had been uttered by a human being. My body reacted to a compulsion that swept me up the staircase so fast that when I paused in the gallery my breath was locked in my lungs. Three doors were closed; a fourth was ajar. I inched the gap wider, saw a room so dim that at first I could make out nothing but contrasting blocks of shadow. As my eyes adjusted to the quarter-light a bed defined itself, a bed in which someone was lying. And, on the far side of the room, a crouching man was fumbling under the pillow of a second bed.

As my hand thrust open the door I was struck by a suspicion so incredible that my mind refused to give it credence. At the creak of the door the man straightened, swung about. For a split second I was confused by what could only be a delusion of recognition, instantly blotted out as I stared into the muzzle of a gun he was pointing at me. He straightened, took a single step. "What the hell . . ."

His brusque demand was cut short by a cry from the other bed, weak, pitiful but recognisable. "Liz! Liz!"

I ran, stumbling over my feet. The light streaming from the staircase and into the room revealed a shrunken face with hollowed cheekbones, parched, cracked lips, eyes sunk pitlike in a skull. Arms, the stick-arms of the hospital child, reached out for me. I held her, stroking the long amber hair, torn apart by rage, pity, anguish and disbelief, knowing nothing except that Olivia was desperately sick, and behind me was a man with a gun.

Over Olivia's head, which I pressed to my breast, I saw that without making a sound he had moved to the opposite side of her bed. His hands hung empty by his side. I wondered if the gun had been an hallucination induced by shock, or conjured out of the dimness of the room. But, no, I was certain it had been there.

"Liz?" he murmured with a querying note.

The little claw hands fastened on to me. "Yes, Liz. Mother Clare's Liz." Her eyes, even paler now, as though illness had stolen what little depth of colour they had, devoured me. "My Liz, too. Everyone should have a Liz in their lives."

"Yes, indeed!" His glance lightly brushed my face, rekindling that teasing sense of recognition. "I'm Patrick Harlow."

The self-effected introduction told me nothing except that he wasn't Olivia's new husband.

Footsteps became audible. A breathless voice spoke from the door-

way. "Goodness me, what have we here?" In a vaguely theatrical gesture, she pressed her hand to her drooping bosom: a tall, pear-
shaped, middle-aged woman with a stoop, wearing a blouse that had
come adrift from her baggy tweed skirt, peering at me through spectacles mended with sticky tape that had slid half-way down her nose.

Olivia released herself from my grasp, sank back on the pillows.
"Maidie, this is a very old friend of mine, Elizabeth Ashley. I've told
you about her. I've known her forever." She began to gabble as
though frightened she would run out of breath. "She's on her way to
Venice and looked in to see me." The claw hand grabbed mine, and
her eyes threatened and implored. "Didn't you, Liz, on your way to
Venice."

In a chaos of ignorance, I could do nothing except nod my head.

The woman held out her hand, but her glance was evasive. "Well,
how nice! Just what Olivia needs, the company of an old friend. I'm
Audrey Maidstone, but everyone calls me Maidie." Her hand
dropped to her side, and she looked at the man, who watched and
waited and didn't speak a word. "Sorry, dear boy, that I've been such
a time, but half-way through my letter I dropped off." She giggled,
turned to me. "It's the heat, you know. Though I should have got
used to it by now. Sometimes I think I shall sleep my wits away."
She cocked her head. "If this sounds dreadfully rude, you must forgive me, but will you be staying the night?"

"Yes," Olivia answered for me. "Liz will be here for lots of
nights."

Maidie pushed a damp strand of her hair, which must once have
been gold but was now faded to grey-blond, behind her ears. "Well,
how was I to know! No one ever tells me anything. You see," she explained to me, "we have a problem with the bedrooms. Dozens of
them, enough for an army, but so few of them are fit for human hab-
itation. The ceilings aren't safe. They could fall down and concuss
you during the night, and we wouldn't like that to happen, would
we?"

Patrick Harlow interrupted. "No problem, Maidie. Give Miss
Ashley my room. The ceiling there looks reasonably sound. I keep a
sleeping-bag in the car. That will suit me fine."

But Maidie disapproved. "Cramped up in a car all night! I don't
fancy that idea. Surely . . ."

Olivia fretted: "Maidie, don't fuss." The protest had exhausted
her, and she subsided on the pillows, closed her lids that were as

dark as though they'd been stained with walnut juice. "Make some tea."

"Of course, dear." As Maidie reached the door, she voiced a mild complaint. "Actually, I thought it was Mimi's turn to make the tea today."

Patrick Harlow, hands in his pockets, strolled to one of the front windows, unbarred it, opened the shutters, stood looking outwards, apparently wishful to disassociate himself from what went on behind him.

Olivia's lids parted. With a beseeching gaze she whispered: "Liz, I didn't write to you. I didn't. It's a surprise visit. Promise me. I didn't ask you to come."

"Promise," I whispered, as though we were conspirators, and momentarily she relaxed. Seconds later, the tide of anguish flooded back. "And don't leave me, Liz. Don't leave me."

Again I promised. At that moment if she'd asked me to snatch the moon from the sky, I'd have said yes.

The cracked lips stretched into a travesty of a smile. "Thanks." The whisper was so faint as to be hardly audible. "I feel safe now you're here."

The lids sealed themselves together, and her grip on my hand slackened, abandoning me to panic, rage and a black numbing bewilderment. Safe from whom? From a tyrant of a husband? If so, where was he?

Without drawing my hand from Olivia's feather-weight grasp, I turned, not seeking help, more a thread of enlightenment. Patrick Harlow, one arm braced against the window sill, was studying me with a contemplative gaze. As our glances touched, he switched the angle of his body, left me with his back. He was tall, lean to the point of thinness—I could see his shoulder-blades through his cotton shirt. His hair was thick, a light sable, shaped with a master's hand into his neck. Cobalt blue eyes, watchful but unrevealing of a single thought that passed behind them. His fine-edged face suggested intelligence plus an assurance so imperturbable that it could only be inbred or utterly bogus. Also, I reminded myself, a man of violence in that he'd threatened me with a gun. The flash of recognition hadn't been mutual. So somewhere I'd seen him, but he hadn't seen me, or seen me and not found me worth remembering. Sotheby's? Christie's? A country sale? A party? Memory obstinately refused to yield an answer.

I wondered if he'd overheard Olivia's plea, but thought it unlikely in view of the wide space that separated us. That is what Olivia's bedroom consisted of: emptiness dotted here and there with pieces of shoddy furniture. Her bed was of fumed oak, so was the dressing-table, surmounted by a circular looking-glass corroded at the edges by mildew. There was a bedside table with a bottle of medicine and phials of pills, a pottery water jug, a finger-marked glass and a couple of grubby paper-backs. Another table stood at the foot of the bed, its varnish marked by overlapping rings. On the farther side of the room was the second bed, in which I'd surprised Patrick Harlow either hunting for or hiding a gun; the bed was similar but not identical to the one in which Olivia was lying; a wardrobe that required wads of newspaper to keep it upright, and—scarcely believable—a marble-topped Victorian wash-stand with a hole in the middle to support a jug and basin, plus half a dozen plastic chairs, identical to the ones grouped round the crippled marble table in the salon. The sheets on Olivia's bed were coarse cotton, machine-hemmed; I found myself giving thanks to someone that they were clean.

I did not hear him until he paused on the threshold like a second-rate actor intent on drawing applause for his entrance: Leo, neither dead nor, apparently, divorced from Olivia. I had a sensation of falling into an unknown depth, plus nausea and a longing to gulp air. His dark slate glance fastened so instantly on me that I knew that if he had astounded me, I was no surprise to him. He'd known he would find me at the villa. And since any approach to it was channelled through the village, it was an easy guess that he'd been warned of my arrival by the keeper of the taverna. Warned! The word had a near sinister ring that compressed my fears into a tight knot.

Three years had thinned what little flesh there was on his bones, emphasising his faintly Mephistophelean appearance. Though his mouth formed into a smile, his eyes were ungiving of any emotion except cold calculation. I suspected if he'd had the power he'd have struck me dead. Without it, he inclined his dark head. "Elizabeth! What a surprise!"

Olivia leaned forward, and I rose from the chair to make room for him. Panting, she held out her stick-arms. "Darling, isn't it wonderful! Liz is on her way to Venice, and broke her journey to come and see us."

He pressed a kiss on the dome of her forehead, then raised her fingers to his lips and ceremoniously kissed them. "Wonderful indeed! How fortunate she had our address." The cold-as-ice slate glance divided itself between me and the watcher at the window, who now stood with one elbow braced against the sill, coolly observing, as though he was in a stall at a theatre watching a play. Neither spoke to the other.

Leo turned his grey gaze on me, aped concern. "But it distresses me, and I am sure Olivia too, that you should arrive at a moment when the hospitality we can offer you is far short of what is due to a guest." He sighed dramatically. "If only you'd informed us ahead of your arrival, we could have warned you that until the reconstruction work on the villa is completed, we lack the amenities that a guest has a right to expect."

Olivia plucked at his sleeve. "Darling, it's all fixed. Patrick has offered to move out of his room. Liz can have that. And Liz understands." She appealed to me. "You do, don't you?"

Before I could answer, Maidie, pink about the cheeks, mingled strands of yellow and grey hair hanging damp in her neck, eased a tin tray into the room. Patrick Harlow relieved her of it. "Dear boy, how very kind of you. I haven't got as much puff as I used to have. On the table at the foot of the bed, if you'd be so good."

Olivia reached for Leo's hand. "How is the Contessa? What did the eye specialist say?"

"He was cautiously optimistic. For the time-being he advises against surgery. She is to continue with her eye-drops, but he has increased the dosage, and he wishes to examine her again in two months. Meanwhile, she is resting. The examination exhausted her. Maidie . . ."

"Don't fret. I've seen to her, tucked her up. And Mimi has promised to keep an eye on her. Now let's all have a nice cuppa. I'm sorry there's no cake, but praise be I found some biscuits. Patrick, fetch a chair and sit by Olivia's little friend."

"Thank you, Maidie, but if you'll excuse me, I'll remove my belongings from my room, leave it free for Miss Ashley."

"I don't want to push you out."

He gave me a charming, completely meaningless smile. "Oh, I assure you it causes me no inconvenience whatsoever. It will be ready for you in half an hour."

"Oh, Patrick," Maidie urged, "have a cup of tea first. It'll revive you no end."

He patted Maidie on the shoulder, smiled affection spiced with humour on her that wiped away the aloofness from his face.

"Maidie, dear, I haven't your addiction to tea. So if you'll all excuse me."

He walked towards Olivia's side. I watched tenderness, almost a lovingness, touch his mouth. Suddenly memory clicked and I felt a trip of the heart, a moment of desolation for which there was no explanation, no excuse. He touched one of the little claw hands. "See you."

"Please," she whispered, and her eyes followed him until he was beyond sight. Leo watched, his lips formed into a set-piece smile. Then he walked to the window Patrick Harlow had opened, barred the shutters, leaving only the half-open window on the east side to light the room. He opened a bottle, shook some pills on to the palm of his hand.

Olivia grimaced, protested like a fractious child. "No, they make me so sleepy, and I'm coming downstairs tonight. Oh, Leo, I am. I want to so much. Please, darling."

He frowned doubt. "Dr. Spinosa wouldn't approve. *Caro*, you're not yet strong enough. In a little while you will be, and then you may come downstairs."

"No. Tonight." She clamped her lips against the pills he held to her mouth. "Leo, it's months since I've been out of this room. I hate it. I can't bear it." Hysteria threatened as tears burst through her lids.

From the other side of the bed, I could see only his profile. It expressed a doting concern. An amateur actor's face, with a small talent? Or an adoring husband? He leaned over her, smoothed the amber hair that was darkened and clotted with sweat. "Hush, my little angel. You know it makes you ill if you upset yourself." He sighed with patient resignation. "But you shall have your treat. To save you exertion I'll carry you down the stairs and up again. Does that make my darling happy?"

She nodded, whispered: "I love you."

"And I love you, my little one. Come, take your pills."

She swallowed them, sipped once or twice at the tea served in a cracked cup, then lay back on the pillow, her eyes dazed, unfocussed. "Where's Mimi?"

"With the Contessa." Maidie's sniff was tinged with scorn. "After she's put some clothes on, I hope. How that girl can sleep for hours broiling herself in the sun, I'll never know. It would bake my wits to a crisp."

Maidie wielded the tea-pot, handed round the stale biscuits and chattered nonstop. Olivia fell asleep.

In a suave, patronising manner, Leo went through the motions of fulfilling his duty as a host, enquiring after my mother's health, and what kind of a journey I'd had, mere conversation-fillers that would not have deceived a child. When Maidie began to gather up the cups, he suggested—though it was clearly an order—that I might like to go to my room, adding that he would sit with Olivia, and that dinner was at 7:30.

"Prepare yourself for the worst," Maidie cautioned as she led me round the half-circle of columns into a spider's web of passages. Some of the flooring was rotten, and where the plaster had not stripped itself off the walls it was mottled with grotesque patterns of damp. She showed me into a cell-like room furnished with bare essentials: an iron bedstead, a set of drawers, a hanging mirror, one chair, but I thanked heaven there was a wash-basin. Patrick Harlow seemed to have swept it clean of his possessions in a remarkably short space of time.

"I'll fetch some clean sheets," Maidie said, as she mopped her face with a man's grubby handkerchief. "Just give me a minute."

"There's no hurry. And the room's fine. Everything I need." I unlatched the window, looked down at the terrace. The girl who was presumably called Mimi had disappeared. All I could see was a raggy outline of what, long ago, had been a formal Italian garden of yew and box, statues and pools, now half buried under a jungle of growth.

"I'm afraid the hot tap doesn't work. Only the cold."

She was so downcast, I tried to relieve her of one worry. "In this temperature who needs hot water!" I turned to see her sitting on the edge of the bed, pleating a portion of her sagging skirt into folds. Suddenly, in a gesture of defiance, she thrust her glasses higher on her nose. "I'd better confess, clear my conscience."

"Of what?" I sat down beside her. Though scatterbrained, a compulsive chatterer, she was an endearing woman, possessed of that instant likeability that springs from a nature that is essentially kind. Or that was my instant judgment.

"Can't you guess?" When I shook my head, she blurted out: "I posted the letter to you. Not, I may say, without a great deal of soul-searching; in fact, I wrestled with my conscience for over a week before I took the plunge, posted it. Of course, I didn't read it. I'm not a pryer, but I could guess what was in it." For the first time since we'd met she looked me straight in the eye. "She asked you to come to her, didn't she?"

"Yes. But surely there was nothing wrong in that?"

"I hope not." She stared morosely at the rubbed toes of her shoes.

"When did she lose the baby?"

"In April." Her voice shook. "It was a boy. Stillborn."

"Where? Here?"

"In Sicily."

"How long have you been living here?"

"Since June. We arrived on the eighth. Of course, she was still weak as a kitten, pining, and the journey exhausted her."

Questions that screamed for answers were a log-jam in my head. I had to battle to curb my impatience, sensing that if I pushed her by asking too many—or the wrong ones—she'd clam up. "Wouldn't it have been wiser to leave her where she was?"

"Certainly not." Her instant denial was both sharp and emphatic. "In any case it wasn't practical. There were too many . . . well . . . well . . . complications. Besides," she ran on in a more confident tone, "the air here is so good, and there are the most beautiful gardens, world-famous, or there will be, and watching the villa being restored to its former glory will provide her with a stake in the future."

As her eyes rose to my face challenging me to contradict her, I smiled. She flushed. We both knew that she was repeating parrot-fashion phrases that had been put into her mouth.

The joke lived no more than an instant. "Olivia is pretty sick, isn't she?"

She moistened her lips. "At first, after we arrived here, she showed signs of gaining strength. Then, about a fortnight ago, it seemed as if she began to lose heart. I suppose that is why she wrote to you, though it must have cost her a tremendous effort. A line at a time! Not to have posted it would have been like disappointing a sick child."

I could have demanded why Olivia couldn't write as many letters as her fingers had strength to pen, but I refrained. Plotting which question to ask was like threading my way across a minefield. "Leo spoke of a doctor. What is his opinion?"

"Dr. Spinosa? He calls once a week, on a Wednesday, oftener if we need him. He says her mental state is a bit more stable than it was, but that physically she is still at a low ebb. His orders are absolute rest and quiet, no excitement, and day and night nursing. The Contessa, Mimi and I nurse her during the day, and Leo takes over at night. Fortunately, he's a light sleeper, wakes if she as much as turns over in bed." She gave me an admonishing glance over her sliding glasses. "I wouldn't like you to run away with the idea that Olivia lacks for anything. She is cherished, yes that is the word, cherished. There is nothing any of us wouldn't do for her. Time is the best healer, that's what Dr. Spinosa says, and I believe him."

She heaved herself up. "I'd better be fetching the sheets, and then I'll see about dinner. You'll be hungry after your journey. Maybe I'll be lucky for once and persuade Mimi to give me a hand! That'll be the day!"

My mind was stuck fast on two words—"mental state"—but I couldn't bear to back-track. I persuaded myself that Maidie was slip-shod with words, that "mental state" to her meant the natural depression that is the aftermath of any protracted illness. Instead I asked: "Who is Mimi?"

"She's the granddaughter of an old friend of the Contessa's. Their families have always been close. That's how it is in Sicily, everyone is either bosom friends or mortal enemies. All a bit childish to my mind. But Mimi's a clever girl. Very good linguist. She translates at conferences. You know, where the delegates wear head telephones and hear only their own language. When we went back home to Syracuse she looked us up, and being temporarily without a job, stayed with us for a while and helped Leo with his business affairs. Later, when she was tipped off about a translator's job in Paris, she left us. But when Olivia lost the baby, she came flying back to help with the nursing." She scrupulously added a postscript in case she'd been guilty of unfairness: "She's a capable girl, smart too, though ask her to give a hand with a meal and you'll get a black look, I can tell you. And she has a convenient knack of forgetting any chore she doesn't fancy, and that's most of them." She shrugged her shoulders good-naturedly. "Still, we're none of us perfect, are we!"

"Anything but. And the Contessa Olivia mentioned?"

She gave a merry laugh. "Why Leo's mum. Oh, I see! Well, of course she's not a real contessa. It was the nickname her husband gave her. 'His little Contessa!' I can hear him now coming through the front door, calling up the stairs: 'And where's my beautiful little Contessa this evening?' Very nice man, Mr. Johnson. Kind to every-one and genuine, if you know what I mean. That counts a lot with me: genuineness. She was fond of him, even though after he died she did change back to her maiden name. Still, I don't blame her, it made her less like a stranger in her own country."

"Why did Leo change his?"

"To match up with his mother's. It made it awkward forever

explaining why mother and son had different surnames. And it wasn't as though Olivia objected."

As she walked towards the door, I said: "I'll come with you. I need my bag from the car."

"Right-ho. I'll show you the bathroom." She giggled. "Only cold water in the shower and sometimes that gives out. We find ourselves in some right old pickles, I can tell you. Good job I was a girl guide in my youth. Taught me to be resourceful. I'm a dab hand at clearing out stopped-up drains."

Patrick Harlow was standing at the end of the marble table when I entered the salon, a girl by his side. She was wearing a rose kaftan with garlands of hand-embroidered flowers on the neck and wide sleeves. The glistening fall of dense black hair reached nearly to her waist.

Patrick Harlow introduced us. "I don't think you two have met. Elizabeth Ashley, Mimi Angelo." She held out her hand first, a formal smile flickering for a split second on her mouth. "A friend of Olivia's from England, I understand. Hello!"

She had sparrow-bones but the covering of flesh was satin-smooth, the colour of dark honey; her eyes were green with unusual flecks of yellow. There was a stillness about her, a composure that held the eye, plus a kind of flawlessness, a girl so coolly self-contained it was impossible to imagine her at the mercy of any strong emotion. I marvelled that, even at a distance, spread naked on a towel, I had ever counted her a child. Poise such as she possessed did not develop until one was out of one's teens. I guessed her age to be somewhere in the mid-twenties.

As I released her feather-weight hand, I asked: "Do you think Olivia will be able to come downstairs for dinner?"

"Why not!" Her voice was crisp, assured. "She will be under no strain if Leo carries her. It will probably boost her morale. Have you known her a long time?"

"Since we were children."

Patrick Harlow touched my arm, and I instinctively looked down at his hand. Tanned, long-fingered, sinewy. "Until Leo arrives, I'm acting as barman. What will you have?"

I chose a Martini & Rossi, and as I lifted the thick tumbler, he raised his to me and for the first time at close range we mutually took stock of one another. What he learned about me, I don't know. All I knew about him was that he had looked at Olivia with loving tenderness and that he was prepared to defend her with a gun. Also that he was a handsome devil.

When Leo's footsteps sounded on the staircase, we automatically moved to the door to provide an impromptu guard of honour. He bore Olivia high in his arms, like a trophy, the pale violet chiffon negligee so fine, so exquisitely embroidered, edged with cobweb lace, that it literally floated like an amethyst cloud on the air: a fairy garment hand-sewn in a couture house that must have cost a fabulous sum; yet Olivia lay between coarse sheets and drank from a cracked cup. Leo, playing to an audience, lifted her higher, and the silver kid slippers, too large for her wasted feet, dropped to the stairs. I picked them up, also a ring that had slid from one of the skeletal fingers: a solitaire diamond as big as an acorn that was a blaze of blue fire in the palm of my hand.

Ceremoniously he eased her into one of the plastic chairs. Mimi produced a rug and wrapped it over her knees, as Olivia gazed about in a dazed rapture that painted a feverish glow on her cheeks. "It's like being readmitted to heaven, like a dream, a beautiful dream."

We were standing round her grinning our pleasure, when a woman garbed in flowing black silk made a stately entrance. She had a heavy bust and broad hips but both were brought into proportion by her regal carriage and the height of her elaborate coiffeur of black satin hair. Her magnolia skin was matt without the faintest blemish, her delicately tinted lips full sculptured, a little pouting either with arrogance or petulance. Her right hand rested on the ivory handle of a stick and she wore dark glasses. But however impaired her sight, I felt her pinpoint my presence from the threshold.

Leo hastened forward to lead her to the patched armchair at the head of the table. He waited until she was comfortably seated before he presented me. "Mama, this is Elizabeth Ashley, an old friend of Olivia's. She is en route to Venice and is paying us a short visit."

She regarded me impassively, not a muscle of her face moving, as she appeared to be deliberating what words were appropriate to welcome me. She settled for the commonplace. "How do you do, Miss Ashley."

Olivia leaned towards the matriarch, who by some divine right took her place at the head of the table. "My dearest friend, Contessa. Almost a sister."

"Indeed!" the Contessa murmured, as though the information could be of no interest to her.

"Champagne!" Leo clicked his fingers like a stage *maître d'hôtel.* "Where's Maidie? Mimi, find her and tell her we're waiting."

"No need to shout. I'm here." Maidie gazed at Olivia, crowed with delight. "Why isn't that a sight for sore eyes! My lovely girl, sitting up!"

"Maidie, the champagne!"

"It's where you left it, dear boy, in the cellar. You've only to carry it up. Those steps do my old knees no good at all."

Leo departed with scant grace.

"Now who's going to give me a hand carrying in the food?" she demanded, placing a bowl of salad on the table. "I'm sorry it's not a feast, as it should have been for Olivia's first meal downstairs, but I'm not one of your cooks that can work miracles with a bowl of rice."

Patrick Harlow put down his glass. "One volunteer coming up."

Olivia pulled at my hand. "Liz, come and sit by me, so that I can really believe you are here. Tell me about Mother Clare. How is she, better or worse?"

I told her, exaggerating the slight improvement a new treatment had effected; added that she sent her dearest love and was longing for news of Olivia.

The smile was so sad, so yearning, so without hope that my heart emptied. "My happiest dreams are about her."

"She dreams of you too." I did not add that they were dark, haunting dreams that lived on into the daylight.

She stared at her wasted hands that were as pale, as deeply veined, as the Carrara marble. "Without her what would have become of me . . ."

The Contessa interrupted peremptorily, her English as carefully enunciated as though it were still a foreign language to her. "It will do no good to dwell on the past, my child. It is the future that is important. That is why you must force yourself to eat. Only food will give you strength, and once you have regained that, your health will return."

Olivia darted an apprehensive glance at the trays being carried by Maidie and Patrick.

Maidie carolled: "It should have been caviar and roast swan, with a syllabub to follow. Instead it's melon and cannelloni, with a nice ripe piece of Brie."

"And champagne!" Leo held two bottles aloft.

We toasted Olivia. She drank thirstily but no more than nibbled the food the Contessa urged upon her. Leo sat at my side. He spoke in a low tone, his voice inaudible to anyone but me. "Suppose you explain why you are en route for Venice."

The dark grey eyes blatantly mocked my deceit. It was an outright challenge, leaving me with two alternatives: to play the role of an innocent guest who had arrived by chance, or to admit Olivia had written to me and demand an explanation for the appalling condition in which I'd found her. But I'd given her my promise, so, in fact, I'd no option but to play along with the Venice lie.

"Does one need an excuse to see Venice?"

"You mean that you're a tripper armed with a bag of corn to feed the pigeons?"

"Feeding the pigeons and visiting a couple of antique dealers for my boss."

"What are their names? I may know them."

I laughed, and saw his face tighten into malevolence. To mortally offend him when I hadn't an inch of sure ground beneath my feet was poor strategy, but, to a degree, irresistible. "Sorry, I can't divulge names. You might be an interested party, a collector, prepared to outbid our offer."

"I forgot that antiques are your trade!"

With every shutter in the room latched, the only illumination came from the crystal chandelier. I glanced up. "That's a magnificent piece. It looks Venetian. Is it?" Deliberately I stared at the metal fork in my hand. Any hard pressure would have bent it.

"My wife is not fittingly housed! That, I assume, is what you are implying."

"It crossed my mind." I sipped the champagne that was served in thick, chain-store tumblers.

His breath exuded hate, so intense that part of its base must surely be fear, so raw and elemental that for a moment it infected me. "In a year's time, if you should by chance visit us, you would have cause to form a different opinion."

"You intend to restore the villa?"

"Yes. Every inch of it."

My amazement was genuine. "It's a mammoth job. It will cost a fortune."

A narrow smile licked his lips as hate gave way to malice. "What leads you to assume I don't possess one?"

"I don't. All I know is that Olivia does, or will do so on her twenty-fifth birthday."

"And every right, don't you agree, to spend it how she chooses?"

"Of course. But ill as she is, I'd have thought her recovery might have been speeded up by a few modest comforts. For instance, a damp-proof bedroom, running hot and cold water, walls that aren't splattered with bullet holes."

Across the table Patrick and Mimi were talking desultorily, with long pauses, like two near-strangers who have little in common. If she had a flaw, I thought, it was a lack of humour in that she never lost consciousness of her supreme importance to herself.

I had spoken too loud. The pressure of their glances switched to me, and that of the Contessa, her eyes veiled behind the tinted glasses. Maidie, head bent, continued to eat, and Olivia sat with one hand pressed to her breast as though to soothe a physical pain.

Leo leaned forward, addressed his wife in a firm voice of sweet reason. "Little one, it seems that Elizabeth is distressed that I am subjecting you to hardship and discomfort that could retard your recovery. I think you should reassure her."

Her glance that she slowly willed to meet his was so appalled, poised on a knife edge of terror, that I was struck with guilt. "Not that," I burst out. "I expressed myself badly. Any house that has been unoccupied for a long period, which I imagine this has, must inevitably suffer from a little damp and . . ."

Leo's voice overrode mine. "Darling, put Elizabeth's mind at rest. Assure her that it was by your wish that we moved into the villa as soon as the legal formalities were completed instead of waiting, as I pleaded with you, for the restoration to be carried out. That was so, wasn't it, *caro?*"

"Yes." It was the tiniest of sounds, barely audible.

"There, I hope you are both reassured." His glance, both vindictive and triumphant, flew to Patrick and back to me. "No coercion, no pressure, not even the gentlest persuasion." He demanded confirmation from Maidie and Mimi. "That is correct, is it not?"

"Olivia couldn't wait to move in," Maidie agreed.

Mimi added hers. "She refused to enter a nursing home, even stay in an hotel while the work was being carried out. She wished only to be in the villa, oversee every stage of the restoration."

The matriarch set her final seal on the argument. "It was Olivia's wish, but naturally we consulted Dr. Spinosa and obtained his approval."

Olivia fainted, her head falling on to the marble, the overturned tumbler spilling champagne over her hair, soaking the long amber strands. Maidie gave a shrill cry, jumped up, while the other three silently went into a course of action so automatic as to suggest they were following a familiar routine.

Leo picked up Olivia, Mimi rescued the slippers, covered the flaccid arms, the stick-legs with a rug, the Contessa rose, dabbed her mouth with a lawn lace-edged handkerchief and, entirely composed, sailed forth at the rear of the cortege that was leaving the room. When the sound of their footsteps mounting the staircase faded, Patrick Harlow and I were alone, facing one another across the marble table.

CHAPTER 3

His glance stayed riveted to the door through which Olivia had been borne, like a dying nymph, his profile clenched in a bone-deep bitterness. I remained imprisoned in shock until my hand accidentally moved a piece of cutlery. The sound touched off an awareness in him of a fact he had temporarily forgotten: my presence.

His first words were evenly balanced between taunt and accusation. "You're hardly the soul of tact, are you, Miss Ashley?"

Under the down-beating light I examined his face. A split second before he spoke, the dead memory cell had flickered into life. I remembered where I had seen him, in what context. It followed that I must absorb from the structure and composition of his features every facet of character they revealed. Indigo eyes, brown-gold lashes. His mouth was mobile, devoid of meanness, but maybe a little overproud. Above all, it was a face that proclaimed its intention of giving nothing away.

I broke the contact, slanted my glance to the far end of the room. In my head I heard the sound of anger rising, gaining momentum, cut it off. "It was the truth."

"Granted." I sensed his wry smile though I refused to acknowledge it. "Also a declaration of war. All your guns firing simultaneously. Not always sound tactics!" A hand reached for my plate. "Why don't you abandon that mess of congealed cannelloni for the Brie?"

Talk of food seemed an unforgiveable irrelevance. I ignored it. "Speaking of guns . . ."

"Ah, yes," he countered, "on that score I plead guilty. I owe you an apology. I'm sorry I scared you."

It was an inadequate apology, tossed off carelessly, as though he'd committed a minor peccadillo. "Not only an apology, an explanation."

"Simple. I needed to discover whether or not Leo kept a revolver under his pillow. He does."

"So you pointed it at me! Why?"

His glance was mildly amused, as though suddenly he had relaxed his guard. "Friend or foe, you could have been either. A spy or a conspirator, an attractive girl who'd sneaked into the villa to cadge a night's lodging. You must see," he pressed, as though I were guilty of obtuseness, "that I couldn't afford to take chances."

I said slowly, enunciating each syllable: "All I'm capable of seeing right now is that Olivia is dying."

He made a factual correction. "She could die."

"In a grandiose hovel, reeking with damp, literally falling apart! What's going on here? What is this place?"

His answer was calm, factual. "A small, very private hell-hole. A hide-out. And if a hide-out is secure those in need of one don't give a damn if it's falling about their ears."

"Why do they need a hide-out?"

A tilted smile tipped one corner of his mouth—a smile I was to learn by heart—as he reached for a half-full bottle of champagne, poured some into a tumbler. "If you won't eat, try a drink. You look as though you need it."

I sipped once, put the tumbler down. "You haven't answered my question."

"Forgive me, but this isn't the time or place; too many eaves-droppers around. How did you find Olivia?"

"She wrote to me, persuaded Maidie to post the letter. Venice was a fiction Olivia dreamed up, presumably because she's terrified of Leo finding out she wrote to me. Why? Why shouldn't she write to me?"

"The key-stone of Leo's strategy is to keep her isolated, incommunicado, unreachable. Letters could breach his defences."

"Then how did you find her?"

"Bribery, though not necessarily corruption."

"Who did you bribe?"

"A youth in Syracuse who was booked on a flight leaving for Chicago precisely thirty minutes after he'd whispered the address to me. It was Aunt Marianne's idea. She has a touching faith in the miraculous power of money, that it will buy you the earth, that is if you happen to covet it."

I was startled. Marianne could surely only be Marianne Carstairs. "Mrs. Carstairs! Do you know her?"

"She's my father's sister. At the moment anxious, extremely apprehensive on Olivia's behalf as it's over eighteen months since she's been able to establish any contact with her. Uncle Hayward is a semi-invalid, mostly confined to a wheel-chair, but her physical and mental energy is unimpaired, especially now she's convinced that Leo is the crook she always suspected him of being and is rarin' for action. But they've retired to his mother's estate, and it isn't too easy for Aunt Marianne to abandon Uncle Hayward and fly to Europe. So, she ordered me to seek and find Olivia. Even with professional help, which I hired, it took a while. The Marianis returned to their home base in Sicily eleven months ago, but by that time I caught up with them, they'd flown and I was at a dead end until I happened on the youth I mentioned."

"When did you arrive here?"

"Ten days ago." He lifted his tumbler of champagne, raised it and beamed a smile of warmth and goodwill directly into my eyes. The effect on me was electric, as though for the first time I was seeing him whole, fully dimensional. In essence it was no more than I was prepared to hand him my trust, but at that moment it seemed an infinitely more valuable gift. "Actually, despite the reception I gave you, I couldn't be more delighted to see you. It means that you can take over and I can move on."

Well, anyone can miscalculate, but my mistake was that I'd allowed myself to be snared by a handsome presence and one beguiling smile. He was neither friend nor ally, but a man who, having fulfilled Mrs. Carstairs' order, was about to duck and run.

"You're bowing out, leaving her to die!"

A blistering anger transformed his face into a different mould. His lips parted fractionally as though he was about to shout, then as I waited, he controlled it, spoke in a carefully enunciated undertone. "Suppose we line up the facts, cut the melodrama. Olivia is a prisoner, watched day and night on a rota system. There is no telephone; no direct postal delivery. Mail is left at the taverna, brought up here, delivered to Leo for his personal scrutiny. I suspect the doctor who attends Olivia isn't a registered doctor but some stooge dressed up to look the part. And God knows what drugs are in the pills they pump into her. No, I'm not proposing to abandon her, merely to arm myself with space to manoeuvre outside what amounts to a fortress, establish a few basic facts that will ensure that Olivia does not die."

He leaned back in his chair, his gaze hooded, his voice implacable. "Does that put you straight?"

Looking at him, my dominant thought was that only a hair's

breadth existed between a passion of anger and a passion of love. It was a simple equation. Patrick Harlow was a man possessed by love otherwise he wouldn't be where he was, self-charged with a mission to save Olivia's life.

"Quite straight."

There was a whisper of silk touching silk, the tip-tap of sandals moving over tiles. From the doorway Mimi's glance by-passed me and focussed with a prim half-smile on Patrick. "Leo has sent me to apologise for your disrupted meal. Unfortunately, when she is excited and overemotional, as she was tonight, Olivia suffers from sudden, and rather alarming, fainting attacks." The speckled gaze, limpid and coolly uninvolved, homed on me. "Your unexpected arrival, pleasant though it was for Olivia, was too much of a strain."

It was a reprimand, but I had no intention of apologising. She was too intelligent to believe my arrival had been a chance one. "How is Olivia now?"

"Her pulse has steadied and she is sleeping. Maidie will be down in a few minutes to make you some coffee." With deft grace she lifted a platter of peaches, put it beside my hand. "Will you excuse me? I have a file of contractors' estimates to check." She ignored me, favoured Patrick with another of her delicate little cat smiles, a queenly half-nod.

On her heels, Maidie bustled in, hair adrift from its bun, the front of her blouse damp. "Oh, you poor dears! What a horrid shock for you. Not to worry. Olivia is sleeping like a baby. As soon as I've recovered my breath I'll make us a nice pot of coffee."

Patrick rose. "Not for me, Maidie, I've an errand to run."

"At this time of night!"

He glanced at his wrist-watch. "Maidie, dear, it's precisely nine o'clock. A little early for my bed-time, don't you agree?"

She scowled at him. "Where are you going?"

"Prowling." Seeing the incensement on her face, he laughed, amended: "In search of some fresh air. I haven't sniffed any since early this morning."

"The door will be bolted . . ."

"Maidie, Maidie!" He touched her shoulder in a gesture of reassurance. "Bars and bolts present no problem. I shall lower one of the front seats and sleep in the car." He gave her a wicked grin. "And stop your fussing. Remember I'm a grown man, not a delinquent to be checked in before dark."

Across the table he wished me a casual good night. For all I knew, it might be good-bye. A man arming himself with ambiguity, secrecy, maybe intending to vanish into the night. Also a man with a mission. His departure left me deflated, without any firm ground beneath my feet.

"It's not," Maidie complained, "that I don't trust him; it's that I'm never quite sure what he's up to. Nice lad, but a bit of a dark horse to my way of thinking. The road's not safe at night, and he knows it. So where is he off to? That's what I'd like to know. It's not as though he's a drinker. Very moderate, all things considered. Maybe he's picked up some girl down in the village." She brooded over her doubts, rubbing her knees. "Give me a minute and then I'll make us some coffee."

"Unless you want some, let's forget it."

She beamed relief. "Actually, I prefer my cup of Horlicks to take up to bed. But I'll . . ."

"No, truly I don't want any."

She sat at ease, her lids drooping, a killing fatigue deepening the lines on her face into runnels. Though it was only nine o'clock it was cruel to keep her from her bed, but there was no one else who could throw any gleam of light on the pitch blackness of my ignorance.

"How long have you been with the Contessa?"

She perked up. "If you're asking me for the story of my life, I think I'll treat myself to my fifth and last cigarette of the day." She took a battered packet of ten from a pocket, extended it to me. "You're very welcome to one."

I said I didn't smoke.

"Sensible child. Not only a wicked waste of money, but it clogs your lungs with tar. Alas, I fell a victim to it so many years ago I can't give it up. An addict!" She gave an unrepentant giggle. "Of course, the Contessa being allergic to nicotine, I can only indulge in my little vice when she isn't around. It's such a relief she's got the visit to the eye specialist behind her. It's all been very worrying." She squinted through the smoke she didn't inhale. "I suppose I'd better start at the beginning. About five or six years after the war it would have been, when Leo was beginning to toddle about on his little fat legs, that Mr. and Mrs. Johnson took the house next door to ours in Cheetham, a superior residential area of Manchester. Very select. Friendly he was from the start, holding up Leo to the fence so that we could have a chat. And very understanding and sympathetic about Daddy. He was an invalid, you see, with a dicky heart and trouble with his legs. Straightaway Mr. Johnson made me promise if

I needed any help I'd to call on him. Of course, I never did, but it was a comfort to know he was there.

"After a while he got round to explaining about his wife, that she was an Italian lady, from Sicily, where he'd met her on holiday. She found it hard to adjust to English ways. The shopping bothered her, and she felt the cold in winter so cruelly that she refused to go out, even with Leo in his little push-chair. And he'd be obliged if sometimes I could slip round and have a chat with her, try to make her feel more at home. Well, with Daddy and a sizeable house to run— right to the end he was a stickler for having everything kept the way it had always been—I hadn't much spare time, but he was such a nice man I was only too happy to help any way I could. You could see that he thought the world of her, worshipped the ground she walked on.

"At first she didn't take to me and I had a rare old job getting a civil word out of her, but gradually we came to understand each other. And when Daddy died, between one sip of whisky and the next, Mr. Johnson was goodness itself. If he'd been my brother he couldn't have been kinder. You see, because of his bad heart, Daddy had retired early, which meant he'd had to eat into his capital, and there wasn't more than a few hundred pounds left. Poor darling, he'd even been obliged to mortgage the house.

"And it wasn't as though I had a profession to fall back on. To keep house, as I'd done since Mummy died when I was sixteen, was all I knew. I was pretty much at my wit's end I can tell you when Mr. Johnson came up with this idea that I should live with him and his Contessa as a companion-help. One of the family. The Contessa had never been one for housework, not being used to it, you see, in her own country where there'd been a flock of servants at her beck and call. What she liked best was to sit doing her embroidery and listen to Italian songs on the gramophone. It suited us all to a tee; never a cross word. And then when Mr. Johnson was taken in an accident on one of his building sites, that's what he was, a masterbuilder, she decided to go back to Sicily, make her home among her own folk. I'll never know why, but she asked me to go with them. I didn't hesitate a tick. I knew it was my one chance in a lifetime to see the world, and I grabbed it. I've never regretted it. They say act in haste, repent at leisure, but it wasn't like that with me. Seeing the world, that's the best thing you can do with your life, that and looking after someone who needs you. The places I've seen, you'd never believe it. Half the capitals of Europe, the U.S.A., South America;

there was one time we went to the Virgin Islands! Imagine! Leo being an only child, naturally mother and son were very close, thought the world of one another. Wherever he went, and his business affairs took him travelling, he never left her behind, or not for long, which meant that I went too. So I'm the lucky one, and don't I know it!"

She blinked, gazed about her, as though it required an act of will to reorientate herself in the present. "Of course, we've got to get this place to rights. I can understand you were a bit shocked at the sight of it, that's why you said what you did. But it will be a palace by the time Leo has finished with it. A palace!" She glared, as though challenging me to contradict her. I had no wish, no energy, to do so.

She yawned, stood up, and I began stacking the crockery for her. But when I offered to carry one of the trays into the kitchen, she would have none of it.

"I don't mind admitting it's a shambles back there. And with you being used to a nice home, it might give you a turn. Cockroaches crawling all over the place! But they don't worry me because we used to be plagued with them in the cellar at home. They're not so bad as they were; Mario brought up some poison the other day and that's killed off three dust-pans full. Do you think you can find your way to your room?"

I assured her I could, said good night, and then as I turned away, she gave a tut-tut of annoyance. "There's me forgetting, mind like a sieve. Would you be sure to keep your shutters latched? Leo's very strict about that; a rule of the house so to speak. We being so isolated, you see, we can't take chances. Gypsies, vagabonds, sneak-thieves, you never know these days, do you? And then there's the mosquitoes and maybe a bat flying in. Filthy creatures, smothered with lice. So you won't forget will you, dear?"

I promised.

I was at the door when her glance focussed on me, suddenly alert, prying, her voice sharp-edged. "Fond of her, are you? Olivia, I mean."

The question caught me by surprise. Fondness was an imprecise word that could be applied to a pet or a bar of chocolate. The emotions that Olivia had triggered off in me were shock, agonising pity, inner chaos and others I couldn't instantly name. "Why, of course I'm fond of her."

There was a tiny pause, then she gave me an admonishing nod. "I know she looks poorly, but there's no need for you to fret. Once the workmen get cracking, she'll pick up. So you run up to bed and have a good night."

Dismissed like a child, told to be a good girl! I was too tired to care.

I ascended the grand staircase into a silence so absolute that I could hear myself breathe. I paused by the door of Olivia's room. Not a whisper of sound, though the keyhole was a minute window of light. Leo with a gun under his pillow keeping watch over a beloved wife, or Leo guarding a fortune that would fall into his lap when Olivia was dead? Fatigue, the aftermath of shock dulled my wits so that contradictory images revolved in my head, like clips of films that cancelled one another out. Hide-outs, bogus doctors, a gun under a pillow . . . The events of the day had stupefied me, destroyed my normal thought processes. I discovered that your eyes could spell out a truth so appalling that your mind rejected it.

The room had absorbed so much of the day's heat it was like an oven. To keep my promise to Maidie would have meant a sleepless night. For ten minutes by my watch I opened the windows, unbarred the shutters, leaned out. No bats, no mosquitoes, only the murmur of cicadas, the wink of fireflies. No moon, the starlight muted, emphasising the blackness of the trees that crept like an encircling tide round the decaying villa, lying in wait for the day when it would dissolve into a heap of rubble which the trees would claim as their own preserve.

When I'd sealed myself in, I counted back. It was nearly seven years since I had hidden behind the hawthorn tree and spied on Patrick Harlow making love to Olivia. A long section of time for passion to endure, but I found nothing odd in the obstinacy of the human heart. I would love David until I died.

I was up and dressed when at eight o'clock Mimi brought me a breakfast tray. I protested that she shouldn't have bothered. I'd have come downstairs.

"As we all have our coffee at different times, it's more convenient this way." Dressed in spanking clean blue jeans and shirt, shining ebony hair tied back in a pony tail, she exuded a refrigerated super-efficiency, plus an air of not having a second to waste—at least on me. Though she spared one to enquire perfunctorily: "I hope you slept well."

I said I had, which was the truth, though at the moment of waking I'd been overthrown by anguish at the tormenting memory of Olivia's near fleshless form being borne from the table.

She also had a parting message, or maybe she counted it an order. Leo wished to see me in the salon after I had finished breakfast.

I sat by the window which, whether or not it was permitted, I'd opened, sipping the tepid instant coffee, nibbling the *biscottos* that were a substitute for toast. In the translucent morning light the original design of the formal gardens was discernible in shadow form. Through giant yews untrimmed for a quarter of a century, and the tapering cypresses, I glimpsed a pool, ghostlike statues of Grecian goddesses, interlaced with brilliant patches of colour where shrubs and plants had been abandoned to make havoc of what had once been a traditional pattern of elegant symmetry.

I found Leo sitting at the head of the marble table, a spread of papers before him. "Ah, Elizabeth. Good morning." He indicated a plastic chair, his manner brisk, purposeful, suggesting a schoolmaster about to address a rebuke or a stern warning to a rebellious pupil, except that the hand-made shoes, fine black wool slacks and a white silk pullover hardly fitted the part.

It pleased his ego to keep me waiting. Eventually, when he had tidied the papers into a neat pile, his opening shot was the one I'd anticipated. "How did you come to possess Olivia's address? Who gave it to you?"

"Her bank in London. When my mother began to fret because it was so long since she'd had news of her, I telephoned them."

"And they supplied you with her address?" The cynical line of his mouth, the snake-eyes accused me of lying, but he could not prove it.

"Yes."

"After I'd issued an order that it was not to be divulged to anyone."

"Why the secrecy?"

He leaned forward, drew a narrow cigar from a case in his hand, lighted it, as though in urgent need of a tiny prop. "Because of the nature of Olivia's illness, which is part physical, part mental, the treatment for which demands that she should be protected from intruders and busybodies. To put it brutally, her fainting attack last night was triggered off by your sudden appearance at her bedside, the effect of which must have been made painfully clear to you."

"It was you who offered to carry her downstairs."

"A request she would never have made if you hadn't walked into the villa uninvited and unannounced. I was, naturally, aware that the effort was beyond her strength, but to have thwarted her wish to make a supreme effort on your account might have had an even worse result. I was called upon to balance one danger against another. Such a position is intolerable."

A single word stuck like a burr in my head. "Could you explain what you mean when you say she is 'mentally' as well as physically ill?"

He extinguished the thin cigar, suggesting he no longer needed its support. For a long moment he gazed at me with a relish I found obscene, as though he were savouring ahead the shock he was about to administer. "That she has made three attempts to end her life."

My reaction was total disbelief; I had to fight hard to suppress the recoil of horror he had pleasurably anticipated, but I succeeded, mouthed a platitude. "She lost the baby. Many women who have lost a child, particularly a first child, suffer from severe depression, even despair."

"Really!" he mocked. "I wouldn't have thought you were sufficiently informed on medical matters to proffer a diagnosis of my wife's illness. An illness that is complex and deep-seated, which, if she is to recover, requires specialised treatment. And, above all, protection from every disturbing element that is liable to subject her to stress. I am not asking for your co-operation. I am demanding it for the reason that I will not permit her life to be put at risk by you. Dr. Spinosa will be visiting her this morning, and until he has examined her and she has rested, you will not be permitted to see her. Have I made myself plain?"

If he could be blunt, so could I. "How did she try to kill herself? You said she had made three attempts."

"Throwing herself from a height. A fortnight ago she managed to reach the gallery where a section of the balustrade was weakened. It was an attempt that came within an ace of success, which is why the balustrade has been securely roped off. She had already made two previous attempts that I find too painful to recall." The deep grey eyes examined my face for a reaction. It was not the one he wanted. "You appear to disbelieve me?"

"If you're speaking the truth she should be under the care not only of a medical practitioner but a psychiatrist. Is she?"

I watched the venom strike his eyes. "My wife's health, what specialists I choose to attend her, do not concern you. The mental imbalance from which she suffers has its roots in the past, a subject I do not propose to discuss with you. Having made the nature of her illness plain, I must warn you that if you attempt to flout my orders, involve her in emotional scenes which drain her strength, inflame her brain, you will not be allowed into her room. Have I made myself plain?"

"Yes." I rose from the chair, tested my legs. Surprisingly they seemed tolerably steady. As I reached the door, he called: "I imagine you know that Harlow proposes to leave us this morning?"

"Yes." Anything more complicated than a one-syllable word was for the moment beyond me.

He added with a sly laugh: "Rather a coincidence, don't you agree, one uninvited guest departing as another uninvited guest arrives? You might call it a take-over!"

He couldn't have expected an answer, and I certainly had none to give him. A man secretly gloating that his wife was out of her mind! Revulsion struck so deep it made me physically sick. Buried deep was a knowledge that I should have challenged him, but instead of standing my ground I'd slunk away. Victory for him, defeat for me. I vowed it would be only a temporary one.

When I rounded the corner into the gallery, I heard a click, glanced over my shoulder. Patrick Harlow was standing with his hand on the porcelain knob of the door of Olivia's bedroom, his face averted, his head bowed in a pose that suggested either indecision or despair. If he'd turned his head slightly to the left he would have seen me, but he did not. The seconds dragged and multiplied, but perhaps they did not add up to as many as I imagined they did as I spied on a man who believed he was alone with himself. With a conscious jerk he drew his tall form upright, walked at speed to the head of the staircase and disappeared.

One task lay inescapably ahead of me: a letter to my mother. Leaving wide spaces between the lines, I winnowed it down to a dozen scrawled sentences that were so innocuous they would not alarm her. I was staying with Olivia; she'd been delighted to see me. She and Leo, with Leo's mother and her English companion, were living in a villa half-way up a mountainside. Olivia sent her dearest love. I'd write again in a couple of days.

Inserting it in the envelope I was struck by a qualm of doubt. My mother had a keenness of perception that on occasions amounted to second-sight. The only event in my life I'd been able to keep from her was David—and death had cheated her of that.

Maidie would probably have a supply of stamps; certainly, Mimi. I

chose not to ask a favour of either, but to drive down to San Giorgio
and buy my own.

Patrick Harlow was leaning against the Jensen, watching me descend the steps that threatened to collapse under the weight of each
foot. When I was within earshot, he said: "Good, there you are! I
was just coming to look for you. We must get ourselves sorted out."

Though he spoke with a brisk purposefulness, I had the feeling I'd
experienced the previous evening, that to him I was someone whom
he saw slightly out of focus. Then, as though he'd blinked and
cleared his vision, he demanded: "Didn't you sleep?"

My reaction was to accept the excuse offered, but I hesitated so
long that he ran out of patience. "What's upset you? Leo?"

"He's been brain-washing me, or attempting to. He swears Olivia
has made three attempts to kill herself."

When he didn't instantly refute the lie, I raged: "She isn't the sui-
cidal type." Again I waited, but the silence between us held. "She's
been ill so long that she's lost hope, is terrified of dying. But if you're
scared of death, you don't kill yourself. And never if you're in love
and loved."

His glance probed mine, warily as though I'd touched a hidden
nerve. "You sound very sure of your theory."

Momentarily I'd forgotten that though I'd seen him with Olivia
in the pavilion, he hadn't been aware of my presence, nor had he
glimpsed his own tell-tale face as she'd been carried unconscious
from the salon. "Do you believe she's a potential suicide?"

He said, picking his words with precision, staring beyond me into
some indefinable mid-distance: "Not while she is in her right mind.
But out of it . . ." His shoulders moved to express doubt. "There
exist hallucinatory states on the borderline of insanity that can be
triggered off by drugs. So the answer is, I don't know." He looked
down at my hand. "You've a letter to post, so why don't we drive
down to the village?"

He guided me towards the Fiat with as much care as though I
were liable to fall flat on my face. "We'll need both cars. Are you
okay to drive?"

When I said yes, he examined my face before he conceded: "All
right, but take it easy."

He parked in the piazza that surrounded the church, and we
walked side by side to the tobacconist on the corner. He waited outside while I bought stamps and then took the letter from me and

dropped it into the post-box. I was grateful for his silence, to be walking as though with a friend in a narrow village street.

"A shot of brandy would do you good."

"I'm fine. No brandy, please. I don't care for it much at any time, and certainly not at ten A.M."

"It's eleven in London, quite a respectable hour for drinking. And brandy's the best morale booster there is. I'm afraid we've no choice of venue. There's only Mario's."

There were four tables outside, split into two groups. All empty. Patrick chose the one farthest from the bead curtain. The man with the physique of a prize-fighter removed some dirty glasses, swabbed down the table. In less than twenty-four hours he could hardly have forgotten me, but the slit eyes between puffy lids betrayed no sign of recognition. Apart from a grunted *buon giorno,* which fleetingly revealed his gold teeth, he did not speak. I decided he was battling with an almighty hang-over.

Choice or no choice, it struck me as highly suspect for us to be seen together. I said so. "You mean Mario will report back to Leo! Naturally. That's his job, petty espionage. If we sat huddled in the car, climbed into the hills, stowed ourselves in a cave he'd still tail us, or order one of his minions to do so. So we may as well make ourselves reasonably comfortable; moreover you need that brandy. All we have to do is to keep our voices low; he speaks some English but doesn't understand as much as he'd have you believe."

"Does he deliver the post to the villa?"

"A youth brings it up, Mario's nephew, the son of an older widowed brother who helps Mario and Rosetta—she's Mario's wife —run the taverna. Leo and Mario are buddies. They have drinking sessions at the villa. Two last week."

When Mario had set the glasses before us, retreated to the far side of the bead curtain, Patrick put the brandy into my hand. "May I suggest not only low voices, but emotions firmly pegged down, otherwise we're beaten before we start. Drink up."

I obeyed, suspecting he needed to apply the stricture to himself as much as to me. As the brandy slipped down in trickles of fire, I looked across the street where, in a shadow-filled courtyard, women bending over a giant trough filled with water gushing from a pipe were washing clothes by beating them against the stones. It could have been a biblical scene except that each woman was armed with a giant-sized pack of detergent.

His enquiring glance was spiked with impatience. "Any improvement?"

"Yes." Conscious of the stress and impatience riding him, of words, maybe pleas, building up inside him, I asked: "Where are you moving to, an hotel?"

"No, to a base that should provide more privacy than an hotel. Behind Caromezza there is a warren of small houses climbing the foothills, literally piled on top of each other. They were little better than hovels until some enterprising developer recognised their potential, did them up and sold them as miniature villas to a higher income bracket. There's a honeycomb of them, connected by winding alleys that twist like goat-tracks. Very picturesque; more important, as the walls are solid rock there is no risk of eavesdroppers, and without a high degree of technical expertise telephones can't be tapped. Enquiring around I ran to earth the owner of one, an artist, who is off to Jugoslavia for a month. He wasn't keen on letting it, but I applied a little pressure and last night he agreed. I move in later today."

"What writers of spy stories call a safe house!"

"But then we're not writers of fiction, are we! We're concerned with live flesh and blood, in the removal of Olivia from a hell-hole to somewhere she'll receive the expert medical care she needs if she is to remain alive."

He was right. I deserved the reprimand. All the same, with Leo's image firm in my mind's eye, I wondered if he was not indulging himself in the belief that the task he'd set himself was relatively simple to accomplish.

As though he'd caught a whiff of my scepticism, he went on: "Oh, I admit it would be child's play for any interested party to track me to the door, though they'd be unlikely to get beyond it. The owner possesses what, rightly or wrongly, he believes is a Picasso. To protect his treasure he has spent a small fortune on burglar-proof locks, grills on all the windows."

The bead curtain rattled but no one emerged. Even so, I lowered my voice to a near whisper. "But *how* do you propose removing Olivia from the villa?"

He by-passed the question, either that or he hadn't heard it. His words were so muted, he appeared to be speaking to himself. "We're like a couple of theatre-goers who've missed the first act, come in half-way through the second, desperately trying to sort out the plot." His glance raked my face for a reaction. So far as I knew there wasn't one. My emotions were as firmly pegged down as he could have wished.

"So, we have to make-do with the few hard facts we possess, act on them. Olivia desperately ill, a prisoner in a villa crumbling about her ears, subjected to third-rate medical care, maybe treated with drugs that will kill her; or just as likely with worthless placebos made up of sugar and paste. We have Leo, the nature of the man, with an insatiable greed for wealth, bedazzled by a vision of himself as a millionaire tycoon. A would-be Midas without the magic touch, in that everything turns not to gold but to debts. A chronic absconder of debts, essentially a lone wolf. That's been his life-style from his late teens. You could say it all adds up to an imbalance of the mind if not outright insanity. He'd pull the whole world about his ears rather than relinquish his dream of riches and power.

"Then we have Uncle Hayward. Two years ago, before he developed Parkinson's disease, he discovered that not only was Olivia consistently drawing her allowance months ahead of time, but using the trust as a guarantee for substantial loans. Nothing illegal there, except that Uncle Hayward, who in those days had his ear pretty close to the ground, found that the loans were being negotiated through a shady finance company that demanded an extortionate rate of interest. With the idea of protecting Olivia, he employed a private agent to investigate Leo's activities. By the time the investigator had caught up with him, the capital he had borrowed and invested in a quasi mineral company was a worthless heap of share certificates. He'd been played for a sucker by a gang of professional sharks who'd filled their pockets at the expense of a financial ignoramus who'd accounted himself a genius at playing the stock market. In fact, Leo's business acumen is nil; I doubt if he possesses the know-how to balance the books of a newsagent. The venue for that particular disaster was Argentina. Hounded by debt-collectors, Leo moved on to Caracas where, robbed of his get-rich-quick dream, he became involved in some highly suspect deals, most of which failed. Where money is concerned, he certainly has a death-touch. One was linked with a gun-running racket. The authorities picked him up and, along with Olivia, his mother and Maidie, discreetly deported him. From there on the investigator lost track of him; also Uncle Hayward became too ill to pursue the search for Olivia."

"If they were deported, Olivia must have known the reason, that Leo was a criminal?"

Now it was he who stared at the washer-woman on the far side of the street. "Where Olivia's concerned, Leo possesses a silver tongue, near miraculous powers of persuasion. Probably as related by him to her it emerged as a story of unwarranted victimisation. I haven't a clue how much she knows, or chooses to know. She may have deliberately schooled herself to a blindness to facts she prefers not to admit." He moved his head, and his indigo glance looked straight into mine. There was a glint of cynicism in it and, unless I imagined it, a shadow that suggested he found the cynicism painful. Then a corner of his mouth tilted, either in amusement or self-derision. "If they're all in a flap, you can't blame them! With a fortune in their sights, it's an awkward moment for a nephew of Olivia's trustee and a proxy sister to appear on the scene."

The implications were so far beyond the depths a normal mind could plumb that I side-stepped them, concentrated on a practical issue. "If Leo is penniless, how could he buy the villa?"

"I doubt if he did. I've some evidence, though not sufficient, that the villa is owned by a syndicate who are hatching plans they have no wish, at this stage, to divulge to the public: to transform it into a luxury hotel and sports complex. It may be that Leo scraped up sufficient cash to obtain a short-term lease, but I've no positive proof. To obtain that I have to run to earth an Italian English-speaking lawyer who's willing to do a bit of devilling. I'm on the track of one and, with luck, I'll see him tomorrow.

"The private eye Uncle Hayward hired has since died, but his records exist, and one man, Lewis, who did some leg work for him, is familiar with the case. He's been in Sicily for the last five days. So far he hasn't come up with an answer as to why Leo, with a sick wife, mother, Maidie and Mimi in train vanished overnight, abandoning all their possessions, except those they could load on to a plane. But he's a bright lad and won't drag his heels."

He looked at me with a spice of pleasure, as though in his mind the future had brightened. "We've got the underpinnings of a good case. First the pills, to locate a pharmacist who is willing to analyse them, prove they are either harmless tranquillisers or, what I suspect, drugs that keep her doped, depress her appetite and confuse her mentally. In other words, slow poison. That's where you take over."

I whispered, appalled: "A doctor who poisons his patient!"

"*If* Spinosa is a bona-fide doctor. From the evidence to date he's either a doctor without a telephone, or he practises under a false name."

I was lost; he had zoomed beyond the reach of my imagination.

For a second I wondered if he was mad. A futile question that cancelled itself out. All love is reckless; most has an element of madness. "You're accusing Leo of murdering Olivia for her money? But why should he? In a couple of weeks it'll be hers, she'll be rich. . . ." My voice dried. He possessed eyes, a high degree of intelligence. He had observed the pitiful little skeleton on the bed, been a witness as Leo bore her downstairs, heard her whispered loving gratitude as he settled her in the chair. I did not have to spell out that Olivia's response to her husband was nearer to love than hate.

"Rich indeed! So why should she choose to hand over a fortune to a husband who, she must realise by now, will squander the lot. As for murder, you don't have to administer poison. You can commit it by neglect with far less risk of paying the penalty."

"That would mean that Leo's mother, Mimi, that Maidie . . ."

He interrupted. "Not Maidie. Her only crime is that she's been brain-washed. In her eyes Leo is still the little boy from next door to be alternately petted and scolded. Mimi and the phoney Contessa? Maybe innocent, maybe not. They're not important except as gaolers. Leo's our quarry. A man who stands to inherit a fortune from a dead wife."

Suspended between belief and disbelief, I marvelled that it never crossed his mind that Olivia might be willing to make Leo a present of her fortune if he spent it on creating the dream villa she coveted. I didn't know. But then neither did he. He was committing himself to a gamble loaded with risk.

He leaned forward, bent his face closer to mine. "It's becoming a habit, my apologising to you. But I'm sorry if I threw you in at the deep end, took it for granted we were moving along parallel lines— that what has become apparent to me in ten days had become so to you in a few hours. Forgive me. Perhaps in such a situation one is guilty of overplaying the drama."

"In this case, is that possible?"

"For me, no. For you, maybe yes. Your eyes are misted with doubt."

"Female caution. And shock!"

His smile was warm, genuinely contrite. The sliver of ice that was fast closing over my heart melted. In a black hour a gesture of friendship was like an unexpected gift. In the dark, villainous world he depicted, I treasured it.

His conscience salved, confidence restored, he reverted to practical issues. "There are three bottles of pills. I need two pills from each for the pharmacist. I don't see any way you can obtain a sample of the medicine."

"You're asking me to steal samples of the pills?"

"Well, there's no one else," he said reasonably.

In that moment I was not sure whether he was a man whose nature it was to demand the impossible, or whether he was blithely passing over to me a task he'd failed. "Yesterday afternoon, when Maidie was out of the room and you were alone with Olivia, why didn't you help yourself to the pills then?"

"Too risky. Olivia drowsed for only a few seconds at a time."

Yet he'd found time to burrow under a pillow for a gun.

"But not risky for me?"

A touch of devil-like humour swept his mouth. "Girls are neater, more dexterous, have a lighter touch with small objects, like pill bottles with snap-tops, than men. Take shop-lifting. Women have a monopoly of the game. How often do you read of a man being hauled before a magistrate for helping himself to a bottle of after-shave?" He switched subjects. "What do you do for a living?"

"Work in an antique gallery in London."

"There you are!" His smile was a beguiling flash of triumph. "That must call for ingenuity, finesse, split-second decisions, and you have an air about you of extreme competence."

"A compliment?"

"No," he said briskly. "I wish we'd time for them. You deserve them. But we haven't. Are you prepared to have a go?"

I saw the dimmed room, Olivia drifting in and out of sleep, if sleep it was, the watching eyes of the guards, the position of the table. The task he'd set me demanded not only ingenuity but a magician's sleight of hand which I didn't possess. I found myself resenting his tendency to bulldoze his way through obstacles, or alternatively persuade himself they didn't exist.

For the first time he used the name by which Olivia, friends of my own generation and David called me. "Liz, we have to take chances, otherwise we might as well pack up."

The plea was so free from reserve, so full-hearted, that its basis could only be love. I kept my face angled away from him, scared that I would see on it the expression I'd spied on from behind the hawthorn tree on the common. With one finger he turned my chin towards him. No love was visible; then he'd had years to practise keeping it under a mask. "Would you prefer to bow out?"

"No. Of course not. But my fingers don't happen to be particularly dexterous. Neither are they neat. Any button I sew on invariably falls off next day."

His answering smile was the first carefree one I'd seen cross his face. "I'll remember."

It struck me as a remark curiously out of context, but I did not challenge it. "All right, I'll try. But don't expect me to guarantee the result."

"Bless you!" He leaned back in his chair, as though he was exhausted and, his battle won, silence was the only restorative.

By now the village street that had been deserted and shuttered in yesterday afternoon's heat had come to teeming life. Women, the old dressed in black with dark kerchiefs covering their hair, the young in short, bright cottons, were shopping, gathered in knots to gossip or just leaning over their balconies calling to one another.

My lack-lustre gaze was captured by an old woman, spindle-thin, bowed at the shoulders, who with extreme care was manipulating a perambulator across a gutter on the opposite side of the street. Boat-shaped, the navy coachwork polished to a high gloss that would have been a common enough sight in Kensington Gardens, the pram stood out in an Italian village street like a strutting peacock among a flock of sparrows. The hood was lowered, the baby propped high against a snow-white pillow-case with goffered frills, protected from the sun by a canopy edged with lace from which was suspended a silver rattle. All that was needed to complete the picture was a grey-coated nannie in a severe felt hat balanced on a bun.

"What's caught your eye?"

"That baby, being paraded in state round the village in a sort of Royal Progress."

He looked baffled. "What's remarkable about a baby in a pram?"

"Not the baby, the pram. Modern mums tuck their kids into fold-up canvas go-carts. That one must be some kind of status symbol. Look how all the women are clustering round it."

"Some proud grannie. Its daddy probably bought it second-hand from tourists who were forced to fly home in a hurry. Anyway, does it matter?"

"No." I was guilty of using the baby who travelled in royal style as a momentary escape from the nightmare of reality. "What happens if I fall down on the job, don't get the pills?"

"You will. But even if you get caught in the act, you've got a ready-made excuse. Women aren't only nimbler with their fingers, they're naturally curious. Nine out of ten presented with an array of pill bottles will examine the labels. That's what you must appear to be doing, picking up the odd one. Then if you're seen, you'll have an alibi. Actually the names of the pills aren't on the bottles, but you're not to know that. The best time is when Maidie is on duty in the afternoon from around two-thirty to four. The phoney Contessa is taking her siesta and Mimi either sunbathes or drives down to the village for supplies."

"And Leo?"

"Oh, he's around. The only occasion he left the villa while I was there was to drive his mother to Milan to the eye specialist. My guess would be that he, like her, takes a nap. And Maidie, fortunately, is apt to drop off into forty winks. But she's a light sleeper, wakes suddenly, ready to leap into action. So be on the alert."

The beads rattled, parted, and Mario ambled over to our table. By now the hang-over was easing and he split a golden-toothed smile between us.

We walked down the street to the piazza. As Patrick held open the door of the Fiat his voice was uncharacteristically tentative. "I realise it's tricky filching the sample pills. But they are crucial evidence. Can you think up any other way of laying our hands on them?"

I felt his height bearing down on me, a head taller than my five feet four; also his throbbing anxiety, that rage of impatience, and wondered if his suspicions were correct, that there might be no way out for Olivia. That Leo might beat him on time.

"No. I'll do my best, but please don't take success for granted."

"I won't." He reached into the pocket of his linen shirt, handed me an envelope. "Inside there is a sketch map. The house is 10, via Rosabella. The alleys, too narrow for cars, form a sort of pedestrain precinct. The best car-park is in the centre of the town behind the Excelsior Hotel. Cross the main square, follow the shopping arcades, and on your right you'll see a street of steps, the via Donatello. Follow the route I've marked. It looks complicated, but actually it's not."

I took the map from him. "When shall I come?"

"I suggest the day after tomorrow, around three o'clock. That gives two chances at the pills. If for any reason you can't make it, I've jotted down the telephone number." He felt in his pocket a second time. "Here's the key—in case I shouldn't be there when you arrive. Go in and wait; I'll make sure not to be away long."

For the first time his glance hung on me with total concentration.

"And for God's sake play it cool. Don't under-rate any of them. Promise?"

I promised, turned on the ignition. In the rear mirror I saw his tall, lean form, standing immobile against the background of reverent shawled women who dipped their fingers in the stoup of holy water before they disappeared into the twilight of the church, watching me until I was out of sight. Praying that his trust was not misplaced, that my nerve would not fail, that my fingers would, for once, prove nimble!

I recalled how he'd deliberately evaded answering my question as to how he proposed to rescue Olivia. Why? Because he didn't trust me, or because he fiercely rejected a fact I believed to be true: that Olivia retained some remnants of love for her husband; alternatively was by some mystical alchemy bound to him, her will rendered powerless. The word "hypnotism" flared in my mind. In the heightened state of my imagination I did not toss it out.

Below the make-shift parking place a small black car passed me. The driver was so short in stature that only his head appeared above the steering-wheel. He drove with exaggerated caution, nervously jamming on the brake when he passed me. Elderly, with a pointed grey beard, a wide-brimmed black hat a size too large that hid the upper half of his face.

Leo, who had seen me drive in, remained poised on the bottom of the steps; his expression, now he had established authority over me, was a mixture of self-congratulation and condescension. "You will be delighted to hear that Dr. Spinosa has examined Olivia and pronounces that, physically, she has gained a little strength since his visit last week." He reshaped his features into husbandly concern. "But her mental state still gives rise to considerable anxiety. Alas, it takes longer for the brain to heal than the body."

There is no visible mark upon a human being's face that proclaims him capable of murder. Leo's eyes, though chill and merciless as an Arctic sea, were no more so than some others. Yet, as he followed at my heels up the crumbling zig-zag steps, conviction was born, not of the mind but of the senses, that if I stumbled and he made contact with my flesh to haul me to my feet, I would scream as though touched by the devil.

In the hall he announced with an air of beneficence that repelled me: "You may see Olivia this afternoon, at three when she is rested. But only on the terms we agreed this morning, that you will on no account excite her, or subject her to the slightest stress. Have I your word?"

I gave it to him as meekly as though I were an obedient child. Playing it cool, as Patrick had ordered. As I mounted the flying staircase to my room, conscious of his eyes following me, the knowledge hardened that I had committed myself to a role in a macabre duel of wits between Leo and a man of obstinate passion whose heart, after all these years, still belonged to Olivia.

CHAPTER 4

Olivia held out the stick-arms as visual proof she was stronger. "I'm ashamed about last night. But it was only a faint, over in a minute."

There were fever spots of colour on her hollowed-out cheekbones, but her voice was a little steadier, not so husky. "In a week or two I'll be dancing up and down stairs." The pale heliotrope eyes between their darkened lids challenged me to disagree, but it was Maidie who answered.

"Of course you will, lovie. As soon as Dr. Spinosa gives the word." Sitting on the far side of the bed darning a hole in the sleeve of a raggy cardigan, she divided a bracing smile between us.

The shutters of the three windows at the front of the villa were latched. One on the east side was slightly parted to admit a wedge of light into the room, remove a little staleness from the air. I chose one of the plastic chairs beside the table laden with pill and medicine bottles, as Olivia gestured at some sheets of thick drawing paper spread across the bed.

"The architect's plans for the villa. I borrowed them from Leo to show you." With the fever spots spreading across her cheeks, she handed them to me one by one. Not architectural plans drawn to scale but amateurish line and wash impressions. With a wild inventiveness the artist had transformed Olivia's bedroom into a courtesan's boudoir, with swags of tasselled curtains, a lacquer bed, Louis XV armoires, occasional tables piled with bibelots, a hideous modern dressing-table with a triple mirror and alongside it what appeared to be a polar-bear skin rug, on which was sketched a small long-haired dog. They were so patently the work of an amateur I wondered if Leo was the artist.

She pointed to the dog. "My Pekinese-to-be, a gentleman from China, only he's too dark. I want a pale biscuit puppy, a little sleeve-dog. Maybe I'll have two."

"Oh, I wouldn't recommend that, dear." With a snap of her teeth Maidie severed a strand of wool. "They can be snappy little beasts. And the Contessa wouldn't take kindly to a dog nipping at her ankles, and certainly not two of them. Besides, she might fall over the little brute."

Olivia chose not to hear. I was completely in the dark as to her relationship with her mother-in-law. The Contessa had been my sole companion at lunch. Various odd remnants of past meals, all equally unappetising, were dotted about the marble table for anyone to help themselves. Her manner towards me was one of overbearing condescension: heavy silences interspersed with pontifical statements, designed to convey to me in manner if not in words that I came well below her on the social ladder. She was a hearty but slow eater, seeming, unbelievably, to relish the limp salad, rings of shrivelled dried sausage and stale cheese. With her eyes masked behind the tinted spectacles, when I rose from the table I had learnt no more than three facts: that she resented my presence in the villa, was anxious to learn when I proposed to depart for Venice and was the doting mother of an only son, exuding pride on every occasion she could find an excuse to speak his name.

Olivia passed me a succession of the line and wash sketches: of a bathroom with a sunken tub, gold lion-head fittings; of a salon which bore not the faintest resemblance, even in dimensions, to the one in which I'd eaten lunch. The last two were of an *orangerie* that reminded me of old pictures I'd seen of the Crystal Palace, and the Italian garden restored to perfection with clipped topiary, silver pools, slender cypresses, high-spurting fountains and an army of statues.

"Now you don't have to use your imagination. That is how it will be. Liz, it will."

I looked up, at a loss for words to describe my reaction to an elaborate piece of fiction, but anxious to soothe her, and met a look that was a desperate plea to believe the evidence she'd laid before me. By reaching for some last remnant of strength all her senses had come vibrantly alive; for the first time since I'd arrived at the villa I was staring at the real Olivia. In a few seconds the image faded, as if she'd taken refuge behind a cloud.

"It's marvellous. Beautiful, all of it." Shaken by the poignancy of that second-long demand for absolute truth, conscious of Maidie's listening ears, words became treacherous. I edged away from them. "What's the history of the villa? Whom did it belong to originally?"

The emaciated face was listless now, uncaring. "Leo did tell me, but I've forgotten. Maidie, do you remember?"

"Odds and ends; it's all so far back I'm a bit hazy. Apparently

until the war it was owned by the Fossita family. Towards the end
the Germans over-ran and looted it. Apart from the marchesa and
her grandson and one old servant, there was no one about to stop
them. They shot the boy and the marchesa died of a heart attack.
Well, you can't wonder, poor soul! I can't remember what became of
the old servant; maybe she got away, maybe she didn't, who's to
know? Anyway, it's ancient history now. After the war there were
years of bickering, as there always is among heirs, as to which one
had a right to the villa. Who won I don't know, but years later it
was patched up and used as a convalescent home because the air's so
marvellous. But something went wrong, maybe it was too isolated,
and they moved the patients away. It had been empty for years when
Leo found it . . ."

With a renewed flicker of hope in her castle in the air, Olivia
picked up the final threads of the story. "Leo took pictures of it for
me, and I fell in love with it." This time she didn't look at me. "The
builders will be moving in any day now. A whole army of them." She
gave Maidie a wan smile. "And we'll stop travelling, hopping all over
the globe. You'll enjoy that, won't you, Maidie, to be settled down?"

"I'll run the flag up the day the builders move out and leave
behind a nice fridg and a washing machine. You can keep your
orangeries, though I grant you they're very pretty."

Soon after that Maidie's chin dropped and her needle went still.

Olivia fretted: "Patrick's gone. I begged and begged him to stay,
but I knew he wouldn't because of Leo. He can't bear to have anyone see the villa as it is now. Pride; all Sicilians are prickly with it. If
he seemed not very welcoming to you, that was the reason." Her
voice began to tremble. "You mustn't be upset. I want you here. Liz,
you've got to stay. Please."

"Don't worry. I will. Maybe Patrick will come back."

She nodded, the curve of a little smile coming to her lips. "He's
special, very special." She lay relaxed, removed from the present to
another place, another time.

"What does he do, for a living I mean?"

"He owns a printing works in Norfolk. It's been in the family for
generations. They run a newspaper too." A ghost of a laugh sounded
in her throat. "A printer and newspaper proprietor! It's so dreary I
tease him about it. But he says it allows him to be his own man and
that's important to him. In his spare time he goes off climbing. He's
crazy about mountains."

If I couldn't visualize him as the proprietor of a printing works and a local newspaper, I could see him roped, slung about with a climber's impedimenta, ice-axe in hand, scaling a mountain. Going a little too fast, a lock of sable hair escaping from a bright woolly cap. Olivia's hands reached out, clutched mine. "Liz, you won't leave me, will you. I get so frightened. Liz, please!"

For the second time I promised. I glanced at Maidie. Though it was impossible to be certain, her sleep appeared to be deepening. I took the risk that was like throwing myself overboard, leaned close to Olivia, reduced my voice to a whisper. "Olivia, what frightens you? Can't you tell me?"

"I don't know." Terror drained the last pigment of colour from her eyes, turned them silver; her voice was wispy, breathless. "Except that I've believed for so long I was going to die, ever since I lost the baby, I can't not believe it. I fall asleep afraid; I wake up afraid. I think I'm going blind or that I can't move, that I'm paralysed." She shut her eyes tight as though to shut out the horror. "It's like some foul disease in my head, as though someone somewhere is willing me to die, like natives who make a wax doll of someone they hate, and stick pins in it. But no one wants me to die. They couldn't . . ."

I tried to soothe her, coax her out of the traumas of fear. I swore that as soon as she was stronger the nightmares would dissolve, disappear forever.

"Will they?" She was avid for reassurance, but her energy was running down to vanishing point. Now she had to gasp for breath between sentences. "Still the same old Liz . . . always knew what she wanted and made a bee-line for it. Never blown off course."

To see oneself in someone else's eyes is like being shown a picture of a stranger, unrecognisable, bearing no relation to the image that faces you in a mirror, because the inner thought patterns are secreted away. The Liz Olivia had known had been before David, before love had swept in a tumult through mind and body, transforming me into a different being. I found it incredible that she detected not even the faintest shadow of change in me. "Ugh, what a horrid little prig I sound!"

She made a fumbling motion of denial with her head, then fell asleep with one hand on the folder of crude sketches, as though guarding something infinitely precious.

Her sleep was shallow, Maidie's no more than a doze out of which the first flick of consciousness would jerk her wide awake. I sat absolutely still, my eyes moving from one to the other. I told myself that

I didn't have to perform the conjuring trick today; I could postpone it until tomorrow. But could I count on them both falling asleep simultaneously two afternoons running?

I was racked by a fever of indecision, at the mercy of conflicting emotions: hate for Leo; confusion as to the role Maidie played. Patrick living in what might prove to be no more than a mirage of blazing hope.

I stared at my hands: short-fingered, incapable of the simplest act of *léger de main*. I heard the ghost of Patrick's voice, cajoling, begging and finally metaphorically going down on his knees. I looked at Olivia's claw hand guarding a clutch of illustrated lies. Damn him, I thought with a spurt of rage, he made it sound so easy when in fact it was like walking a tight-rope stretched across a chasm, the penalty for failure, banishment.

First, I slid the two paper-backs into a slightly different position, topped them with the water glass, fractionally edged the jug nearer to provide me with a tiny rampart behind which my fingers could manoeuvre unseen. Three bottles of pills: one white, one yellow, one blue. I poised my finger and thumb over the blue, lifted it. When it lay clenched in my fist I darted a glance at Olivia, who scarcely seemed to breathe, then at Maidie, who gave one of the little snuffling sounds she made at intervals. Suddenly a spasm jerked her head upright. For a second, I swear her eyes opened and we stared at one another as my heart beat in great bounds of panic like that of a wild animal that has been run to earth. Then, as if she lacked all power over them, her eyelids dropped like a doll's. And the rhythmic sequence of snuffles-snores became audible. The plastic stopper was tight, and when I managed to prise it off, I misjudged the tilt and two of the pills fell on the floor, rolled under the bed with a minute sound that my ears distorted into a machine-gun rattle. When I'd recovered them, replaced the cap, secreted two in a tissue, sweat literally burst through my skin: my fingertips were slippery, and the sound of my heart-beats was louder in my ears than Maidie's snuffles. I had extracted two from the second bottle and had the third bottle concealed in the palm of my hand when, on an instant, Maidie became fully awake, alert, complaining at herself: "All this sneezing in the afternoon does me no good at all." She bent over Olivia, studied the waxen face. Olivia's sleep was broken by Maidie's breath on her cheek. Her lids flew wide, and her half-deranged eyes fastened on me. "Where am I? What's happening?" Then she gave a shuddering sigh. "Oh, Liz. I dreamed you were only a dream." The hand that was nearest to me reached out to cling to mine that was wrapped around the third bottle of pills.

With my free hand I stroked her brow, eased back the clotted hair, until the rigidity of terror loosened its hold. She looked at Maidie, whimpered: "Where's Leo? Why isn't he here?"

"He's working on his papers, getting everything put to rights."

"Papers? What papers? I can't remember."

"You will, love. Have another little nap and when you wake Leo will be sitting beside you like he always does."

Olivia moved her head in denial. "I don't want to sleep anymore." But she did, instantly.

Across the width of the bed I saw Maidie examine the little rampart I'd erected. Casually, with fingers that by some miracle were steady, I lifted the glass, sipped from it half an inch of water, returned it to its place and picked up one of the paper-backs. It was Ian Fleming's *Goldfinger*. I read the opening sentences under Maidie's watching eye. I could not tell, without challenging it, whether or not it was spiked with suspicion.

With my head bent over the paper-back, I heard her retreat to the half-open window. She moved the chair so that it faced Olivia's bed, putting me directly in her line of vision. Did she know the bottle was hidden in my fist, or was it guilt that transformed me into a shaking coward? I hunched over my shoulders, leaned towards Olivia's bed and, below the level of Maidie's sight, eased a length of the cotton counterpane into a deep fold, struggling to control the panic that turned my hands into clumsy, unresponsive lumps of boneless dough, prepared for Maidie to cross the room and gaoler-fashion clamp an accusing hand on my shoulder. I prised the stopper off with my thumbnail, dribbled two pills into the tissue, restoppered the bottle, leaned back in my chair, dabbed my nose with the tissue and tucked it into the pocket of my shirt. But without knowing whether or not Maidie had witnessed my pilfering, was biding her time, my dead wits refused to suggest any sleight of hand whereby I could return the bottle to the table without her seeing.

The only sound in the room was a whisper as I turned, at what I judged were appropriate intervals, the unread pages of the paper-back. It was twenty minutes by my watch before Maidie rose.

She folded up the cardigan she'd been darning, hung it over the back of the chair, affording me a second's flash of time to return the bottle to the table. As though intent on torturing me she walked over to the bedside, examined each individual bottle and phial. She didn't speak; maybe she doubted the evidence of her own eyes; maybe she felt guilty about the nap. When she spoke it was in a tarter voice than any I'd heard her use. "That table needs a duster over it, and a tidy-up. I'll see to it after tea."

And then, her eyes casting themselves in my direction every few seconds, she waited until Leo and the Contessa came into the room.

Neither of them acknowledged my presence as, with Leo's steps matched to hers, they approached Olivia's bed. I moved away. Olivia, awake again, gazed mutely at her mother-in-law, her face waxen, like a doll's. The Contessa bent, held the two hollow cheeks between the thick palms of her hands, spoke to her in Sicilian, then glancing in my direction, announced: "To have received such a good report on Olivia from Dr. Spinosa makes this a very happy day for us all."

Leo murmured something, bent and kissed his wife with lingering fondness. "Darling," she whispered, "part of the reason why I'm better is because Liz is here."

"Yes, *amore mio*, of course," he said in the soothing tone one uses to a small child.

Except that Patrick was absent, tea was a repetition of the previous day's drab ritual. Maidie chatted nonstop, fulfilling her role of half-privileged retainer, half family friend, so that it became monstrous to suspect her of playing a part in the foulest of foul play.

She had unearthed some dried fruit that she'd mislaid, and made a cake. The Contessa assured me that Maidie was an excellent baker and pressed me to accept a second slice, which I refused, and to which she helped herself.

Maidie emitted a derisive snort. "Any Lancashire woman would be downright ashamed of herself if she couldn't bake a decent cake. Though I was a bit short on eggs."

Leo murmured: "Mimi will be bringing you all the provisions you need. If you omitted any items from your list you have only yourself to blame."

"Oh, I wouldn't be too sure about that," she retorted, refusing to be brow-beaten. "It's been known for Mimi to mislay her shopping list before she's half-way to the village."

"Since we have a guest I'm sure on this occasion she will take care not to lose it."

Olivia twisted her fingers together, pleaded: "Darling, do you two have to bicker, even in fun? Look, I've been showing Liz the architect's plans."

He glanced vaguely in my direction. "What did you think of them?"

"Most impressive. How long do you estimate the restoration work will take?"

He made an airy gesture. "Before the workmen move in the fabric must be subjected to extensive chemical tests. It would be inviting disaster to pull down or rebuild until these tests have been analysed. A few weeks, no more, and the preliminary work will begin."

"All I'm praying," Maidie interrupted, "is that they start on the kitchen—that's the heart of the house to any sensible woman. There's mornings when I think I can't face that horrible sink another day. It's not even hygienic."

"I promised you the kitchen quarters should be the first priority. Don't you remember?"

She gave him a dead-pan look, waited until the silence between them conveyed what she wished to communicate, and then announced: "There's nothing wrong with my memory."

I wondered whether they'd played out a little charade specially for my benefit, each supporting the other, and doubted it if only because I desperately needed Maidie to be guileless and innocent, with a heart that loved Olivia.

As soon as I could I made my excuses and left. I skirted the villa, crossed the terrace with its smashed flagstones, edged my feet down a flight of broken steps and entered a wilderness. Yews that had moulded themselves into towering, sprawling hedges. Fallen trees, their trunks rotting. Roses being stifled to death in weeds and saplings, clumps of dried grasses that reared above my head. Cushions of moss, ant-hills and a rectangular pool of scum. Some of the statues were headless, others sprawled like dead bodies in the undergrowth. One was pitted with bullet holes, several in each bulging breast, suggesting she had been used for target practise. Vandalism gone mad, which left a stench of mindless violence on the sunburned air. Beyond a second flight of steps I could see ghostlike traces of terracing; there were even a few unpruned vines, and to my left a silver shimmer of olives. Then nothing but the rising foothills, the trees growing sparser until the bare limestone of the mountains refused them a foothold. Unless you took to the hill-tracks the villa marked a dead end. Protected from the rear, as a hide-out should be.

I retraced my steps by a different route, past a waterfall that trickled down a miniature cliff-face. At its base was a grotto where a tiny virgin smiled down at a baby draped in slime cradled in her arms.

Only the lizards that feigned death at my feet were alive, and an occasional swooping bird. Would bulldozers, an army of skilled men restore it to its former symmetry with silver pools, tapering cypresses? Was there a process guaranteed to mend bullet holes in marble, reunite smashed heads with bodies? Would Olivia ever walk in a garden that would be a three-dimensional replica of the line and wash drawings she handed me? My belief would not stretch that far; not even as far as Maidie's modern kitchen.

As I rounded the corner of the villa, I saw Mimi carrying two heavy straw baskets up the zig-zag stairway. I ran down and took one from her. Perhaps because she resented the chore of domestic shopping, she appeared less coolly self-possessed than usual. There was a fine beading of perspiration on her high brow, and her mouth was a thin, tucked-in line.

"You've scratched your arm," she said, as though the ugly, bleeding line afforded her satisfaction.

"I've been exploring the gardens, comparing the before and after version of the architect's sketches."

Her curious speckled eyes gave me a sideways glance. "One day they'll match up."

It was the sideways glance that tripped her on a jagged step, threw her forward. A package resting on top of an assortment of groceries was jolted out of the skip. Before she could retrieve it, the paper bag exploded, flung its contents at my feet. I bent, picked it up, held in my hands an object so unexpected, so endearing, that I smiled. A teddy-bear, a perfect replica of Pooh.

It was wrenched from my grasp, the paper bag recovered, the teddy-bear thrust into it and jammed into the basket. She grabbed the basket I'd been carrying, the yellow flecks in her green cat's eyes imbued with a life of their own, in contrast to the perfectly proportioned triangle of her face that was taut, waxen. Enraged, her queenlike image despoiled, she beamed savage malevolence upon me. Between her teeth she gritted: "Thanks. I can manage now."

I sat on a corroded stone bench under the salon windows to regain my breath. That immaculate composure shattered because I'd chanced to pick up a teddy-bear! In retrospect the scene became a monstrous absurdity, incredible; yet it had happened. Did she collect teddy-bears and was embarrassed by the disclosure of a childish fondness that continued into adult life? I remembered an old bachelor in the village who had a dozen he arranged cosily in an armchair across his hearth. "They're company," he said, when he'd caught my startled look. "I've always had a fondness for teddy-bears."

He was lonely, my mother explained, with no one to love, and so his teddy-bears were a substitute for human company. But Mimi, sphynxlike, ultra-sophisticated, cherishing a sentimental fondness for woolly bears was so wildly out of character it defied belief. A present for a child? There were no children around. A present to be packed up and posted? Could be. But no conjecture accounted for the viciousness with which she'd snatched the bear from my hand.

Next morning Maidie, grumbling, brought me a message from Olivia. "Nothing will satisfy but that you brush her hair. Getting herself into a rare old state about it. Complains that I don't do it hard enough. Poor lamb, if I did, she'd be as bald as a coot. Don't take longer about it than you can help. She's not supposed to have visitors in the morning. If Leo catches you I'll be in trouble."

Olivia was sitting up, a leaf-green chiffon nightgown with flounces round the neck camouflaging the deep pits in her collar bone. Her eyes were too brilliant, her voice querulously complaining. "You didn't come and say good night to me."

"Leo said you'd fallen asleep and that you weren't to be disturbed."

She snapped her lids together as though to restrain a burst of anger. "I hate being a soggy sleep-soaked log. I hate it. I want to stay awake, be alive." Her eyes opened. "Liz, you've got to help me. You've got to."

"But I will. You know that."

"Then talk to me, pinch me when you see me dropping off to sleep. Slap me if you have to."

I laughed to coax her to laugh. "Leo wouldn't fancy you bruised black and blue."

"No man fancies a half-dead wife!"

I bit back the shock, said firmly: "Which you're not. Dr. Spinosa gave you a good report yesterday morning."

She looked at Maidie, who was wiping down the antiquated washstand, kept her voice low. "I loathe him. I feel sick when he touches me. He knows that I can't bear him pawing me, so all he ever does is to take my blood pressure and pulse."

"You should have a younger doctor, up-to-date on modern treatments. Couldn't you . . ."

A hiss cut me off. "I told you, I loathe doctors. If I was offered what I wanted most in the world, I'd ask never, never to see another doctor ever. They paw and fuss and they lie. Strings of lies."

Maidie turned her head, as though she'd overheard Olivia's last words. She moved to the bedside, began dusting the table, while Olivia clung mutely to my hand. A table that had been swept clean of pills and medicine; all that remained were the paper-backs, a glass and a jug of water, proof that my sleight of hand had been a dismal failure. Observed by Maidie, who'd reported it to Leo. Then why, I fretted, if she'd seen me dribble the pills into my hand, hadn't she snatched them from me, demanded an explanation? Why hadn't Leo accused me of theft? My belief in Maidie's innocence faltered. I saw her slapdash good nature, her little spats with Leo, even maybe the dozes into which she dropped as carefully contrived deception. If Mimi possessed a dual personality, why not Maidie?

Olivia snatched her hand out of mine, held out both her arms, fumbled ineffectually with her legs in an effort to kick them free of the blankets. "Liz, help me up. I'm going to sit at my dressing-table."

Maidie charged round the bed. "Oh, no, you don't, my lady. Seems to me we're getting a bit above ourselves. Doctor's orders have to be obeyed. Bed, he said, until he sees you next Wednesday."

Olivia's pale eyes narrowed to slits, and a contortion of rage made her shrunken face as ugly as a hob-goblin's. "Maidie, don't interfere. I warn you, don't you dare." She held out her arms to me a second time, while Maidie, startled, disbelieving the evidence of her eyes, stood aghast.

It would have been simpler to lift her and sit her on the stool, but she insisted on dragging her feet over the ten paces. Even with her back braced with my arm she hardly made it. Seated, she swayed alarmingly, and her breath pumped itself out of her lungs in agonising gasps.

Maidie resorted to pleading. "You see, lovie, you're overtaxing your strength. Come on now, let's get you back to bed where you'll be nice and comfy."

"Don't touch me, Maidie. Go away. Liz will take care of me." She drew in her breath, waited until her voice gained strength, and then said with a faint echo of the autocracy I remembered of old: "If you hadn't posted the letter to Liz, she wouldn't be here, would she? But she is. So who's responsible for that?"

Maidie's cheeks flamed. "That's a fine way to repay me, I must say. I'm under orders . . ."

"Yes, Maidie. Mine." She dredged up another breath. "So away with you, Maidie dear, and obey my orders."

Neither of us watched Maidie's departure. We were too intent on keeping Olivia upright on the stool. But as the door closed on her mute indignation Olivia gave me a grin made macabre by the effort it cost her. "My first attempt at blackmail. Poor old Maidie!"

"She'll be back, with reinforcements."

Ignoring my warning, her breathing less laboured, she peered at herself in the mirror. "I've dreamed for months of issuing an order and having it obeyed. I'm sick of being a thing, to be cosseted, coddled, treated as if I were made of glass that could be smashed and swept up into a dust-pan and thrown away." She shivered. "Brush my hair. I hate the sight of it; it's hideous."

I tested the bristles of the tarnished silver brush. Mercifully they were old and soft. There was a patch on the back of her head where the hair was so thin her skull gleamed through. Avoiding it, I brushed rhythmically with one hand, while supporting her shoulders with the other.

I was nearly at the end when Mimi stepped through the door, chided as though addressing a disobedient child: "Really, Olivia, you should know better! Dr. Spinosa would be extremely upset at your flagrant disobedience. You know his orders, you're not to be allowed up until after his next visit. Come along"—she held out a peremptory hand—"let me help you back to bed."

Olivia interlocked her fingers in her lap. "Go away," she said, enunciating each syllable separately. "You have your orders. I am never to be left alone. And we all know why, don't we! But I am not alone, am I? Liz is with me. *She'll make sure that I don't come to any harm.* Be good enough to leave us."

The yellow specks in Mimi's eyes, which seemed to act as an emotional barometer, became darts of fire, but her voice retained the coolly dictatorial note of a professional nurse. "You're being extremely foolish. You should know by now if you don't go back to bed, you'll suffer for it. Come . . ."

"This is my room; my villa. You are an employee. That is correct, is it not? A highly valued employee, but an employee nonetheless. That means I'm entitled to give you an order and expect you to obey it. So would you please leave us."

Mimi stared first at Olivia and then at me, visibly weighing the possible courses of action. I thought she might once again lose her temper, but her self-control held. "I'll find Leo. Maybe he'll be able to talk some sense into you before you do yourself harm."

"You do that."

The second Mimi closed the door, she collapsed into my arms. I had to hold her tight or she would have slid to the floor. She leaned against me, the reflections of my alarmed face and her skeletal one merged in the glass. When she had regained enough strength, she whispered: "Now you understand why I need you, Liz. They treat me like a child; a retarded child. If I obeyed their orders I'd be an invalid forever." Her eyes wavered out of the mirror's reach. "I have to fight. I've tried so hard, but I can't do it all alone. I want to, Liz, but I can't." She laid her cheek against mine. It was clammy cold. "You must help me, Liz, teach me to walk, to become strong like I used to be. Oh, Liz, please!"

I stroked her hair that had once been a sheet of silk and was now dry and brittle as straw. "I'll help you. I'll teach you to walk."

She closed her eyes, covered them with her hands. "Liz, don't leave me. They say . . ."

"What do they say?"

"Lies. Things that can't be true . . . that I can't believe ever happened, but they swear they did, that I've forgotten the dreadful things I've done . . . but I wouldn't do them, I wouldn't. I want to live so much."

I held her tight, said, half under my breath, like an oath: "You're going to live."

There must have been conviction in my voice because she looked at me with a perfectly focussed gaze. "I am, aren't I! I'm going to live to be an old, old woman with a score of grandchildren."

She smiled at herself in the mirror, and I thrust terror underground, spread the colourless hair in a fan across her shoulders, brushed it gently. "How's that?"

She grimaced in disgust. "It'll never shine again."

"Of course it will. All it's suffering from is vitamin deficiency. Protein shampoos, a good tonic will soon put the shine back."

"Maybe you should cut it off, leave me to grow a new crop."

"Don't let's lose our heads." I reached for a chipped tray on which lay a small assortment of cosmetics dried up with age, and began on her face. "Remember when I made you up as Ophelia? You were the image of Millais' drowned girl. Even though the river was tinfoil, the

weeds were genuine, I picked them, so was the wreath. You brought
the house down."

"Especially when the boat collapsed and I slid forward just before
the final curtain and nearly crashed into the footlights." Amazed, I
heard the lovely sound of her breathless laugh. For a minute scrap of
time fear was put to rout.

She insisted on applying her own lipstick. "At least I don't look as
though I've been chained to a stake in a cellar for years!" She held
up the stub. "I haven't used make-up since . . ." She shook her
head. "Oh, ages. Could you drive into Caromezza and buy me lots of
cosmetics? And toilet water. Maidie will smother me in talcum
powder. I feel as though I've been plastered with flour."

"We'll make a list, and I'll drive down tomorrow afternoon."

Leo, who possessed the knack of entering a room soundlessly—all
his movements were fluid and economical as though he were forever
conserving his energy, paused on the threshold, his cold hypnotic
glance never touching me, but resting in studied adoration on Olivia.
He tossed her a kiss from the fingertips of one hand. In the other he
carried a glass.

I rose from the stool I'd been sharing with her, and he put down
the glass, cupped her face in his two hands.

"I wanted to surprise you," she whispered. "You must be sick of a
face that's like a death's head."

"My darling, you could never be anything else but beautiful."

To escape from eavesdropping on the love-talk between them, I
walked to the only window that was ever opened, on the east side of
the room, where their voices were inaudible. I sat down in the chair
Maidie used. A combination of revulsion and fear could, I discovered, leave you physically sick. Presently sounds of movement turned
my head towards them. Leo was tucking Olivia into bed. He lifted
the glass from the dressing-table, held it to her lips.

She leaned away from it. "What is it?"

"Fresh orange juice and glucose."

"Nothing to put me to sleep?"

"Never fear, my darling. Orange juice to refresh you, glucose to
give you strength."

She put the glass to her lips. In small sips she drank a third of it,
and then thrust it aside. "It tastes bitter. Everything tastes bitter."

"You imagine it, *caro*. I watched Maidie squeeze the oranges to
make sure they were ripe. And they were, ripe and juicy."

"Bitter," she repeated, "horrible."

She had forgotten I was in the room. He bent over her, smoothed back the hair I had brushed, dipped his head and pressed his lips to hers, playing his part to an audience of one. I heard the door open, the tap of the Contessa's stick. He held out his hand to her, put a finger to his lips to indicate Olivia was asleep, as she joined him at Olivia's bedside.

When I slipped away they were standing guard over the bed, behaving as though I were invisible, or of no account, powerless, not worthy of space in their minds. Pressing my hand for support on one of the columns in the gallery, I stared at the cat's cradle of old and, in places, rotted rope. For a second it was as though the air had darkened round me and that by some form of extra-sensory perception I saw ahead that agony of terror that was lying in wait for me.

CHAPTER 5

To avoid another mind-numbing lunch session with the Contessa, I drove to Caromezza in the morning.

"Enjoy yourself," Maidie said. "What time will you be back? That is, if you intend to come back."

Her face was sour. "Why shouldn't I come back? One of the reasons I'm going is to shop for Olivia."

"Because if you want to know anything in this house, you have to ask. Not that you can be sure of getting a straight answer even then. Don't mind me, there's not much sweetness and light about me in the morning, but I daresay I'll improve as the day goes on. Well, enjoy yourself."

"Is there anything I can bring you back from Caromezza?"

She gave grudging consideration to the question. "Mimi does the household shopping, so I'm supposed to keep my nose out of that, cook what she dumps on me. But I wouldn't say no to a bar of Toblerone and I'm clean out of cigarettes."

Once I'd turned on to the main road, it curled its way to the piazza that was the mediaeval heart of Caromezza: apricot houses with terra-cotta roofs, hotels and shops decked out with flowers as though they were in love with themselves. The air was so clear that the foothills of the mountains formed a background to the twin towers of the *duomo*, and what must once have been a grandee's palace was now down-graded to the Hotel Excelsior. I parked the Fiat and, as a precaution in case the arcades of shops closed their shutters for a three-hour siesta, ticked off the items on the list Olivia had dictated to me, plus three large sticks of Toblerone and two hundred cigarettes for Maidie. By rights I should have bought courtesy presents for Mimi and the Contessa but that was an act of hypocrisy I could not stomach.

I ate lunch in the gallery of a *ristorante* that overlooked a street market, awash with locals and tourists. Flowers gushed from every crevice, wine flowed and two small American boys at the table next to mine put on a charade of tipsiness to divert their parents. Beyond the plaited shades the sun blazed and the white peaks of the snow-mountains were a cut-out against a blue sky unmarked by a smudge of cloud. As the waiter lifted my plate that had been emptied of *langouste*, replaced it by a *casate* made on the premises not in a factory, I marvelled at the sense of ease that lapped over me, so near to happiness that I was pricked with guilt. With Olivia a pawn in a game so hideous and unspeakable that I still could not believe it was not a piece of horror fiction, to be happy was unforgiveable. My sole vindication was that I had prised six pills out of their bottles, had them in my shoulder-bag to give to Patrick, plus a confession that all the bottles of pills had been swept out of sight, ignominious proof that my pilfering had been detected! And yet however hard I struggled to subdue that lilting sense of being a part of a world that was bright and shining, a fragrance of happiness kept me company on my way back to the car-park.

I had locked my shopping in the boot of the Fiat before I noticed the van parked directly behind me. Sludge-coloured, battered. It, or its twin, had been visible in my driving mirror for over a kilometre before I reached the town. A youth was behind the wheel, asleep. He was wearing a blue shirt, a bakers-boy cap tipped over his forehead, leaving only his chin visible. Some aspect of him struck me as vaguely familiar, as though, not very long ago, I'd seen him. It was the black leather jacket spread on the back of the seat that triggered off my memory. There had been a black leather jacket on the bench beside the younger of the two men on the afternoon I had parted the bead curtain of the taverna to ask my way to the villa. But leather jackets were common-form gear for the young and not so young across the breadth of Europe. I retreated to the car, looked hard at him in the driving mirror. The hair was the same dun colour and length, but that proved nothing without a sight of the narrow face, the thin, high-bridged nose. In the end, still undecided whether they were one and the same youth, I locked the car and went in search of the via Donatello.

I climbed up flight after flight of cobbled steps. Once I crossed a bridge beneath which water gushed. Women gossiped from the vine-swathed balconies, the strings of washing that separated them motionless in the heat.

At the top of a web of alleyways twisted left and right confined between the rock walls of the squat houses which had been up-graded by the addition of brilliantly painted doors, tubs of flowers, twinkling name-plates and rubbish—since it was clearly garbage-disposal day—stowed hygienically in black plastic bags tied up with string. The dots on the sketch-map directed me to a right fork, up another even steeper flight of steps. Mostly the hollow ring of my footsteps was the only sound to break the silence but occasionally there were others: a running child pursued by a dog, an old woman who paused, gave me a dead-eyed glance as I verified the name of the alley. Otherwise in the post-lunch siesta period the warrens of little houses were as quiet as sealed graves. I climbed another crooked stairway, looked down into a mini garden where a girl in a bikini sat under a striped umbrella pouring lemonade for two small children. She smiled, the children waved and I went on climbing until I reached another fork. On my right was the via Rosabella. I began to check the numbers. Number 10, I calculated, should be about mid-way. The continuous wall of houses form a curve which screened anyone approaching from the far end. I was abreast of Number 10, about to slot the key in the lock, when he passed me. A youth in blue jeans and shirt, wearing outsize dark glasses, a black beret over his fawn hair. In a moment he was beyond me, leaving me with only his back. Not running, but walking at a high-speed lope so that in seconds he was swallowed up by a side alley.

I stood motionless, aware that baseless suspicion could act as a magnifier, distort judgment. The hair was a common shade, so was its shoulder length. In the car he'd worn a cap not a beret—but that could have been a quick-change act. His face? But he'd passed me so quickly I'd had no chance of checking it. There'd only been his rear view, no different from those of hundreds of youths in the streets and alleyways of Caromezza.

If he was the boy from the taverna, what had been the point of waiting in the car-park when he could not have been certain I'd return to it before I'd identified the number of the house for him? Wouldn't he have kept track of me from the moment I entered the town? Then had he been skulking at my heels while I shopped? Had he watched me eating lunch on the balcony? Questions buzzed like wasps in my head, but there were no firm answers. The harm, if harm there'd been, was done. I slotted the key into the lock. It turned as soft as silk.

The door opened directly into a low, oblong room, white walls hung with modern abstracts, the genuine or fake Picasso awarded the place of honour over the fireplace. Stone-flagged floor, an outsize fleecy white rug. A sofa piled with scarlet cushions, a low modern table, an odd chair or two, a goldfinch in a fancy gilded cage and, on the far side, a teak desk at which Patrick sat, sifting through some letters.

He'd not heard the key turning in the lock, nor my footstep, but a second later he must have caught the sound of my breath.

He twisted his head, and in that first second the mould of his face appeared to have reshaped itself, with fractionally less flesh on it, the indigo eyes buried a little deeper in their sockets. A taut, anxiety-ridden face. Then, as he sprang up, a smile expunged the gravity; maybe it had been no more than a trick of light and shade.

He stretched out a hand and drew me towards the sofa. "How is she?"

I was armed with the answer to what I could have predicted would be his first question. "No visible change. What strength she has lasts for about ten minutes, then she becomes exhausted, breathless, falls asleep. No better than when you saw her, but no worse either."

He smiled relief, appeared to relax, but the unrelenting burn of his anxiety communicated itself to me as clearly as if it had been spelled out in words. "What about a drink? I can make a tolerable cup of tea or Nescafé, or there's a bottle of nonvintage white wine cooling in the fridg. Which do you fancy?"

I chose the wine.

While he was out of the room, I unwrapped the pills, laid them on the table, aligned in their separate colours.

For a long moment he stared at them, then a smile deepened with love spread across his face. "Bless you!" He laughed with a boy's exuberant joy. "So much for clumsy fingers. Was it very hair-raising?"

"Very. And I wasn't wholly successful. Maidie came out of her snooze while I had one bottle clenched in my fist. I'm pretty sure she spotted it missing. Anyway, all the pills and medicine have been confiscated, and now Leo brings in individual doses." Exasperated with myself, I spelled out my fear. "If Maidie saw me steal the pills, wouldn't she have told Leo? And if he knows, why hasn't he accused me of meddling with them? Ordered me out of the villa. It's a heaven-sent excuse. But not a word from either of them."

Meditating, he poured the wine, handed me a glass, the glow of satisfaction still illuminating his face. "Since he hasn't done either, the logical assumption is that Maidie didn't spot what you were up to, or only formed a mild suspicion. Remember her sight is none too good, mainly because her glasses are useless, always sliding half-way down her nose." He grinned. "My bet is that you got away with it.

And good for you!" He lifted his glass. "Now we can get moving. I've laid on a chemist who's agreed, for a suitable fee, no questions asked, to analyse the pills. But I'm still in the dark about Spinosa. Untraceable. It's as though he disappears down a rabbit-hole after he leaves the villa."

He frowned broodingly into his glass and in the silence I was made miserable by the sound of the goldfinch batting its wings ceaselessly against the gilded wire of the cage until I could bear it no longer and closed my eyes against a sight that outraged me. "How can you stand it? A wild bird caged! Why don't you open the cage and let it fly free?"

"Because it would be dead in an hour, either eaten by a cat or its feathers torn off by wild birds." He put his hand over mine, and beneath his touch mine flinched. "It was bred in captivity; it couldn't exist outside a cage. Besides which, its owner dotes on it. One of his conditions in renting me the house was that I fed and watered it every day, followed a diet-sheet that's taped to the kitchen wall. When he's home he lets it fly free each evening. Most of the time it perches on his head and plucks out his hair. He showed me the bald spot. Does that make you feel any better?"

"No. It's a prisoner."

He released my hand. "Then who isn't," he murmured, "at least to some degree. Absolute freedom is a myth."

To brace my courage, I drank half the wine in the glass at a gulp. "May I ask you something?"

"Of course."

"How do you propose to kidnap Olivia? Because that's what it amounts to, doesn't it? Even if you have the pills analysed, prove Dr. Spinosa is a phoney, that the villa does not belong to Leo, that he's a pauper until he gets hold of Olivia's money, how are you going to . . ." I came to an abrupt stop, holding back the words "persuade her to leave him?" and substituted, "free her?"

While I'd been speaking, I'd avoided looking at him; now I did so. He was staring past me, as though I'd faded from his mind. The words leapt off my tongue, ugly, accusing. "Either she still loves him, or she's completely under his thumb, incapable of defying him. I can't see her co-operating in a kidnap, not if she's convinced he's going to rebuild the villa for her."

"I wonder!" His voice was remote, speculative. Then he turned his head, gave me a half-musing, half-mocking smile. "Doesn't love, true or false, provide the perfect cover story?" Suddenly he dipped his head, and the sable look tumbled over his forehead. "Are you saying that I'm set on a hopeless course? Quixotic, impractical? Doomed to failure?"

"I just want to know how you intend to scoop up a sick girl, guarded round the clock, and ride off into the night with her. You must have some outline plan."

His laugh was harshly unrepentant. "I haven't. And I won't have until I've established proof that Leo is systematically engineering the death of his wife."

"How long will that take?"

"Now I have the pills, I hope not more than three days. The lawyer who specialises in property details is in Milan. But his secretary promised to telephone me this afternoon and fix an appointment for tomorrow. What I need from him are the names of the owners of the villa, the date when Leo's short-term tenancy, if he has one, which I doubt, expires."

He smiled. "Now for some good news. Lewis telephoned last night. The day after the Marianis flew out of Syracuse, which is their home base, a man's body was recovered from a ravine. One Valentino Randoli, aged sixty, suspected of being affiliated to the Mafia, though only in a low-grade capacity. As far as Lewis can make out, his job was to keep his eyes and ears open, report what he saw and heard to his employers. In short, a small-time informer.

"Lewis has established that some contact existed between Leo and Randoli. Witnesses saw them together several times, and on one occasion, when Randoli was drunk, they had a row in public during which Randoli accused Leo of cheating, and threatened to inform on him to his bosses. Lewis hasn't so far been able to connect Leo with any crooked deals. In fact, he appears to have cultivated the life-style of a gentleman of private means. But he did make two trips to Morocco, remained there for a week and then returned to Sicily. That suggests, though Lewis is not yet in a position to prove it, that he played some minor role in drug-trafficking. Maybe he set up the routes, checked the transport system, distributed the cash to small-time pushers. We don't know. But being Leo, I'd bet that he'd worked out a plan for cooking the books, creaming off profit that didn't belong to him. If I'm right, he was inviting a bullet through his head from one of his superiors."

"But he got away?"

"Yes, but Lewis is pretty certain the Sicilian police are trying to trace him, and that they are in touch with Interpol. Meanwhile, Valentino Randoli's two sons have left the island."

"Which means?"

He shrugged. "No firm proof, but it suggests they are hell-bent on avenging the death of their father, vengeance by summary execution being a way of life in Sicily."

Hope sprang alive in me. "Then you've got a let-out. Order Lewis to make the Sicilian police a present of Leo's address."

His head jerked up. "A blood bath! Is that what you want. A shoot-out at the villa, with a sick girl, two elderly women, you and Mimi on the side-lines! Not on your life! We're not interested in a dead Sicilian or his two avenging sons. Only in Olivia's survival."

"You prefer blackmail! Threatening Leo with the police?"

"Yes."

"The end justifies the means?"

"A thousand times."

"But there's a time factor, isn't there? One telephone call and the Sicilian police would pick up Leo within twenty-four hours, probably less. With Olivia in the state she is, you're prepared to gamble with time?"

"They could pick him up, release him for lack of evidence. *That's* the gamble I'm not prepared to take. For me there is no choice."

No, for him that was true. Love turned a blind eye to rational argument. His pride, too, was a factor in that I suspected he was hell-bent on a one-man mission. A lone wolf!

He lifted my wine glass from the table, put it into my hand. "What you're demanding is a gold-plated guarantee of success. I wish to God I could give it to you. But I can't. His expression suggested a depth of calm that was without foundation. But implacable resolve, too. "Our only weapon is that we can't afford to fail. It's pretty powerful." The smile came slowly, humour lightening his eyes. "I'm not the wild irresponsible man you think I am. Have a little faith. I'll do all in my power to justify it."

I can't rationalise what happened. A flash of wonder that ignited every sense in my body, a flash that must be instantly quenched. I didn't trust my hand to hold the glass steady, so very carefully replaced it on the table. For seconds the room, his presence beside me, receded and I experienced an ache of longing and loss, as though something infinitely precious had been stolen from me. But what was the loss that emptied the heart and left it a hollow shell? The pain of acknowledgement when it came was searing: it was David, diminishing until he was reduced to a blurred fast-fading shadow, his voice that I had preserved in my ears all these years drifting away into inaudibility. I wanted to scream like a child: David, come back. But I couldn't, and a silent cry burst from my heart, not as an exclamation of despair, but as a desperate plea. "Oh, God!" And a second later I thought simply, on the waste. That all over the world love was wasted.

He leaned forward, scanned my face. "Are you all right?"

I pushed the waste and loss out of sight. "I think, although I'm not absolutely sure, I was followed here." I told him why; described the fawn-haired boy.

He paced the room slowly, with that look of intense concentration I'd come to know. "It's possible, and if they're set on beating a path to my door, frankly there's no way of stopping them. But also short of using a crowbar, which would alert the neighbours, there's no means of entry. As to the outside contacts I make, it's up to me to make sure I shake them off. No, I'm not worried about that angle."

"Then what?"

His deep indigo glance searched for and found my eyes. "Whether I've a right to involve you."

"But I am already involved." For heaven's sake, it had been he who'd forced me into involvement!

He stood with his elbow on the mantelpiece, seemingly examining the Picasso. A little of his cast-iron confidence appeared to have slipped. Suddenly he laughed. It was a bell-like, full-hearted sound. "You know something. Suddenly you've become a weight on my conscience!"

"Shrug it off."

"Too late. Maybe you should stay inside the villa. With Maidie around, no harm is likely to come to you there."

My reaction was to make no comment. My trust in Maidie was ambivalent. She had, admittedly, a mind of her own, but I had a feeling that it might be temporarily in pawn. "It's inhibiting enough to be an unwelcome guest, strictly rationed on the time I'm allowed to spend with Olivia. I don't fancy being a prisoner."

"But you will take care?"

I felt a lightness of mind, a sense of joyousness. This time it was I who laughed at his strictures. "What horrible fate had you in mind for me?"

He frowned. "I don't know, but for God's sake keep an eye on what's going on behind you. Mario and his cohorts are a pretty nasty bunch of thugs."

"So don't go out after dark!"

He said with severity: "I'm talking sense. Don't roam about on foot. Wherever you go use the car. Promise?"

Without the grace of a second's warning, the image of David overwhelmed me. My throat closed up and I was sickened by the fear that tears might trickle ignominiously down my cheeks. I said yes, then leaned over the table to pick up my shoulder-bag. It was an instant in time that was to lie in a crevice of my heart for life. "I promised Maidie I'd be back by five. I've bought some cosmetics for Olivia and I'd like her to have them before supper in case Leo puts an embargo on my seeing her later."

He frowned at the telephone. "Damn that girl of Zambetti's. She still hasn't rung. I'll walk you to your car."

"Please don't. You could miss her call." I was frantic to get away from a smile so falsely concerned that one could persuade oneself that it sprang from the heart's depths. I had made a couple of steps towards the door when his hand clasped my shoulder. "Will you call me from the telephone kiosk in the morning?"

"What time?"

"Say between ten and eleven. Lewis will have reported in by then, and I'll have contacted Zambetti."

When I could give him the latest bulletin on Olivia. I was his spy in residence. A cross between a guard-dog and a protector. "Between ten and eleven," I repeated. We must have exchanged some form of good-bye, but I've no memory of the words we used. I know that I was careful not to touch him, that I was swamped, near to drowning, in an emotion to which I steadfastly refused to put a name.

I looked neither right nor left, certainly not behind me, but walked swiftly, dead-eyed, through the honeycomb of alleys into the main square and to the car-park. The van had disappeared. I would not have paid it any attention if it had still been there with the driver asleep at the wheel. A shutter had descended. On one side was before; on the other after, as though I were divided into two equal parts. I promised myself that the temporary spasm of insanity would pass.

I was about a kilometre from the villa when I heard a whirring noise behind me. The rear mirror revealed an empty track. It was some seconds before I located its source: a helicopter, like a scarlet wasp, alternately dipping and zooming upwards on my tail, once so close that I was scared some dare-devil pilot was about to crash on the car roof. By the time I reached the parking space the helicopter had swung out of sight, though not hearing. I jumped out of the car, searched the sky. It roared in from behind the villa, skimming the roof, then hovered insectlike above the steps, so low that I could see the helmeted and goggled pilot, with a passenger beside him. Twice more the helicopter circled the villa, then, with a lift of its tail, gained height and gradually the deafening rattle died away, lost in the smothering silence below the sloping shelf of trees.

Climbing the zig-zag of steps, I looked back down the valley, but the helicopter did not reappear. The simplest explanation for the exhibitionism was that the pilot and passenger were bored, getting a kick out of playing games with a girl alone in a car.

I slipped both carrier bags into one hand and lifted the iron latch. It moved but the door would not budge from its frame. I dropped the plastic carriers, applied both hands to it, pushed with all my might. It held against me, bolted on the inside. I hammered until my knuckles were bruised.

I stepped back, stared at the three rows of shuttered windows. Since they were never opened, they told me nothing. Instinct set me running, stumbling over the uneven paving, the broken pots, towards the east side of the villa. There the window that was normally half-open during the day-time to admit a slice of light into Olivia's room was shuttered. I stood motionless under the blazing sun, fear curdling. Maidie had demanded to know what time I would be back, a question that suddenly acquired sinister overtones. I was hypnotised by a picture that drew itself in my mind. Olivia, sick, too weak to struggle, being bundled out of bed and into a car—the parking space had been empty—and driven to some new hide-out, more secure than the old, where I would never find her. The flesh began to shiver on my bones.

I raced along the terrace to a block of low buildings that could only be the kitchen quarters. That door, too, held against me, though it rattled in its frame. I shouted, screamed like a mad woman: "Let me in," with not a shred of hope that anyone would.

When the door was flung back, relief transformed fear into a storm of anger. I shouted at Maidie: "Why did you lock me out?"

Maidie, flushed, agitated, snapped: "Silly child. You're not locked out. We always bolt the downstairs doors when we're upstairs. They have sneak-thieves in Italy, too, you know. They'll whip anything they fancy from under your nose."

There was nothing to steal, except a few plastic chairs, cracked china and an assortment of cheap cutlery—it would have required a crane to remove the marble table and the chandelier. And she'd lied. The previous afternoon when I'd abandoned the tea-party, the front door had not been bolted on the inside. That I had caught Maidie out in one lie was frightening: if she could lie once, she could feed me with as many more as she'd been ordered to tell.

She regained some of the breath she had lost. "As you're here, you may as well come through this way, only mind how you tread. I can't vouch for the floors."

I picked my way through a labyrinth of unlit passages, dim, musty-smelling rooms, through a dungeon of a kitchen, into the dusk-filled salon.

"Could you unbolt the front door, so that I can collect Olivia's cosmetics I left on the terrace?"

She did so, and I passed her one of the carrier bags. "Chocolates and cigarettes. And some biscuits. I thought they might come in."

She peered inside. "Well, thanks. A real little lady bountiful. I'm much obliged." Embarrassed, her glance took care not to cross mine.

"These are the cosmetics Olivia asked for. May I take them to her now?"

She hesitated, conceded with a drag of reluctance: "I don't see why not, provided you only stay a couple of minutes."

I followed her worn-down heels up the staircase. Until she opened the door there was no light in the bedroom. She left it open, and I did not close it. The swathe of brightness revealed a scene so static it formed itself into a tableau. Mimi sitting on one side of Olivia's bed, the Contessa facing her. Olivia bending forward, her clenched hands held tight to her breast. Leo standing, dagger-straight, by the closed and shuttered window. Four terror-struck human beings, prisoners behind locked doors, shutting themselves out of sight of a helicopter pilot.

But at least Olivia was there, subsiding in slow-motion against the pillows. For a moment that was all that mattered. That and the mirage of loving that had struck like lightning in the little stone house. But that, I promised myself, would pass like a violent storm and leave me to subside into the peace of memories.

CHAPTER 6

When I went downstairs in the morning, Mario, sober, trendily dressed, was chatting with Mimi, three bottles of scotch balanced in the crook of his arm. Throwing a protective hand round them, he salaamed from the waist. "Ah, the little English miss! The best friend of Signora Mariani. You enjoy your holiday?"

Before I had time to answer, Leo flung open the salon door, impatiently beckoned him inside.

Mimi favoured me with one of her strictly rationed smiles that were measured by fractions of an inch, said in her precise, pedantic voice: "There have been outbreaks of vandalism in the neighbourhood. In future all doors are to be kept locked. When you leave the villa, someone must bolt it on the inside. One of us will let you in when you return."

"What will I knock with, my knuckles?"

She opened the door, pointed downwards. Poking up from the weeds on the terrace was a wooden mallet. The dumb show, the inference that I was not entitled to a fraction of courtesy, maddened me. "As the villa is more or less vandalised already, what is there to tempt thieves to break in?"

"Why Olivia's jewelry!" Her eyes widened in feigned astonishment. "I'm surprised she hasn't shown it to you."

The door shut in my face. I heard the two bolts slide fast against me. I'd forgotten Olivia's jewelry. The diamond as big as a hazel-nut that had slipped off her finger and rolled down the stairs to lie at my feet. Never having owned a diamond, I couldn't estimate its value. David's engagement ring, of seed pearls and sapphires, which had belonged to his mother, I kept in its faded velvet case. It had been found in his pocket by a hospital nurse and Hal Forman had sent it to me.

In the car-park the Mercedes was in its usual place, alongside it a second car. Leaning against the bonnet, squinting ferociously into cigarette smoke, was Mario's wife, dressed slightly more tidily than when she was at the taverna, with a silk scarf tied over her tousled mop of piebald hair. She provided an explanation for the absence of the Mercedes the previous afternoon. It had been serviced, which meant that unless someone was prepared to trudge up from the village one day, down the next to collect it, two drivers were needed. I unlocked the Fiat, wished her *buon giorno*. If she made any reply, I did not hear it. But as I drove off, in the rear mirror I saw her grind out the cigarette under her heel, follow me with her eyes.

I parked the car on the street, almost opposite the telephone kiosk, and as I crossed over, checked the time by my watch. Exactly mid-way between ten and eleven.

Before I lifted the receiver I rehearsed my answer to Patrick's first question, tempering it to cause him the minimum pain and alarm. Leo had not appeared at supper, neither had Mimi. There had only been the Contessa, fussed over by Maidie, and me. Leo, Maidie explained, was with Olivia, trying to coax her to eat.

"My son," the Contessa declaimed, rolling her pasta round a fork, "possesses a miraculous gift of patience. He feeds Olivia in morsels as though she were a little bird and for him she eats when she will take food from no one else. The consequence is that he pays too little regard to his own meals." She frowned, focussed the tinted glasses upon me. "He neglects himself, becomes too thin."

"He does as well as the rest of us," Maidie snapped. "We're not exactly living at the Ritz. And he always was picky with his food, wasn't he?"

The Contessa's face quite literally swelled with incensement as she delivered a withering rebuke to Maidie in her native language. The remainder of the meal passed in silence, the Contessa haughtily disregarding both of us and Maidie in a fuming sulk.

It was Mimi, in a sheath of silk that was a near match to her eyes, who delivered the message. Olivia had expressed a wish that I should unwrap the packages I had bought. As she withdrew, I wondered for whom she dressed herself in couture clothes, laboured at a presentation of herself more suited to a model gliding down a catwalk than an inhabitant of a decaying, vandalised dwelling where dust and mildew were an ever-present hazard to delicate fabrics. I could think of no one but herself. Maybe she was narcissistic.

Leo was seated on the far side of Olivia's bed, his hand cupping her cheek. On the table was a plate of congealed scrambled egg, and some jelly that had melted into syrup. For a napkin he had tucked his handkerchief into her neck.

"Liz, I never thanked you for my presents. Would you take them out of their wrappings, put them on the dressing-table where I can see them?"

One by one I stripped the bottles and jars of their packaging and ribbons, set them out. She moved her head fractionally, kissed Leo's palm. "It's like Christmas, isn't it?"

"Yes, *caro*, an extra Christmas just for you." He made a ceremony of brushing his mouth against her cheek. When he drew back, her eyes clung to him, yearning, supplicating. What Patrick persuaded himself was faked love to provide her with a protective shield to keep a murderer at bay! But surely Olivia was too sick to put on an act? Wasn't it Patrick who dealt in dreams? A chronic habit with lovers that amounted to self-hypnotism. I should know!

Without a second's warning, the smile on her lips froze into an agonised grimace; there was a single choking cry before her body went rigid.

Leo, upright, stood motionless, as though every bone and muscle in his body were petrified. For perhaps two seconds our glances met across Olivia's body. Mine must have been stunned, appalled; his glittered with some demonic expression too evil to name. Then the breath began to heave in his chest, as I heard myself shout: "Do something. Tell *me* what to do . . . how to get hold of the doctor!"

There was a second when he fought against indecision, and then he wrenched the pillows away, tossed them on the floor. "Fetch Mimi. Mimi. No one else. Mimi."

She flew up the stairs, and when I followed her to the bed, she thrust me violently aside. Their treatment was savage, administered in silence except for odd clipped phrases. Three times Leo bent and sucked at Olivia's lips. Mimi massaged her heart, plunged a syringe into the barely existent flesh on one stick-arm. I stood by one of the shuttered windows, not knowing whether they were aware of my presence, waiting through a timelessness that amounted to no more than twenty minutes to learn whether Olivia was dead or alive.

I saw the covers being drawn up to her throat, one pillow replaced under her head, and heard a breath of a sigh that signified life.

Leo literally dropped into a chair like a man whose limbs would no longer support him. The flesh on his face was a sickly white, the hand resting on his knee shaking. Slowly he forced his head up and I saw a face contorted with rage or anguish into a grimacing mask, heard a voice that hissed through the space between us. "Get out, damn you, get out."

I had to wait until midnight before Maidie came to my room. "She's sleeping, over the worst." Exhausted, her hair tumbling down her back, she sank into a chair, began slowly as though her brain was so numbed she could only with difficulty summon to her tongue the words she needed. "I'm not blaming you, but your trouble is that you're not used to her, don't know what she's been through, how she is now, weak as a sick kitten, the slightest exertion liable to set her back. Unwrapping all those bottles and jars, it's more excitement than she can stand. Overstimulation, that's what the doctor calls it."

I'd no means of knowing whether Maidie was speaking out of honest conviction or parrotlike relaying a message from Leo. Drained, what defeated me was why a husband intent on murdering his wife should exert every ounce of strength, skill and will-power he possessed to resuscitate her. Slowly the answer spelt itself out. There'd been a witness. He'd been driven to herculean efforts to convince me of his innocence. I was his alibi, proof to be stored away for the future that he'd fought like a demon to save his wife from death. Olivia had lived because, on a whim, she'd summoned me to unwrap a heap of beribboned bottles and jars.

I was in no mood to pay any regard to Maidie's exhaustion. "Olivia nearly died. Why didn't you send for the doctor?"

Her mouth settled into a mutinous line. "But she didn't die, did she? Leo and Mimi know what to do, massaging her heart, keeping her flat, giving her injections. Besides, the doctor doesn't drive at night."

"Then why not call in a younger doctor who is prepared to visit a critically ill patient after dark?"

Cumbersomely, she heaved herself to her feet, smoothed down her crumpled skirt, damned me with her eyes. "Maybe you should mind your own business. There are people in this house who have gone without sleep for days on end, never stopping to grab more than a cup of tea, to keep Olivia alive. But you're not one of them, which means, in my book, you've no right to interfere, when you know nothing, nothing of what the rest of us have gone through. You're nobbut a silly little schoolgirl." Then, half-drunk with fatigue, she stumped out.

When she brought me my coffee in the morning, she looked as exhausted as she'd been at 1 A.M., but her rage had ebbed, and her glance was no more sour than it usually was at that hour. "She's had a good night, so you can stop fretting. She's out of the wood." She slammed the door behind her.

Imprisoned in the telephone booth, I balanced truth with mercy, dialled the number. A series of tiny pulses started to beat in my bloodstream when the ringing tone ceased, but otherwise I was calm, rinsed clean of my crazed fantasy.

"Liz!"

It didn't help there was a lilt in his voice. I rushed my words, anxious to have the bulletin behind me, to finish on an optimistic note. "I saw Maidie before I left and she wasn't worried. I'll try and see Olivia this afternoon, so that I can give you another ring."

The silence lasted too long before he said: "Yes, do that."

"And something else. When I arrived back at the villa yesterday afternoon, I was buzzed by a helicopter, diving nearly as low as the car roof. It hung about for five or six minutes, then flew off. All the doors of the villa were bolted, all shutters latched, and when Maidie let me in and I went up to Olivia's room they were all huddled together in the dark, in a state of siege. Maybe it was that which triggered off Olivia's collapse."

"Maybe!" Again there was a long pause. "It could have been someone trying to run Leo to earth. Did you see the pilot's face?"

"No. He was wearing goggles. But the helicopter was red. Not much use as identification, I suppose?"

"I'm afraid not. But perhaps it's not important. Things are beginning to shape up this end. Aunt Marianne's now set on taking action herself, working on some plan she's not prepared to divulge until it's finalised, but she promised to telephone later today." His voice hardened with determination. "Between the three of us, we'll have Olivia out of that hell-hole within the next forty-eight hours."

The race of time that fretted my nerves, but didn't affect his, spurred me into a plea. "Wouldn't it speed things up still more if you asked the police to contact Interpol . . ."

"No. If only for the reason that they'll barricade themselves in the villa and no male who isn't instantly recognisable will be admitted. More likely he'd be shot on sight, and his body . . ."

There was a frantic rapping on the glass behind me where a shawled woman was shaking her fist at me. I missed a couple of sentences and then there was an explosion of static in my ear, backed by two ghost-voices gabbling in Italian. Occasionally I caught a word or two, a reference to Lewis, but never a complete sentence.

The static thinned, the ghost-voices became less audible, and his voice rang in my ear. "I can't hear you, Liz. Can you hear me?"

"Now I can . . ." But I'd spoken too soon; the waves of static were back, interspersed with his groans of frustration. For a few seconds the background noise subsided to a level above which he was able to shout.

"God, this is hopeless! We're getting nowhere. Meet me for lunch tomorrow. By then I'll have heard from Aunt Marianne and had another report from Lewis."

I must have said yes because he had just time to give me directions where to meet him before the ghost-voices came to life, screamed at one another. I repeated to myself: turn left at the main road and approximately one kilometre ahead I'd see a lay-by. He'd be waiting there for me at noon.

The shawled woman had become tired of waiting, disappeared, perhaps to find another telephone. So I stayed in the kiosk, leaning against the shelf that was dotted with pimples of chewing gum, piled with torn directories, regarding an image of myself I did not recognise, at the mercy of a tumult of emotions, among them only one that was not pain: a lovely undiluted joy. Wasted. The single thread of reason that had not been trampled to death jeered this was the pay-off to a loneliness I had never admitted: that one fell in love with the first man who appealed to those inner senses that ruled the heart. In my own eyes I'd become a compulsive victim of instant love. The diagnosis arrived at, all I had to do was to cure myself.

It was only in a visual slow-motion that I became aware of the baby-carriage being eased down the steep cobbles into the main street, the fringed canopy tipped back, the old woman leaning forward to coo and cluck, her lips stretched over toothless gums. I examined her black felt slippers. Except for the soles, they were unclouded by dust, proof that she hadn't walked from one of the villas tucked away in the clefts of the hills.

The baby was a charmer, with jet black silken curls, round satin eyes, dimpled arms emerging from a minute white shirt. A boy, at a guess around six months old. The old woman put on the brake to retrieve some object he'd tossed out of the pram, held up a blue kid shoe, clucked with mock disapproval before she thrust it to safety under the *broderie anglaise* cover. Where the alley turned into the main street the baby threw out a second missile. It landed behind the old woman, so that she had to manoeuvre the pram backwards up the cobbles, grunting as she bent her knees to pick up a teddy-bear and wave it chidingly at the baby before she tucked it, too, under the coverlet, whereupon the baby vented its frustration by howls of rage that brought half a dozen women, even a couple of men, to cluster round the perambulator, hiding it from my view.

As I crossed the street in a diagonal line, I saw Mario's wife, arms akimbo, stationed on the edge of the pavement, not watching the domestic scene round the baby, but me. My glance made only a lightning-quick contact before I walked on, down to the piazza, but even so it left behind an imprint not only of sly malice, but of a dark, secret amusement.

I sat in the car. Even though it was identical, there was no possible means of proving that it was the teddy-bear that had burst out of its paper bag at my feet. There must be thousands of teddy-bears in English stores and, for all I knew, they could have become a current fashion in Italy.

But somehow, plausible as the theory was, it refused to stick. The viciousness, the quivering undercurrent of fear with which the teddy-bear had been snatched from me on the steps outlined an alternative. Mimi buying a teddy-bear for her own child. Mimi's baby, not living with her at the villa, but farmed out, near at hand, instantly accessible. If I was right, and belief struck deep, who was the father? I tried to pin together the details of Mimi's history as told me by Maidie, but as there had been little to hold my interest, memory failed me. Boarded out because the villa, unhygienic, without even the basic necessities of hot water and fresh air, the rooms in a constant twilight, was not a fit home for a treasured child? There wasn't a cut and dried answer; there probably never would be.

I hammered on the door with the mallet and waited five minutes for Mimi, in a pale apple-green shirt and white slacks, her raven hair piled high on her head, to unbolt it.

She tossed off one of her crisp orders. "Leo would like to see you. He's in the salon."

She preceded me, opened the door, stood on the threshold. Lithe, with a ramrod-straight back, the perfectly balanced stance of a ballet dancer or a gymnast; the disciplined perfection was not easy to equate with doting motherhood.

"You wanted to see Elizabeth."

Formal though the words were there was a subtle unfamiliar note in her voice that turned my head as I stepped past her. For a second, no more, I looked into eyes that except for their colouring were at odds with the ones I knew: lustrous and tender. Two glances that touched were guilty for one second of flouting the rigid constraint they must have imposed upon themselves. Certainty was instant, intuitive. I was left aghast and enraged that I had been so guileless, so gullible.

Leo sat in the chair at the head of the table. At noon every shutter was closed, the light from the chandelier creating a heat that was like a life force pressing against my skin. From among the remains of uncleared crockery on the table, he seized a pair of dark glasses, covered his eyes. When he did not speak, I sat down in a chair halfway down the table. "You wanted to see me?"

I looked into the blank, opaque circles and for a fraction of a second saw his nostrils quiver. His voice was curt, dismissive. "Even you must admit that your visit to Olivia has been disastrous. I cannot permit you to stay here any longer. Please make arrangements to leave as soon as possible."

I felt a single thump of panic. "You're ordering me out of the villa?"

He nodded.

"Why?"

"I should have thought that would have been obvious, even to you. Despite my warnings you deliberately encourage her to overtax what little physical strength she possesses; for instance to leave her bed when she is forbidden by the doctor to do so. Last night she nearly died. That she did not do so was entirely due to my efforts and Mimi's.

"Furthermore, you have offended and insulted Maidie, a woman who has never spared herself in nursing Olivia. And you behave discourteously to my mother. More than enough justification for me to ask you to leave us as soon as you can book your air flight back to England."

There was only one straight thought in my head, to play for time; I didn't need much. "If I've unknowingly been discourteous to your mother, I apologise. And I'm sorry that Maidie is upset. I did no more than suggest that as Dr. Spinosa doesn't drive after dark, it might be a good idea, in an emergency, to call in another doctor."

He clenched his knuckles and beat them on the marble. "Your behaviour is not only inexcusable, it is as ignorant and ill-informed as that of a child. To someone in Olivia's precarious mental state, to summon an unknown doctor in the middle of the night would be to invite the tragedy which all of us strive to avoid. I have already made the precise nature of that tragedy plain to you, have I not?"

"That she might attempt suicide?"

"That she *has* attempted three times to kill herself. That is the fear we live with night and day, to which you callously pay no regard."

If he could put on a charade, so could I. "Yet she talks of the future, of the villa rebuilt, restored, of buying a Pekinese. And, all the time, she fights to gain strength. Surely that suggests she wants to live?"

He jerked himself out of the chair and advanced on me. For a second I believed he was going to strike me, but he stalked in slow movement to one of the shuttered windows; he stared at it as intently as though its blankness provided him with a view. Then he wheeled, rasped: "I fail to understand why you are determined to remain here. It can't give you any pleasure to see her, except, perhaps, a macabre satisfaction in knowing that her life will probably be much shorter than yours. Is that your revenge?" His laugh rang with malice. "That charming idyll of devotion between two children never existed, did it? It was a myth. Certainly Olivia cherished no fond memories of you. Why should she? You were insanely jealous of her and resented every gesture of affection your parents bestowed on her." He began to walk back to the table. "So why try to sustain this touching, trumped-up fable?"

The fact that he was right stung like a whiplash. Olivia, child and teen-ager, had been blessed by a gift of drawing the eye, holding it, a fluent witty tongue that could charm and tease. Until I'd reached my late teens, when the flesh thinned on my bones, I'd been tubby, withdrawn and uncommunicative, with dingy brown hair, stubbornly determined never to compete with her floating fairy-gold hair, opaline eyes and nymphlike grace. Of course, I'd been jealous.

Nevertheless his accusation was a half-truth. Snapshots flicked like fast-turning pages through my head. Christmas, birthdays, village fairs, picnics. One, above all, as clear and precise as if it had been etched with a fine brush.

We'd taken a short-cut home through Brenham Wood, nearly tripping over a rabbit caught in a gin-trap. Somehow we'd prised the iron jaws apart, tearing our fingers until they were a mess of blood and flaking rust, and all the while the rabbit's luminous eyes never left us as it pleaded for release from pain. There was matted blood on its shoulder and one paw was mangled. Olivia carried it, cradling it in her arms. If we walked fast, but not so fast that it would harm the rabbit, we'd be home in twenty minutes. Mr. Jason, the vet, lived three doors farther up the street; we'd catch him at his evening surgery. We had reached the lane, were five minutes from home when Olivia stopped, gave an anguished cry. Between one second and the next the rabbit had ceased to be alive. In silence we stumbled back into the wood and, because we couldn't bear that the damp earth should muddy and clot the soft fur, smudge with dirt the eyes that death hadn't closed, we wrapped it in my cardigan before we scooped and dug in the leaf-mould with our hands, buried it and weighted the little grave with stones so that the foxes couldn't disturb it. Then we'd walked home hand in hand.

This time I did not have to lie, only honestly try to explain what I myself could not wholly rationalise. "Of course we were jealous of one another. Olivia's parents had suddenly been blasted out of her life; it was natural that she should cling to mine. And I, just as naturally, resented having to share them with her. Children are by nature savages, but mercifully for themselves and everyone else, they grow up. We shared a roof, a life-style, a school, which means, now we are adults, we have memories in common."

"Really!"

"And now you are ordering me out?"

"Yes."

"You don't think my leaving, without warning, will distress Olivia?"

"Momentarily. Perhaps. But that need not concern you."

With an effort I made myself look at his face. I experienced a curious, eerie sense of transference, as though we'd switched identities. I saw myself as I appeared to him: a nobody who had burst uninvited into his fortress, whose eyes and ears threatened to rob him of a fortune, of a woman he loved. And his son. To earn these gifts he had to make a sacrificial offering: Olivia. With an effort, I plunged through the horror, came out the other side. I saw Olivia's emaciated face, the stick-arms, his treachery—and maybe hers if Patrick was right—and found the will-power to do something which I believed was beyond me. I smiled at him, manoeuvring for time, not much, but enough—until tomorrow afternoon.

"Very well. I'll drive down to the airline office in Caromezza in the morning and book myself a seat on the first available flight." Then I held my breath.

"Good!" He rose to his feet in a signal of dismissal. With victory achieved, the rigor of hate lessened its hold on his flesh. "There are invariably cancellations. You shouldn't have any difficulty. Let me know when you will be leaving us. Let's say within the next twenty-four hours."

It was a longer time-span than I had expected. I was nearly trapped into thanking him.

Mimi gave me permission to see Olivia for fifteen minutes. The only light in the room was a low-powered bulb that hung above her bed. She lay flat, her arms extended down her sides, palms upwards, supplicating mercy, like an effigy on a tomb. For a long time she looked at me, as though all hope had been quenched, that she was abandoned. Whatever dreams she had cherished, whatever deception, if any, she had practised, had been reduced to an ash of despair.

I touched her hand, conscious of Mimi, who efficiently, with the minimum of physical effort, was making the bed in which Leo slept. "Are you feeling better?"

She nodded. "I keep wondering where you are. What you do all day."

"Sit in the sun, drive down to the village, sight-see, wander round the garden. It's bliss to do nothing."

Her lids closed for a moment as though she needed a respite, then they opened. "Where's Patrick?"

"I don't know."

The lids folded together again, and I thought of tomorrow, when I must put my dream to death.

She moved her head fretfully on the pillow. "It's so dark. Mimi, please open one shutter. Please!"

Mimi smoothed and reshaped a pillow. "I will when the sun's not so bright."

Between Olivia's closed eyes tears slid down the hollows of her cheeks. I took the bottle of toilet water from the dressing-table and with puffs of cotton wool sponged her forehead and throat.

"Thank you." She whispered with such a depth of grief and resignation that my heart emptied of all emotion except one: fear. Then, as though it was as heavy as lead, she stretched out her hand. I held it while she drowsed.

Mimi touched my shoulder. "Leave her to rest."

But the withdrawal of my hand from hers woke Olivia. "Liz," she whispered. "Come back. Please come back."

I touched her forehead. "I'll be back."

At the door, I glanced over my shoulder. The single bulb highlighted the bed as though it was the centrepiece on a stage. The passion of longing written on her face was so piteous that for a moment it was beyond me to turn my back on her. But with an adroit step Mimi moved ahead of me, opened the door, put her hand firmly on my spine and propelled me into the corridor.

They didn't want Olivia to die, not so long as I was in the villa, but suppose she cheated them?

CHAPTER 7

We walked across a paved courtyard dappled with the shadows of walnut leaves, the air perfumed with the sweet scent of broom and the feather-fronds of plumbago draping the russet walls. A fountain spun dew-drops in the sun, and he put his arm on my shoulder to draw me beyond their reach. The inquisition on Olivia had taken place in the lay-by. When I reached the end, he swore in intolerable revulsion: "The bastards, but for you being in the room, they'd have let her die."

And yet now, no more than an hour later, as we walked through sun and shade, we seemed, by a small miracle, to be removed to a timeless plane where grief and pain did not exist, an emotional enigma I could not resolve. The walls of the hotel foyer were of rough-hewn stone; old Persian rugs were silky beneath our feet. Beyond was a blaze of sun, and at the foot of a curving flight of steps a lake, picture-postcard blue, slotted itself into the contours of the rearing foothills.

"Will this do?"

I nodded. For a blessed moment all that counted was that he'd side-stepped the hideous present to make me a gift to flood the eye with delight. "Perfect."

"We'll eat on the terrace. At night it's packed solid with customers. There's even an orchestra with a fiddler who serenades favoured patrons. But at lunch-time it's less crowded and they space the tables so no one is within earshot of anyone else."

I trod the steps slowly, my hand trailing through geraniums, flying over the trumpets of the morning glories. Mid-way across the sheet of azure silk was the green hump of a minute island, its domed summit crowned with a church, the campanile a peak of russet tiles.

The waiter, who was old, gentle-faced, but who possessed shrewdly observing eyes, came to meet us and led us to a table near the lake-edge overlooking the lapping water. The waiter knew Patrick's name, and when he left us to fetch the drinks, I said: "You must be a regular patron."

The tilted smile removed the aftermath of rage from his face. "Maidie does her best, but you must admit after a couple of days the food begins to pall."

"Maidie doesn't receive much in the way of supplies, does she?"

"No." He waited until the old man had put the drinks and the menus before us. "With Leo broke, on the run, they must be desperately short of cash, which means that someone is subsidising them. Probably Mario."

I thought it more likely to be Mimi, but refrained from saying so. He lifted his glass to me and for a split second I learned the precise meaning of a fool's paradise. It darkened the edges of my mind and created a desolation within me.

He touched my hand. "Choose what you'd like to eat, and then I'll bring you up to date. The evidence we need is piling up fast."

I stared at the menu that was the size of a spread newspaper, scrawled all over in violet ink. "But fast enough? We're running out of time."

"We don't need much."

I closed the menu for the simple reason my ability to concentrate was reduced to nil. "Would you choose? Anything. Melon, maybe a salad."

A swan and a clutch of pewter-grey cygnets nudged against the stone wall. I crumbled a roll and fed it to them; they acted as a calming agent.

I felt rather than saw his gaze hanging on me. "Right, let's start with the chemist's analysis of the pills. The white ones are prescribed for patients who are severely mentally disturbed, liable to become physically violent, mainly used in psychiatric wards, not normally handed out by private doctors, as the precise dosage has to be varied according to the patient's condition at the time they are taken, the effect checked. The yellow ones are a barbiturate sleeping pill. A normal dose, unless the patient has been conditioned to them over a long period, would be one pill. Leo doles out two. The blue one has a digitalis base to stabilise various heart conditions. Again, the exact dosage has to be precisely calculated. Overprescribing can be as dangerous as underprescribing. As I suspected, a lethal brew."

When the revulsion had ceased, I asked: "Have you run Spinosa to earth?"

"No, but when I questioned the chemist there was a shifty look in his eyes. I swear the name rang a bell. Faced with the police, he'll talk. And Leo holds no lease on the villa. Zambetti is having further searches made, but it would appear that an unknown party has granted him temporary squatter's rights. So no legitimate title to the villa; no permission to tinker with the fabric. Then, he never had any intention of carrying out a major job of reconstruction. That was a mirror image he conjured up to pacify a dying wife."

A silence fell between us, until his spirit lifted. "Now for Aunt Marianne's master plan. Characteristically dramatic! Uncle Hayward's illness is subject to remissions—temporary, but for the last few days he's been well enough for Aunt Marianne to discuss Olivia. It was his idea that he should relinquish his trusteeship and appoint a younger, fitter man in his place. The legal formalities have been rushed through and Charles"—I missed the surname as a boat with an outboard motor left the pier and zoomed towards the island—"is flying to Milan, due to touch down at two o'clock tomorrow afternoon. Charles will be bringing with him a consultant-physician in whom Aunt Marianne had implicit faith. I'll pick them up at Milan and we should be in Caromezza in a couple of hours." He gave me the smile that tipped the corner of his mouth. "Does this new development boost your confidence?"

"It sounds like the backing we need."

"Then there's Lewis. He's asked for another twenty-four hours to follow developments in Sicily. Meanwhile, he's discovered that the police are holding a man in custody whom they believe was in contact with the two Randoli brothers shortly after their father's body was recovered. They're trying to get him to talk. So!" His face was alight with hope, triumph glimmering on the edge of his personal horizon. "With Olivia's trustee and a doctor on hand we'll have Olivia out of that hell-hole fast. If, as I imagine he will, Leo obstructs us, we'll call the police and lay the evidence before them." His smile of satisfaction was unrepentant. "All right, blackmail. When it comes to a choice between whether Olivia lives or dies, I've no conscience. Have you?"

"No." But the denial lacked conviction. My faith in lightning success was not as firm as his. I could not fault the line-up, the strategy, but I was still, with nothing but intuition to guide me, fearful: afraid that the current that was sweeping Olivia towards death was faster than he suspected, that he might find himself looking down at the corpse of the girl he loved.

I concentrated on practical issues. "Leo is armed with a gun he'd have no scruples in using. It was you who said you didn't want a blood bath. So how are you going to break into the villa?"

He smiled, and I dropped my eyes from a face that had suddenly become dangerous. "No blood bath. You'll undo the bolts for us."

"But afterwards, when you're inside the villa, supported by Olivia's trustee and a doctor, how do you snatch a desperately sick woman from her bed and drive off? I doubt if she would survive the shock. And whatever you say, Leo would put up a fight. With everything to lose, he's no choice." And though I didn't spell it out, Leo possessed three allies. For all Patrick knew Mimi could have a gun and be prepared to use it.

"Olivia will be in an ambulance. Look behind you, to your right." I did as I was bid. "Higher."

What my eye found was a line of a stark white building that followed the curve of the mountainside. At that distance I could see no road, no detail except that it was large and must command a spectacular view.

"The Clinique Zola. Among the six best in the country, probably the best. This morning I made an appointment with the head physician. Naturally, I couldn't divulge all the facts, and he was obviously puzzled and a mite suspicious, but I finally exacted a promise that he would reserve a room for Olivia from tomorrow evening. The address from which Olivia is to be collected by ambulance will be telephoned him." His deep blue gaze was confident, yet demanding, wanting me to applaud his strategy. "Liz, tomorrow night Olivia will be up there, under expert treatment by a first-class team of doctors."

He leaned back in his chair as the waiter served the omelettes, salad, poured the wine. He had made his declaration; now he was waiting for my applause. However hard I struggled to suppress it, that pin's head of doubt bedevilled me, nagging that somewhere, buried out of sight, there was a fatal flaw in his plan. Its precise nature eluded me, but the whiff of danger was a scent of foulness in my nostrils.

"All you have to do is to draw the bolts. Thereafter, the three of us will be responsible for Olivia. Before we leave the via Rosabella, I'll have phoned for an ambulance to follow us. There's no margin for failure."

Only Leo firing from the gallery, picking them off one by one.

I told him about Leo's edict, that yesterday he had ordered me out of the villa and told me to book myself the first plane seat.

I'd expected to shake him, but his response was unperturbed. "So the planes are fully booked. You have to wait a couple of days for a seat. That's all the time we need."

"I'm supposed to be at the airline office now. He could contact them, ask whether I've confirmed my return flight, even demand to see my plane ticket, which would be date-stamped."

"Telephone?" he queried, and shook his head. "That would mean leaving the villa; he's hardly likely to take that risk."

"Or send Mimi as his errand girl."

"Yes, I suppose he could." A frown lined his forehead, then cleared. "It's a marginal risk we must accept. At the end of the tourist season the planes are usually fully booked. Tell Leo you've got a cancellation for the day after tomorrow. My bet is that will satisfy him."

By now we'd both abandoned all pretence of eating. I could feel that my doubting irked him, but I couldn't suppress it.

"I know it's rough your going back there, but the success of the plan hinges on your being inside the villa, the bolts drawn, when we arrive tomorrow evening." As if I didn't know, he added: "It is Olivia's life that's in the balance."

And his. The naked truth sprang alive in me. Faced with a choice, I would not have saved hers at the cost of his.

Unable to speak, I bent my head. His voice soothed, placated. "I've worked out a time schedule. You arrive at the via Rosabella at five. Charles and the doctor will probably want you to brief them on a few points. You'll be reassured by meeting two highly responsible middle-aged men who're not likely to indulge in gun-play. They know their job and are invested with the authority to move Olivia to the Clinique. Fifteen minutes after you've left, we'll follow you and you'll unbolt the door. Okay?"

"You make it sound as simple as pie!"

"That's what it is." He sighed but not very deeply. "At least you can pin your faith to Charles, who can recite every article of law ever laid down, and a doctor who, since Aunt Marianne picked him out, you can bet your life has every known medical degree."

"I don't fancy the idea of seeing the three of you blown to pieces."

"Not a chance. Even Leo would find three corpses on his hand embarrassing." With no warning, he ran his finger over the crown of my head. "How does one make one's peace for putting a girl through hell? I wish I knew. But try not to hate me quite so hard. I swear I'm not given to heroics, making wild leaps in the dark. In fact, on balance, I tend to be rather a sober citizen."

His finger rhythmically stroked my hair. "It's so glossy that in the sun I can almost see my face in it."

I tried to block my ears but they stayed listening. "I've known you second-hand for years, since I first met Olivia when she'd been around twelve, but you don't bear the faintest resemblance to the picture I had of you."

"Small wonder. I've grown up!"

"She used to talk about you and your mother and father, end-lessly, almost obsessively. I pictured you as self-sufficient, a bit bossy, head-girl of the school type with long flaxen plaits! Gretchen to the life. And here you are, not an inch over five feet four with clear little bones, dark hair and smoke-grey eyes instead of sky-blue ones. I got you all wrong."

"Maybe she did too."

"Could be. Why did you answer her cry for help?"

"My mother was worrying herself sick. Also, I suppose out of some submerged instinct of loyalty which, when it comes to the crunch, you can't duck. And the baby she lost."

He was watching me with an expression that was almost, I deluded myself, tender and caring. A tiny margin of time that was infinitely precious because I knew it would have to last me a life-time. There'd be a reckoning, but not now, not this minute. All that mattered was that his eyes rested on me with that expression of won-der that is sometimes—but not this time—the forerunner of love. Radiance lit up my being. A second later, as I silently cried David's name, summoned up his face, it turned into a blurred shadow, and I was alone in an arid desert of loneliness that stretched beyond sight.

"Though she would never have admitted it, I've a suspicion she envied you."

On an evening seven years ago I had stood under a hawthorn tree and watched him making love to Olivia. Had I envied her?

He smiled, and I found myself smiling back. "Families! I was a late child, atrociously petted and spoiled. My elder brother loathed my guts. I don't blame him. Maybe he still does, though we rub along well enough when, very occasionally, he makes a trip to Eng-land from his farm in South Africa."

I watched the approach of a middle-aged woman, plump, superbly corseted, with dark mahogany hair, her mouth a curve of benevo-lence. Patrick stood up and held out his hand. "Ah, signora. Good to see you. This is a friend of mine, Elizabeth Ashley. Liz, Signora Lim-betto, the owner of the hotel."

She gave me a warm, composed smile. "I hope very much you enjoyed your lunch, Miss Ashley." She scolded Patrick: "But you didn't choose any of the dishes of which we are most proud."

"We'll be back to do justice to them."

I said: "What a superb view!"

"Yes." Her eye swept over every inch of it. "My husband and I came here twenty-two years ago. It was his dream to take an old, disused farm-house and transform it into an hotel where people could eat fine meals and behold the beauty. He accomplished his heart's desire before he died—and that is not granted to every man or woman. Now my son is training in an hotel in Rome, and my daughter is studying languages in London, in Hampstead. Do you know that piece of London?"

"Very well. Is she happy?"

She made a gesture of mock horror. "She works hard for five days and spends the other two buying herself clothes. She has no tidiness, no sense of co-ordination and no feeling in her fingertips for texture. And the shoes! I tell her that she will be a cripple. But does she care!" She turned to Patrick. "You are still interested in the Clinique for your friend who is ill?"

"Indeed, yes. I'm grateful to you for suggesting it. I met the top physician yesterday, and the necessary arrangements have been made. The patient will probably move in tomorrow."

She waited a few seconds, but then when he didn't elaborate, she went on: "It is an excellent *clinique*, the best we have. Whatever care and treatment your friend requires will be provided. The air is so splendid, like cool wine, and all is quiet."

As she rose, Patrick took her hand, held it while he spoke. "I'm grateful. Someday I'll explain how grateful."

I watched her back retreating. "What a very charming woman."

"Charm and guts and compassion. I discovered this hotel the day after I'd arrived at the villa, had seen Olivia and been shattered. She was immensely kind. When I asked her for the name of the best private hospital, she gave it to me and asked no questions."

On the way back to the lay-by he named the peaks of the mountains, slowed the car to gaze at a monastery, drew into a roadside stall and bought a bunch of roses, which he laid on my knee, and told me he'd let the goldfinch out of his cage two nights running, allowing him to fly free. He even rubbed a place on his scalp where the bird had tweaked at his hair. "And he's got a name, Sinbad. It's written on his diet-sheet in the kitchen."

When I transferred to the Fiat, he bent down, his face so close to mine through the open window I could feel his breath. "I hate you going back to that damned villa."

"But I have to, don't I?"

He nodded. "Keep reminding yourself that by tomorrow evening it will be over. Olivia will be safe."

I lifted my glance away from his, slanted it through the windscreen, as that wariness, that blind, eerie sense of foreboding, resurfaced. Take care, I wanted to scream. For God's sake take care. But all I could do was to reangle my head, smile at him. That was allowed; he was an easy man to smile at.

And then, like an echo of my silent cry, I heard him plead: "Take care. Promise Leo you'll leave the day after tomorrow. Be a good, meek little girl who does what she's told." The smile came back. "Not easy, but try hard."

He held on to the rim of the door until I had put the car in gear. "Five o'clock."

"Five o'clock," I repeated after him and turned the car on to the road. He had spoken the two words as though they had come straight from his heart, which they had in that I had a vital role to play in Olivia's survival.

Maidie rammed home the bolts on the door. It was only four o'clock but the interior of the house was saturated in twilight. "There's a pot of tea in the salon if you fancy a cup."

"I'd like to see Olivia."

She stalked ahead of me into the salon, sat down in the Contessa's chair. "She's having a nap. You'll have to wait until Leo says it's okay." She poured me a cup of tea. I refused the powdered milk that was mixed so thin it was almost transparent.

"You could pick yourself a lemon."

"Not worth the effort. All that bolting and unbolting, don't you find it a bore?"

"It's better than having a gang of hippies wander in and help themselves to anything they fancy." She sighed, blew her nose. "What the world's coming to, I don't know. It never used to be like this." She eyed me over the edge of her cup. "Leo says you're leaving us tomorrow."

"Not until the day after tomorrow. There's no vacant seat on the plane till then." I watched her face; she watched mine.

"How's she going to take your leaving her?"

"I don't know. It was Leo's idea."

She stared past me. "He thinks you blame him." She made a help-less gesture with her hands. "All this, it humiliates him, hurts his pride for you to see the villa as it is now, no more than a dump. He never could abide, even as a child, being made to look small. He has to keep his end up. It's his nature, he can't help it. Like it's yours to speak your mind, whether you know what you're talking about or not." She sighed. "I must admit there are days when this place gives me the willies and this is one of them."

Her glance travelled over me. "All dressed up! What have you been up to?"

"Driving down to Caromezza and back. The airline office."

"What would you call that colour?"

"Amber." To coax a smile, I joked. "My best. A boost for my mo-rale."

Some clothes belong forever to a particular occasion, woven into the background, absorbing memory, so that it lingers like perfume. In my wardrobe at home there were some that evoked days or nights spent with David, of months when I'd bought clothes as though money were fairy-gold, not to be counted.

She set her cup in the saucer, dabbed her eyes to blot out a spurt of tears. When she dropped her hand to her lap, it shook as though she were smitten with ague.

"Maidie, you're worked to death, tired out."

"Maybe." She blew her nose with a trumpet sound. "But it isn't the first time and it won't be the last." She stuffed the grubby hand-kerchief up her sleeve and resolutely set her face against sympathy. "I daresay you mean well, but there's a mortal lot of things you don't understand. Ah, well, you're young, you can't be expected to. That's a complaint only time will cure."

As she collected the cups and tea-pot and balanced them on a tin tray, I sifted the evidence for and against her into two piles: gullible and brain-washed, or Leo's willing stooge? Denied a firm answer, I asked: "Has Mimi ever been married?"

She gave me a startled look. "Not that I know of. What makes you ask?"

I ignored the question. "If she's never been married, has she ever had a baby?"

There was a dark hole where her mouth fell open. I'd underes-timated the horror and revulsion with which her generation regard an illegitimate child. She grabbed the tray, tipped it awkwardly so that a stream of liquid flowed over the table. "You've no right to suggest such a wicked thing. Scandalmongering, that's a thing I could never abide in anyone."

And with a rattle of china, she made for the kitchen, steaming with righteous indignation.

Leo was standing mid-way along the gallery, hands in his pockets, balancing alternately on heel and toe in a rocking movement, lying in wait for me. "Have you booked your flight home?"

"Yes, but there wasn't a vacant seat until the day after tomorrow."

For a moment he looked sullen, then he shrugged. "That means I must ask you to take particular care not to flout my orders, upset Maidie, be discourteous to my mother and Mimi. To be precise, to behave yourself." Quite suddenly he laughed. It was so rare a sound coming from his lips that I was startled. A curious elation, like an electric current, emanated from him. "Meanwhile I do not propose to tell Olivia of your departure until you have left. At all costs she must be protected from the emotional scenes in which you involve her. One effect of her illness is that she has little sense of time and . . ." Quite out of character he lost the thread of what he had been about to say and gave me a sharp tap on the shoulder. "She is looking better today, so we will have a celebration drink. Come and join us."

"Now!" It was barely five o'clock.

"Yes, now." He swept me ahead of him, exuberant, impatient. "It's never too early for champagne."

The switch of character mystified me: as though he had turned a somersault. It couldn't have been induced by my promise to be out of the villa within forty-eight hours; it had been there, bubbling beneath the surface, before I'd mounted the stairs.

Under the overhead light Olivia lay with her eyes closed. It was the explosion of a champagne cork flying towards the ceiling that ripped them open, caused her to gasp, clench her fists in terror.

Leo held the bottle high. "Champagne! You are better, *caro*, so we celebrate. Champagne has medicinal qualities. Isn't that so, Mama?"

The Contessa, overlapping the chair on the far side of Olivia's bed, nodded like a mandarin. "Doctors recommend it for convalescents."

Mimi, playing the role of a dutiful handmaiden, presented Leo with a tray of tumblers.

Leo raised Olivia from the pillows, supported her sagging head with the palm of one hand, while with the other he held the bubbling champagne to her lips. She sipped three times, then shook her head. Smiling, he wiped the dribble from her chin.

Her eyes roved blindly about the dimmed room, as though her sight was failing. "Liz? Liz?"

I moved close, bent and touched her forehead. "I'm here."

Leo put a tumbler of champagne into my hand, raised his own high. "To my darling, because she is so much better today."

"Liz!"

I placed my tumbler on the tray, slipped my hand over hers. "I wondered . . ." I watched the confusion thicken, blank out memory. "I've forgotten . . . I've . . ."

Mimi brushed me aside, took her pulse, timing it on a watch that had no second hand. "It's fine," she reported to Leo, who was refilling his glass. "Almost back to normal. But maybe she should rest now."

I heard my voice shout: "She's cold. Like ice. She should have hot water bottles, more blankets to keep her warm."

No one answered. No one looked at me. I might have been guilty of uttering an obscenity. I shouted louder: "She's cold, down to her bones. She needs more warmth."

Leo murmured: "But surely you remember that her hands are always cold, and her feet. Her circulation is so poor that she is never warm. That's why I call her my little frog." The smile of simulated compliance was so hateful that I shut my eyes against it. "But, of course, we will try to make her warmer. Mimi, there must be a wrap somewhere, a shawl."

She went to a drawer, obediently drew out a shell-pink mohair shawl, spread it over the stick-arms, drew it up to the hollowed throat. What frightened me was his confidence, as though, at last, he'd turned his back on the dark side of the world, made buoyant by brightness that lay ahead.

He helped his mother to her feet and ceremoniously kissed her cheek. "I'll sit with Olivia for a little while, Mama."

"But you'll come down to supper? You eat too little, neglect yourself . . ."

"I'll be down."

She pressed his hand to her breast, murmured an endearment. When he had seen her into the gallery, he made a moue of reproach at me, lifted the half-full tumbler of flat champagne. "It's a sin to waste champagne. Drink up."

I did so only because it relieved me of the necessity of speaking to him. Mimi remained standing by the bed on which Olivia slept, so still she scarcely seemed to breathe, like a tiny replica of a death.

At supper, while Mimi kept guard over Olivia, Leo sustained that mystifying charade of goodwill towards me: as though he was slightly high, not on drink or drugs, but self-esteem, with victory waiting in the wings. He pressed me to eat, drink, to laugh at his jokes, praised Maidie's cooking, which this evening was a *frito misto*. She scoffed at his praise. "You might as well call it fish and chips and be done with it."

"It's good," I said, and it was, though fragments of it stuck in my throat, congealed like flannel on my tongue. Under the blaze of light from the chandelier Leo sat like a man listening to applause sounding in his head. His gaze when it crossed mine was exultant yet mocking, as though he possessed some delicate antennae that monitored my brain and revelled in its secrets.

He chided: "You have no appetite! I thought all well-brought-up English girls were taught to clean their plates. Isn't that so?"

"Not after they've left school."

The Contessa said disparagingly: "It is a foolish vogue the English follow to keep themselves thin. That is why they are all anaemic for lack of good nourishing food, walking skeletons."

Leo patted her hand. "Then you are fortunate, little Mama, to have such a perfect figure."

She preened herself, then lapsed into Sicilian until Maidie's patience snapped: "For heaven's sake, let's get the place cleaned up before we start talking about the furniture."

Leo took her to task. "My dear Maidie, everything will proceed according to the time-table we've drawn up, stage following stage in an orderly sequence. Naturally Mama enjoys anticipating the future. You mustn't rob her of that pleasure."

The voice of deceit weaving for my benefit and his divertissement, tissue upon tissue of lies, rose and fell on my ears, leaving no memory behind it. I looked at Maidie, huffy and tired, and as I did so her face began to recede as if enveloped in mist. The Contessa appeared to be leaning forward towards me, as the chandelier above my head waltzed in circles. The truth struck like a hammer blow. I was tight. For a second shock cleared my head, and I became aware of a ring of eyes pinned on me, as I fought with my wits to add up the glasses of wine I'd drunk. Two . . . two . . . only two. One of champagne, one of Chianti. Then the fog thickened, stupefying me until I couldn't even add one to one.

I struggled to my feet. In my mind I heard myself say aloud: "If you'll excuse me . . ." but I never knew whether the words had left my lips.

I was lying on a bed in a darkened room, the sole light thin veins of sun that pierced the interstices in the shutters. I leapt up, and an agonising pain struck the base of my skull. When I opened the window the sun half-blinded me. I was dressed. There was one sandal on my foot, the other on the bed, entangled in a blanket that someone must have spread over me. On the rickety table was a breakfast tray. I touched the coffee-pot. It was stone cold. I looked at my watch. Four o'clock! Panic was so fierce and unnerving that the room swayed. Then I held the watch to my ear. It had stopped.

In a frenzy, as though each second's delay spelt untold disaster, I cleaned my teeth, sluiced my face in cold water, changed the crumpled amber dress for a pair of slacks and a shirt, slid my feet into espadrilles, obsessed by time, made clumsy by the fear that half-suffocated me so that I didn't hear Maidie open the door.

"Come to, have you? Maybe with a bit of a headache!" She looked highly diverted, in better spirits than I'd seen her for days.

"What's the time?" And when she didn't immediately answer, I shouted: "Maidie, please tell me the time."

"For goodness sake!" She looked at her watch. "Just coming up to ten o'clock."

Relief made me feel faintly sick. I sat down on the bed. She patted my shoulder. "Don't get in a stew. The world hasn't come to an end. You got a weeny bit tiddly. Happens to the best of us. All that champagne, then the wine, and eating like a mouse. What do you expect?" She tested the temperature of the coffee. "I'll make you some fresh."

She went away and came back, poured me a cup of coffee, placed a limp, burnt slice of toast into my hand. "Drink the coffee, have a bite of food, and you'll be as right as ninepins in an hour. Daddy," she confided, "at official dinners occasionally took more drink than was good for him. You see, a man's thought a sissy if he can't take his liquor. Many's the time I've had to mix him a raw egg with Worcester sauce and pour it down him. I'd do the same for you, but we've run out of eggs, and where you'd find a bottle of Worcester sauce, heaven knows. Go on, drink the coffee, and then the best cure is a brisk walk. That's what I'd do with Daddy, walk him round the garden. Gets the circulation going, and that works wonders with a muzzy head."

The coffee helped. At least I was capable of sustaining a modicum of coherent thought. "Maidie, did you notice how many glasses of wine I drank?"

She gave a tut of exasperation. "All that traipsing to and from the kitchen, frying up more chips for the Contessa! I've only got one pair of eyes, you know. Anyway, what's it matter? You had a drop too much. It's not a mortal sin."

There she was mistaken. A sin had been committed though not by me. "How is Olivia?"

"Right enough. Not that she's ever at her best first thing. Picks up during the day."

I asked myself whether you could become so inured to a ravaged, shrivelled body, a dying spirit, that you became blinkered against an immutable fact: death like a slow tide advancing remorselessly, stealing mobility, invading brain cells, stifling breath itself. The answer was yes. It happened to thousands, maybe millions, the crazed hope that was the sole defence against abject fear, a shaking of a fist in defiance of the Almighty. Either that or Maidie was a superb artist in deceit.

I stood for ten minutes under the feeble shower that yielded only a trickle of water. I even shampooed my hair. When I was dressed I combed it into shape, sitting in a wedge of sun. At a snail's pace the remaining areas of mist cleared, and my brain began to function. I concentrated on the dinner table, placing each item of food and crockery in position. There had been two bottles of Chianti at Leo's right hand. One full, one with the level of the wine only an inch above the wicker basket. But no amount of effort would rekindle the memory of from which bottle Leo had poured wine into my glass. The movements of his hands had been so fluid that they deceived the eye. But an impression remained that the wine in the bottle of Chianti nearest to him had been at almost the same level as when I sat down at the table, diminished, say, by one glass.

That I'd been drugged, put out of action from nine in the evening until ten next morning was an established fact. But why? Panic sprang alive. What had been accomplished in the night that had required me to be drugged into stupor?

Olivia! I ran along the crumbling corridors that stank of mice and decay, as though out of sight fungi were greedily eating away the bricks and stone. Without so much as a tap I thrust open her door.

The Contessa and Mimi, one on either side of the bed, were sponging the skeletal body. From where I stood I could count the ribs.

Her expression coldly incensed, Mimi advanced on me. "How dare you burst into a private room without knocking! Please leave at once."

Then, faintly, Olivia called: "Liz . . . is that you?"

"I looked in to see how you were. I'll be back after you've had your bath."

And I was out of the room before Mimi could touch me. For a few seconds, I had believed that they were sponging a corpse, that Olivia had cheated them by dying. I waited until I stopped trembling, and then went to find Maidie so that she could bolt the door behind me. She was in the kitchen, working on a table by an open window—breaking one of Leo's rules. I thought, with a prick of hope, maybe she's just dumb, can't see farther than the end of her nose. She gave me a guilty look. "Lets out the smell of cockroaches. I'll shut it in a minute. You still look a bit peaky." She dusted the flour off her hands. "Out with you, and no lazing in the sun. A good brisk walk. And lay off the wine at lunch-time."

I had no intention of eating lunch, of sharing a table with any of them, not as much as exchanging a word with Leo if I could avoid it.

I sat on a crumbling stone bench, surrounded by nymphs and satyrs, the Greek goddess with bullet holes in her breast, not knowing how to fill time until I could climb into the car, drive to Caromezza, walk through the web of alleys to the stone house.

For comfort I counted the hours. In less than three the man called Charles and Mrs. Carstairs' doctor would be touching down at Milan airport. In five they would be together in the stone-floored room with the scarlet sofa and the chirruping goldfinch. I looked farther ahead, but after I'd seen myself unbolting the door of the villa there was a total blank. For something positive to do, I upturned my shoulder-bag, spread its contents on the stone seat and checked through them twice. Nothing was missing. There was the open space for the date on my airline ticket, but I could not believe I'd been doped so that Leo could examine it.

When, at last, I went indoors, it was Mimi who performed the ritual of unbolting. I asked her for permission to see Olivia. She granted it, limiting me to ten minutes. I spent them under the Contessa's morose, unyielding gaze, the eyes behind the dark glasses never shifting their guard from me. She did not speak. Neither did Olivia. She slept, with a barely visible movement of her shrunken breasts. The mohair shawl had been removed. When the ten minutes were up I tip-toed to the door. You can hope so hard that hope becomes a prayer. I prayed, not specifically to God but to any beneficent power on earth or in heaven, that Olivia would not die before nightfall.

In the end I cheated the clock, left the villa an hour earlier than I need have done. To fill in the empty waiting time, I bought my mother a clock in a pretty porcelain case, and Eustace an antique coin. It could be a fake, though I believed it was genuine; in either case he'd gain immense satisfaction in proving or disproving its authenticity.

It was 4:45 when I started to climb the steps threading through the honeycomb of lanes, ten minutes later when simultaneously I rang the bell and slotted my key into the lock. For a second or two the key stuck, and I had to give it a firmer, sharper twist.

When I closed the door behind me, let my eyes travel over the room, I learned for what purpose I'd been rendered deaf and blind. I knew. And a world that, though it could never be mine, was precious, crumbled into ash. And for Olivia it spelled out the final extinction that is death.

CHAPTER 8

The only sound to breach the silence was the cheeping of the goldfinch, the frenetic beating of wings against the wires of the cage. The white rug had been kicked into a heap, the contents of the desk spewed on the floor. The hand-set of the telephone was smashed, books had been swept from their shelves, left where they fell.

The kitchen and bathroom were undisturbed. In the bedroom the mattress had been dragged from the bed, thrown back at an angle on the tangle of blankets and pillows. The chest and wardrobe had been rifled, clothes ripped from hangers, tossed as though by a whirlpool about the room. Vandalism by men with a lust for violence and . . . But I refused to admit that most terrible and final of all words to my mind.

At the rear was a glassed-in addition to the house so dazzling with light that my eyes automatically blinked, then focussed on an easel, a palette, paint-stained rags, two jars of brushes and canvases stacked against the walls. Like the bathroom and kitchen, it had escaped destruction, proof that, even in the dead hours of the night, time had been rationed. I tried the door that led out to a minute patio. It was locked.

I returned to the sitting-room, where the Picasso and the other paintings still hung in their places on the walls. I moved a pile of books from the sofa, bent and with an involuntary gesture straightened the white rug. One corner was splashed with dark red, the stain seeped deep into the fur. At my feet a marble urn that had been entangled in the folds of the rug rolled clear. It was smudged and splattered with dried blood, a little mat of sable hair. Horror pictures collided in my mind, then clarified into one so three-dimensional and precise that it was engraved there forever. I not only saw Patrick dead, but I could feel him dying, the ferocity of his rage at being trapped into defeat, of having life brutally beaten out of him.

My fingers were so numbed and clumsy that it took me a long time to find the key in my handbag. One of the teeth was coated with a minute sticky substance. I held it to the light and identified it: chewing-gum. Thrust into a pocket after it had been stolen from me while I'd been doped into insensibility. Then, later, just as stealthily returned.

For a moment guilt outstripped every other emotion. I fought it savagely. Guilt, remorse, even anguish were futile time-consuming emotions when there was not one second to waste. For relief, I allowed myself the fleeting luxury of hope. They could have kidnapped him; he could be lying trussed and gagged in some hovel. Commonsense resurfaced, preached back at me. Patrick wasn't a diplomat worth a ransom. Leo and Mario, maybe the boy, weren't a bunch of political fanatics. To them he was no more than a man who threatened their greedy dream. To protect it had they beaten him to death?

I buried my head in my hands, shut myself in darkness. After a while I saw not light, but an infinitesimal easing of the darkness. Patrick hadn't for the last twelve hours been acting alone. Olivia's new trustee, the doctor chosen by Mrs. Carstairs, had touched down at Milan three hours ago. Charles . . . in my ears I heard the splutter and throb of the outboard motor that had obliterated his surname. No matter, I insisted, he was a director of a London merchant bank, notable in his own sphere, traceable. With no one to meet them off the plane they would have hired a car to drive to Caromezza, and with no spare room in the tiny house, Patrick would have booked them into a top-class hotel: the Excelsior.

The spur of positive action steadied my nerves, released the adrenaline in my body. I picked up my handbag, then laid it down to refill the pots in the goldfinch's cage with water and seed.

In the courtyard of the Excelsior coaches were disgorging their passengers. Two travel couriers, one German, one American, were shepherding them into the hotel foyer, while porters unloaded the baggage. I had to wait in line while those ahead of me were allocated their rooms, handed their keys.

When I reached the reception desk the clerk asked for my voucher. A cool, alert-eyed young man, a professional to his fingertips, he listened in silence while I explained I wished to know whether a director of a London merchant bank, which I named, had checked in that afternoon with a companion who was a doctor.

"Their names?"

I had one Christian name but no surnames. While he carried out a perfunctory examination of his register, the queue behind me shuffled and sighed with mounting impatience. When he lifted his head, his eyes registered the grime on my hands and, although I wasn't aware of it, a smudge of dried blood on my chin. He was courteous but coldly dismissive. "We have no record of the gentlemen you describe having been booked into this hotel." He motioned to a German couple, with two small children, who were behind me.

For a moment I stubbornly held my ground, pleas that no one could resist building up in my head: a brutal beating-up, a girl who would die if help did not reach her by nightfall. But who would believe me? Certainly not the immaculate young man who would have counted a raised voice a near scandal. "But they're booked in here, I'm certain of it. There can't be many American doctors, a London banker. If you could . . ."

The rest of the sentence dried on my tongue. I was wasting time on a lost cause. He clearly suspected me of employing a trick to prise out of him information to which I was not entitled; perhaps of molesting the hotel's guests.

The three telephone booths in the foyer were engaged. I had to wait fifteen minutes before one was free. It took another ten to obtain the number I wanted.

A male voice answered: "Benson, Chief Security Officer. Can I help you?"

"Could I speak to the chairman's secretary?"

A guffaw sounded in my ear. "You must be joking, miss! At half-past six! There's only me, my security staff and the guard dogs."

I gave him Mr. Carstairs' full name. He'd never heard of it. I explained that a director of the bank whose Christian name was Charles had recently flown to Miami to consult with Mr. Carstairs about their ward who lived in Italy and was now critically ill. I urgently needed to be put in touch with him. Could he give me his surname?

"Sorry, miss. All the files are locked up. Anyway, security staff don't have access to them."

When I begged for the chairman's name, home telephone number, he said good-naturedly: "Now, miss, if you know anything about merchant banks, the class of people who work in them, you'll know that's classified information, as much as my job's worth to hand it out to anyone who rings up out of the blue and asks for it. Let's face it, I don't know you from Adam, do I? Tell you what, if you leave your name and number, I'll see it's handed to the chairman's secretary tomorrow morning."

I thanked him, put the telephone back on its rest.

That left Mrs. Carstairs. Mrs. Hayward Kingston Carstairs. With two distinctive Christian names there should be no delay in tracing her number. I obtained it within half a minute from International Enquiries. Before I could dial it I had to line up at a counter to cash a traveller's cheque. Twice while I waited, the reception clerk's glance slid in my direction, keeping a check on me, prepared, if necessary, to have me discreetly escorted out of the hotel. When I asked for the Carstairs' number, the operator apologised: there was an hour's delay. I asked her to book the call and wondered what on earth I should do with the wasted time.

In the cloakroom the mirror reflected a barely recognisable face, streaked with the grime that had been transferred from the spilled books to my hands, and a smear of blood on my cheek, beneath which my skin had turned an all-over dirty grey tint. In the crowded cocktail bar a youth was paging Mrs. Redmond. For a moment I thought, Why not? I knew the answer. If I went down on my knees to the reception clerk he would never demean a guest by having him paged by his Christian name.

To fill in the hour I sat in one of the shopping arcades, ate half a sandwich and drank three cups of coffee. When I dialled the operator a second time, all she had to offer me was another apology; there was now an indefinite delay on calls to Miami. If I'd leave my number with her, she'd ring me back. I thanked her and said I'd call later.

By now I had exhausted every shred of my capacity for waiting. A shocked brain distorts vision and reason, jumbles priorities. I was obsessed with the belief that I must return to the villa and make certain that Olivia was still alive. That not to do so would be to default on a promise I'd made to the man who'd loved her.

When I reached the villa the rising moon threw a faint luminous glow behind the mountain peaks, but the rest of the world was in darkness. As I switched off the ignition, I was struck by an omission so incredible that in retrospect it seemed beyond self-forgiveness, tantamount to lunacy. I'd been blind to the logical, obvious course: to walk into the nearest police station, report the ransacked house, the blood-stained rug, the missing occupant. Blinded because the evidence of violence and spilled blood had put my wits into a coma? That was not quite the whole truth. There was Olivia, a duty to which I was shackled. Clawing my way up the crumbling steps in the dark, there was a new bitter taste on my tongue. Hate and grief and a terrible rage tore at me but in the end I stood where I believed I should be: waiting outside the door of that dark and secret place.

I listened while the screeching bolts were withdrawn. Light streamed in a swathe from the salon, making a flare-path in which Leo stood. He grabbed my arm, drew me forcibly into the domed hall, rebolted the door.

The self-confidence was still there, the tincture of arrogance that had been his unenviable birthright, but it was thinner, as though pin-pricks of doubt were beginning to wear through the fabric to harass him. I wondered if he knew where I'd been, accepted that he did, and didn't care.

"You're late," he snapped. "We've finished eating. Where have you been at this time of night?" And when my numbed brain refused to produce an answer, he demanded: "Where?"

Like a miracle the words formed on my tongue: "Buying presents to take home." But I didn't have them with me. A long time ago I'd put them in the Fiat. "They're in the car." I turned my back on him, walked towards the staircase.

The half-open door of the salon revealed the Contessa, in her usual position of matriarch, seated at the head of the table. Mario was on her right, the empty chair from which Leo had risen on her left. Mimi and the fawn-haired boy were opposite one another. Not deigning to notice my presence, the Contessa continued to eat a peach. Mario awarded me a lascivious smirk, the boy a sly hooded look and Mimi's sphynxlike profile ignored me.

Leo called after me: "Olivia is asleep. You are on no account to disturb her."

He kept his finger on the two-way switch until I reached the gallery and then, having checked that I'd passed Olivia's door, flicked it off, leaving me to fumble my way through the darkness. I waited until his voice mingled with a burst of laughter that erupted in the salon, then I kicked off my shoes, retraced my steps and soundlessly eased open Olivia's door.

Maidie was dozing by the bedside under the naked bulb that had been draped with a square of dark silk. Olivia's breathing was irregular, for long moments barely perceptible.

Maidie's head had fallen on to her chest: a woman on the verge of old age, burnt out with fatigue. She was a pitiable sight. But I had no pity to give away. Whether or not she was Leo's bond slave, she was the only ally I could hope to win. I touched her shoulder.

She scowled, resentful at being caught napping on duty. "Oh, you're back, are you!"

I stared at her face under the dimmed light, seeking the minimum of words to shock her into a confession of the truth. "Maidie, Olivia's dying. You know that. As long as she lies here, she hasn't a hope of getting better."

Her mouth sagged open. "You wicked girl." Anger, outrage, was suppressed to a hiss. "I'm sick to death of your interfering, sneaky ways, forever poking your nose into other people's business. You've no right to say such things."

"Maidie, Olivia is dying."

"All she needs is quiet and rest." It was a shouted whisper, no hair-crack of pity, no remorse, only an obduracy that defied me.

"You obey Leo's orders, repeat what he tells you to say, though you know he's lying. Why, Maidie, why? You can't want Olivia to die."

She stared back at me, not with fright, but with hate. Then she shook her head, as though she needed to clear it, drew in her breath. "Calling me names. Accusing me!" For a moment indignation choked her. "As if it's easy to keep someone alive who doesn't want to live."

"Maidie, that isn't true. In your heart you know it isn't. What's Leo done to you? Hypnotised you, bribed you? Why do you hide in a house that's a prison? Why, when a helicopter flies over the villa, do you all behave as if you're terrified out of your wits? You know I wasn't drunk last night. I'd been drugged so that Leo could steal a key out . . ."

I had spoken too loud. Olivia's eyelids dragged themselves apart, and her bewildered gaze moved from one to the other of the two figures who were fighting over her in whispers. "Is it night? I hate the night . . . the dark . . ."

Maidie swooped and wound her arms about her, cradled Olivia's head against her breast, kissed away the tears that were beginning to slide down the sunken cheeks. "There, my lamb. Maidie's here. I won't let anyone frighten you. Maidie will take care of you."

I'd gambled and lost. I walked out of the room, along the corridor to my own. The roses on the table were as fresh as when he'd laid them in my arms. For a moment I allowed myself the luxury of lightening my misery by recalling a love that had been stillborn.

I changed into slacks, a heavy jersey, crepe-soled shoes that would make no sound on the marble staircase. Police stations in every country in the world operated round the clock. The only shred of luck I craved was that the salon door should be closed. It was denied me. When I stepped into the gallery, I stared with lost hope at the triangular wedge of light that spread itself brilliantly over the marble floor I must cross to reach the door. I listened in vain for laughter, any sound of speech that would drown the screech of the bolts, but there was none. I had to descend to the curve of the staircase before I caught the sound of muted half-savage voices intermingling, one cutting out another: two males, two females speaking Sicilian. Once Mario's voice leapt into an enraged protest, which Leo's sharp riposte instantly reduced to a growl. Before I could force one bolt from its socket, it would be transformed into an alarm bell that would bring them racing into the hall.

I crept back to my room and lay on the bed. It wasn't final defeat. All I had to do was to wait until they were asleep, then drive to the telephone call-box in the village, dial a number. Minutes dragged into hours, an endless treadmill of time. Midnight. Beyond. It wasn't until nearly one o'clock that my ears caught the sound of slow footsteps mounting the staircase. Three voices reduced to undertones: Leo's, the Contessa's and Mimi's. I heard Olivia's door open and close, then Mimi's and the Contessa's steps recede. Another lag of time before Olivia's door opened again and I heard what could only be Maidie's feet shuffling along the corridor. That left Mario and the fawn-haired youth unaccounted for, but they might have left earlier.

I waited a quarter-hour by my watch before I thrust my arms into a coat, took a pencil torch from my handbag, crept to the head of the staircase. The wedge of light had been obliterated. In its place was a narrow band of semi-lightness that beamed through the salon door, which was a couple of inches ajar. I trod in snail-like steps and, when I reached the ground floor, pressed myself against the wall, listening to irregular, half-choking snores. At an oblique angle I could see into the salon. The chandelier had been switched off, two candles lighted. It was the fawn-haired boy who was snoring, his head supported by his crossed arms; with a wavering grasp Mario was holding aloft an empty glass, his mouth gaping in a succession of cavernous yawns. Lurching, he stumbled to the head of the table, grasped a bottle of whisky by its neck, tipped the contents into the glass. When, with his back to me, he subsided into a chair, nodded into sleep, I began to slide my feet across the hall. I had not covered more than a yard when there exploded about my ears a tornado of sound: of heavy implements smashing glass, splintering wood, a rending, screeching demolition illuminated by blinding, arclike torches. Where, on either side of the door, there had been shuttered windows, there were twin oblongs of space that had been punched clean of glass and wood by flailing crowbars. Through them two men leapt, made blank-faced, hairless, phantom-beings by the stockings over their heads.

The staircase light flashed alive, and from the gallery Leo took aim, fired a shot that made my ears sing. Blots of yellow flamed from Mario's gun as the boy screeched, held up his hands in gibbering terror. One dehumanised man knelt on one knee as if about to pray, lifted his gun and I watched Leo tip forward, and then silently, with a sort of grace, slide down the curve of the staircase, the gun his lifeless hand could no longer grip rattling on the marble. Mario, lurching forward, fired and the nearest of the two hairless men screamed, clutched his arm, as his double fired twice at Mario. Then, running, they leapt on to the window sills, vanished.

Though not conscious of movement, I found I had retreated to the door leading into the double-cube room; that my forehead was pressed hard against its panelling, the only sound that of breath being laboriously drawn in and out of my lungs. I turned, like a sleepwalker, not prepared to believe the holocaust I had witnessed. There had not been enough time . . . seconds only. But surprise, a lightning attack, and an instant retreat had paid off. Leo, spread-eagled on the curve of the staircase, staring dead-eyed at the cupola, was the spoil of victory they'd left behind.

I crept deeper into the hall. Mario's unwieldy body was hunched into a foetal position, the gun gripped against his chest, blood seeping through his fingers. Of the fawn-haired boy there was no sign.

The wail was Maidie's, an anguished keening. Bare-footed, clad only in a flannelette nightgown, her lank hair dripping over her shoulders, she stumbled at a run down the staircase to Leo. When I reached her his head was cradled in her lap. There was no blood, no smashed skull, only a neat hole in the middle of his forehead, a single bead of scarlet.

"Dear God!" It was a prayer she wailed over and over again.

Crouched beside her, I'd heard no sound, but her ears had been sharper than mine, and gently lowering Leo's head to the marble, she lurched to her feet. The Contessa, no longer statuesque, her face, naked without glasses, hands outstretched, shuffled, stumbled, sobbing: "My boy . . . where's my darling boy. Leo, Leo . . ." Before Maidie could reach her, her hand fumbled for the rail, found only the makeshift tangle of rope, grabbed it, then appeared to trip before the solid mountain of flesh, clad in a billowing cerise dressing-gown, crashed forward.

An isolated death can be assimilated, but a massacre overloads the emotions, numbs all sensibility. I felt no grief, no fright, no shock. Maidie squatted at the Contessa's head. Ugly, stertorous noises came from her throat, her eyes rolled back in their sockets, brown glistening eyes that I was seeing for the first time. She had appeared to trip and fall, but now it became plain the stumble had been the forerunner of a stroke.

Olivia! I ran to her room. Under the shaded light I placed my hand over her heart to check the faint beat. I wrenched a blanket from Leo's bed, spread it over her, went back to Maidie. Her face, minus her teeth, her gums showing, was barely recognisable.

"Brandy! That's what she needs to pull her round. It's in the kitchen, in a cupboard behind the door."

As I ran, my brain involuntarily did a sum. Three of us, but there should have been four. I had to search through ranks of bottles until I found the brandy. I picked up a cup, and without flinching skirted the curled-up mass of Mario's body, edged past Leo's neatly spread-eagled corpse and with a steady hand poured brandy into the cup, handed it to Maidie. She raised the Contessa's head, which her neck could no longer support. A sip went down her throat, the rest dribbled on to her chin. Maidie gently wiped it away with the hem of her nightgown.

"Maidie, I must find Mimi."

She gave no sign that she heard me, and I had no time to waste on repeating my message. With no knowledge of the whereabouts of Mimi's room, I had to search two corridors, all the while marvelling that she had slept through the hurricane of smashing glass and wood, the blasting of guns. I saw myself shaking her out of sleep, capsulating a horror story that was still without reality for me. A light behind a transom acted as a guide. I opened the door. She was standing beside the bed, packing a suitcase. Heaped on the bed-rail were a chinchilla coat, a mink wrap, and she was sliding a leather jewel box into the case. She wore a tailored flannel suit, a silk scarf knotted about her throat, her hair brushed satin smooth, her make-up immaculate. Lying beside a Gucci handbag were a pair of doeskin gloves, a passport and a thick wad of dollar bills. From some vantage point she'd looked down on the sprawled lifeless bodies, turned her back on them and set about salvaging her hoarded treasure.

Her glance barely acknowledged my presence as she continued with her packing, deftly forcing the last items into crevices. Her imperturbability, clenched noninvolvement in the holocaust below tapped a crescendo of rage in me. I shouted: "Leo's been murdered. The Contessa is dying in Maidie's arms. For God's sake, we need a doctor, the police. Go and fetch them; you can bring them here faster than anyone else."

As though she were deaf, she folded a silk nightdress, laid it in the suitcase, snapped the locks.

I grabbed her arm. With strength that did not match the small body, she wrenched it free. The cat's eyes were on fire. "Who's been murdered and why is your doing, not mine. If you want the police, you fetch them." She spat in my face. "Leo's dead, I know. And I know who killed him. You and Patrick Harlow!" I stared into a triangle turned into a devil's face by relentless hate. "So go to hell with my blessing, both of you."

She draped the chinchilla coat and the mink wrap over her arm, picked up her handbag and suitcase.

I stood with my back against the door. "Who were they, the men with guns?"

"Men of vengeance with guns who'd never have tracked Leo down if you hadn't led them to him. That makes you a murderer." For a fraction of a second the skin of her calm shivered as the steel of her will threatened to crack. Even so, it was stronger than mine in that I moved aside to let her pass.

I followed her along the corridor. When she reached the gallery, she stepped wide to avoid Maidie, who was crouched over the Contessa. Maidie grabbed her skirt. "Mimi . . ."

Mimi snatched it from her grasp as though Maidie's touch was unclean. She did not slow her steps, not even glance downwards as she by-passed Leo's body. I stayed with Maidie. Mimi pulled the bolts, turned the handle, did not even pause to close the door behind her.

For a fleeting moment that single tell-tale glance of passion I'd witnessed as I walked past her into the salon resurfaced. Either she was a stoic, or a woman who on a split-second decision could plunge a dagger into the heart of love, kill it stone dead.

Though I had a sense of foundering, the front of my mind was tabulating priorities. I ran to my room, wrenched a pillow and two blankets from the bed. I did not know where Maidie's room was, and had no time to waste on a search. I picked up my coat. My shoes were too small, but I bent down the canvas heels of a pair of espadrilles.

As I eased a pillow under the Contessa's head, Maidie whispered thankfully: "She's coming round." Her glance defied me to contradict her. "She's as strong as a horse, always has been."

Was that, I wondered, Maidie's only sin, overoptimism on a mammoth scale? I spread the blankets over the Contessa, persuaded Maidie to slot her arms into my coat, managed to force the espadrilles on her feet. Then I kneeled down beside her. "She needs a doctor, Maidie. That means I must drive to the village and telephone. I won't be away a second longer than I can help."

She gave me a shaky nod, looked away. "You might as well know, I suppose, that you were right about the baby. She's gone to get him. That's why she wouldn't wait. Carlo, she calls him. She has to keep him in the village because with Olivia losing hers it would have been too cruel for her to see another one around the villa. That's what Mimi and Leo decided. I never did hear who the father was, but that's how it is with girls nowadays. Don't think nothing of having babies before they're married." She looked down the staircase at Leo's body and was overwhelmed by ugly, rending sobs. She clapped her hand over her mouth to stifle them, mourned: "In a way he was my little boy, so bright and clever, top of his form nearly every term. And handsome with it. There was nothing he couldn't wheedle out of you if he set his heart on it." Gently she stroked the Contessa's forehead. "She mustn't know. We've got to keep it from her somehow until she's better. It'll break her heart in two."

When I reached the door I stood there, my limbs shaking under me, as though I'd been beached on a strange shore, and all the props of my life had been wrenched away. I thought I could not take one step, but I was wrong. I descended sixty-two. One day I'd counted them.

I parked the car outside the telephone kiosk. Between the tall dark houses, where there was only an occasional prick of light, the cobbled street was a sheen of moonlight. Somewhere a baby cried. With one foot out of the car, I peered up the narrow alley as though I expected to see Mimi wheeling the baby in his splendid carriage. But except for a cat that wound its sinuous body round my legs, the street was empty.

The telephone numbers for the *posto di polizia* and *ambulanza* were printed on a torn card pasted on the wall above the telephone. I dialled the police station. A sleepy voice answered. Mine sounded unnaturally high. With no thread of syntax remaining in my head, I repeated three times: "*Urgente. Due vomini morti. Est-que vous parlez français ou inglese?*"

The line went dead, and a moment later a second voice, sharper, more authoritative, demanded my name and address. I repeated them twice. "*Ambulanza urgente. Immediatamente.*" There was a sound of shouts in the background as unintelligible questions were fired at me. I repeated "Villa Fossita" until I was too exhausted to utter another word, and then put the telephone back on its hook, wiped the perspiration off my face, shivering at the touch of the cool night air on my skin. Momentarily I was physically and mentally bankrupt, incapable of the smallest action. Four cars were parked in the Piazza; one was a grey Mercedes. I speculated whether Mimi would appear, then decided it was of no consequence one way or the other. She wasn't likely to spend a word, a gesture, or a second of her time on the dead. She had wiped the slate clean, turned her back on a world that had nothing left to give her. As I passed the narrow twisting alley, my eyes registered a blur half-way up. It could have been Mimi and the old nanny with a wrapped bundle in her arms. Or it might have been two drunks supporting one another.

I drove back through the silvered lunar landscape, and when I switched off the engine, I could hear the sirens screaming up the hill. I waited for them to reach the car-park. Three cars and an ambulance, more uniformed men than I could count leaping on to the gravel, the rear door of the ambulance being ripped open, a stretcher being wheeled out.

I pointed in dumb-show to the villa, and two policemen went ahead of me. There were others racing past me as I toiled up the jagged steps. By the time I entered the hall, Mario's body was decently straightened, covered with a blanket, and they were bending over Leo. I had to scramble round them to reach Maidie. In the gesture of a mother protecting a child, she was clasping the Contessa's head to her body, her mouth shaking.

The ambulance men fetched the stretcher. One spoke to Maidie, gently prised the Contessa's head from her grasp. She began to cry.

"Maidie, she must be taken to hospital."

She wiped her eyes, blew her nose and somehow managed to pull herself together, even finding a couple of hairpins with which she skewered her hair into a bun. "Then I'm going with her. I'm not having her come to her senses surrounded by a lot of strangers. You'll have to stay with Olivia."

In my coat that did not meet across her bosom, her heels project-
ing out of the espadrilles, the grubby flannelette nightgown round
her ankles, yet imbued with a poignant dignity, she followed the
stretcher downstairs. Only when she'd disappeared through the door
was I aware of the policeman's hand on my shoulder.

I wrenched myself free, beckoned him frantically to Olivia's room.
"*Dottore*," I repeated over and over again. He stood beside the bed,
a middle-aged officer, with a protruding stomach, heavy jowls and a
ponderous manner. I wrenched the dark scarf from the light. "*Malat-
tia . . . dottore urgente*," I beseeched. He bent over her, delicately,
respectfully put his ear against her chest. Two policemen stood by
the door, watching. With his ear still over Olivia's heart, he asked:
"*Inglese? No Italiano?*"

I shook my head, and because my legs had lost all power to support me, I sat down on Olivia's bed. The movement forced her lids
open, but in a second they were sealed.

He walked to the door, issued an order to one policeman, who saluted and disappeared. For a moment he stood frowning, pulling at
his lower lip, as though in consultation with himself, then he walked
out of the room, leaving a single policeman to guard the door. Time
ceased to have a dimension. There was nothing for me to do but sit
on Olivia's bed, watch the breath at long intervals come in soundless
puffs from her lips. I believed I was watching her die; yet all I saw
with the eyes of my mind was the ransacked house, the blood on the
white rug, the goldfinch battering against the gilded wires of its cage.
Maybe I dozed, maybe I was suspended in a state of catalepsy, but I
was unaware that the middle-aged, pudgy policeman had returned
until he placed a ruled pad on my lap, forced a ball-point pen into
my fingers. By gestures, a spattering of Italian I could understand, he
made plain that I was to write an account of what had happened,
and that a *dottore* would be arriving. Then with a nod he left me,
and the young policeman fetched himself a chair and sat, hands
folded across his chest, on guard over me.

I printed my name, my home address. Olivia's name, Leo's, Maidie's, Mimi's and the Contessa's. At the bottom of the list I
wrote Patrick Harlow. I drew a line, wrote Mario followed by a question mark to indicate that I did not know his surname, and lastly
"Boy, 18–19 years old. Name Unknown."

That was as far as I got when Olivia whispered: "Are you writing
to Mother Clare? Tell her . . ." The two words sapped the last dregs
of her strength.

I glanced behind me, wondering if the policeman had left us. But he was still there, a young man with glistening black hair, a full-lipped mouth with a blaze of white teeth, who emitted a succession of gaping yawns he could not stifle, and in spasms blinked his eyes fiercely to keep awake. I was thankful that Olivia's vision had shortened so that she was not even aware that he was in the room.

CHAPTER 9

I must have dozed, though consciousness was never more than a millimetre away. A man in plain clothes stood on the far side of Olivia's bed, short, compact, muscular, with a narrow clenched face, black hair clipped short. He was studying the notebook in which I'd written the names and addresses of members of the household, which must have slid to the floor while I slept.

He dipped his head slightly. "You are Miss Elizabeth Ashley, an English lady. That is so?"

His English was phonetically correct though his enunciation was stilted. "Yes. Are you a doctor?"

"No." His glance, which evinced no visible emotion, returned briefly to Olivia's unconscious form, then focussed on me. "A doctor will come soon. I am Vittorio Umbino, what I believe you call a detective inspector, of the Caromezza Police Bureau. You are a blood relation of Signora Mariani?"

"No. A friend."

"Is she related to either of the two men who were murdered?"

"She was the wife of Leo Mariani."

"And her nationality?"

"British. Whether she changed it after her marriage, or retained dual nationality, I don't know."

There were sounds of cars arriving or departing. He moved with near-silent steps to the windows, threw open the shutters. "The doctor has arrived. His name is Allende. He is an excellent physician. For a time, when he was young, he studied in one of your London hospitals, so he is able to speak English." He returned to the bed. "How long has Signora Mariani been ill?"

"Since April, when she suffered a miscarriage."

"She has been living here since April?"

"Since June. Before that she, her husband and his mother had been living in Sicily, in Syracuse."

"She has been treated by a doctor?"

"Yes. Dr. Spinosa."

"Spinosa?" he queried, then shook his head. A rap sounded on the door, and the policeman posted there opened it to admit a tall man in a conventional black suit, so thin he appeared emaciated. Inspector Umbino spoke to him, introduced me, and Dr. Allende indicated he wished to be allowed to examine his patient. We moved away, stationed ourselves on the far side of the room, not speaking, not even watching him.

When Dr. Allende had drawn the blankets up to Olivia's chin, he made a beckoning motion to Umbino. They spoke in murmuring undertones that didn't reach me, and then Umbino issued an order to the policeman at the door. He saluted and I heard his footsteps leaping down the marble staircase.

Dr. Allende crossed to my side. "I do not think I have to tell you that Signora Mariani is seriously ill, a very sick woman. She is in a state of severe dehydration, and her heart is exhausted. If she is to live she must be hospitalised at once. Inspector Umbino is summoning an ambulance by radio telephone. Meanwhile, would you please give me the name and telephone number of the doctor who has been attending her. It will be necessary to consult him."

"Dr. Spinosa. I'm sorry I do not know his address or telephone number, nothing about him except he visited her once a week."

The thin flesh on his brow corrugated into a frown. "I have no knowledge of such a doctor practising in Caromezza. You are certain the name is correct? Or was it perhaps that he came from a distance?"

"I don't know."

The expression on his thin, ascetic face censured my ignorance, then enlightenment dawned. "Ah, yes. Spinosa. I recollect now. I understood he was retired from medicine." His tone became professionally brisk. "That is something with which we will not concern ourselves at this moment. Our immediate task is to remove Signora Mariani to hospital."

"A room has been booked for her at the Clinique Zola. They are expecting her."

"By whom was the room booked?"

"By Patrick Harlow, a close friend of Signora Mariani."

"And where is this gentleman now?"

For a moment I could not speak. I certainly could not bring myself to recall and describe to him the bloodied little house. "I don't know. But he made the booking, spoke to the head physician at the Clinique. If you contact him I am sure he will confirm that a reservation was made for Signora Mariani."

His eye combed the room: the light bulb suspended on a flex, the broken floor tiles, the coarse cotton sheets, blankets with holes in them, the hideous plastic chairs. "Miss Ashley, I must inform you that the fees at the Clinique are extremely high. Since you do not appear to know the whereabouts of the gentleman who made the reservation, I must ask what guarantee there is that they will be paid?"

"I will guarantee to pay them." I ran to the bed, seized my handbag, which was on the floor, scrabbled for my traveller's cheques, thrust them at him. He counted them, and informed me that they would be sufficient to cover the fees for a one-day stay in the Clinique.

I gave him the name of the bank, Mrs. Carstairs' telephone number, which was written on a scrap of paper in my purse.

His look remained indecisive for seconds as he brooded, then he nodded his head. "I will accompany her in the ambulance and verify that the reservation was made by Mr. Harlow. You do not know where I can contact him?"

"I'm sorry, no. May I go with her?"

Dr. Allende glanced enquiringly over his shoulder at the detective, who shook his head in negation. When the stretcher arrived Dr. Allende accompanied the feather-weight body that a stranger would have guessed was the corpse of a child.

When the sound of the ambulance died, Inspector Umbino dismissed the police guard, indicated a chair for me, sat down, opened a notebook. "You understand that it is my duty to question you, Miss Ashley? I appreciate that you are shocked and much fatigued, but nevertheless it is most necessary."

He employed simple, tersely phrased questions, for which, as my power of concentration was limited, I was grateful. He took down my answers in a painstaking longhand: dates, relationships, details of everyone who had lived in or visited the villa since my arrival. He recorded the zooming helicopter, the private investigator employed by Mrs. Carstairs, the two men who had never reached the house in the via Rosabella, who were probably at the Hotel Excelsior, and as clear an account as I could frame of the holocaust of destruction and murder I'd witnessed in the hall. Only once or twice did he demand a clarification.

There followed a space of silence while he meticulously checked his notes. "For tonight, we may leave it there. I will have more questions to ask you in the morning after you have slept. Meanwhile I will contact Syracuse for enquiries to be made there, and issue orders that Signorina Angelo is to be traced. You have no knowledge of her destination?"

"No." I'd given him the number of the Mercedes, but I had not mentioned the baby. I was sealed in the trauma of stunning shock; Mimi and the baby were reduced to an irrelevance.

He half-closed his notebook, then reopened it. "One further question. This Mr. Harlow you mentioned, you do not know whether he is still in Italy or has returned to Great Britain?"

As an act of self-preservation, I had cravenly blocked off one corner of memory in the vain hope, like a self-induced fantasy, that what was not admitted had not happened. Now I had to tear it down, trample my cowardice to death, or I might never know whether Patrick was alive or dead.

"Would you give me a moment?"

His head made a stiff motion of assent.

In the silence I could hear the beating of my pulses, the slow thud-thud of my heart. It was as though I was possessed by a fever. Yet when I began to speak my voice was under control, the terrors I must translate into words coherently assembled. As he continued to write I had a feeling I had crawled through a dark tunnel from which I'd never expected to emerge.

This time he finally closed his notebook. "You have the key to the house in the via Rosabella? It will be necessary to have it searched at once."

I took it out of my handbag, handed it to him.

There was a long pause during which I believed we had come to an end of the interrogation, but I was wrong. He leaned forward, cleared his throat. "You state that Mr. Harlow and Signora Mariani had been known to one another for some years, that is correct?"

"Yes."

Again he cleared his throat. "Then I must ask you if they were lovers, if the enmity between Mr. Harlow and Signor Mariani was caused by Signor Mariani's jealousy. In view of Mr. Harlow's disappearance, your account of the damage to the house, it is essential that I am informed of this."

Lovers! They had been once; maybe many times. I did not know. I did not want to know. His glance was steely, adamant. "He loved her." The admission spoken aloud, words became easier to speak. "They'd not met for some time before Mr. Harlow visited her. Signora Mariani appeared devoted to her husband. Also, sometimes, to be afraid of him." With no truth to give myself, how could I unravel it for him?

He pressed: "But Signor Mariani resented Mr. Harlow's presence, the attention he paid his wife?"

"Yes."

He pursed his lips, emitted a low grunt, looked at me with the expression of a man making an effort to meet an unwelcome responsibility. "It is late. We must find an hotel where you can sleep. I suggest you pack a bag with the essentials you need. My men need to examine this room and indeed the whole of the villa. There is much work to be done before morning."

He escorted me to the door, hurried me through it. There were sounds of heavy steps, voices in the rooms below, and two carabinieri were climbing the stairs. It was a matter of minutes to tumble my possessions into a suitcase. I was snapping the locks when, like a photograph thrust under my nose, I saw Maidie in an alien hospital clad in a grubby nightgown and a coat several sizes too small, with a pair of bent-down espadrilles on her feet. I had to open eight doors before I found her room. A plastic suitcase with battered corners was stacked on top of a rickety wardrobe. Hanging inside were a couple of baggy tweed skirts, rubbed cardigans, limp blouses and, protected by a cellophane cover, what could only be her best dress: black, its bodice sewn with bugle beads. I packed the lot, plus two pairs of shoes with worn soles, added her brush and comb, dingy toilet articles and underwear, and an old tussore kimono. The tweed coat, the stained Burberry I hung over my arm. In Olivia's room the Inspector was pacing the floor, issuing orders to the two carabinieri I had seen climbing the stairs. At the sight of me, he dismissed them. "You are ready?"

"I will be in a minute. Signora Mariani will require nightclothes, toilet articles."

We both knew it was an act of faith, but he refrained from saying so aloud. "If you would please waste no time." His glance circled the room, spied a suitcase at the end of Leo's bed, which he seized and opened, stood over me while I tossed in the silk nightwear, the cosmetics I had bought her. In the top drawer of the dressing-table, my hand found a leather jewel-case. Inside was the diamond ring, two bracelets, a necklace, some costume pieces, a dozen empty, velvet-lined compartments and an old pipe with a bitten stem. I was too submerged in the present to question the incongruity of its presence.

He lifted the jewel-case from my hand. "It is better I take charge of this. The contents will be listed, and a receipt given you in the morning." He drew me to my feet. "At this hour the likeliest hotel to accommodate you is the Hotel Excelsior."

Some alert cell in my brain must have been working for me while my hands had been folding and packing, to express a need so elemental that I made no attempt to justify it. To preserve myself intact I had to see and speak to someone who had known him, otherwise the mirage of love I'd created and the nightmare of reality would merge into one, become unendurable. "I would prefer to go to the Hotel Fiori."

For the first time his patience showed signs of being exhausted. "It is not practical. There are not more than a dozen rooms; they will be occupied, booked in advance. And at two o'clock in the morning none of the staff will be on duty."

Stubbornly I repeated: "I would prefer the Hotel Fiori. Signora Limbetto will understand. I can sleep on a sofa or even on the floor. I don't need a room."

"You know Signora Limbetto?"

I was gambling on a gentle blossoming smile, a serene imperturbability. "Yes. She is a friend of Patrick Harlow."

"Very well." Abruptly he gave his assent because it cut a corner of time that was precious to him.

He picked up Maidie's suitcase and Olivia's, left me to carry my own and Maidie's coats, and I followed him down the staircase where his men were brushing the walls and the gilded banister with fingerprint powder. I stepped through the front door into a blaze of flood-lighting, saw in the parking space there were eight or nine cars jammed round the Fiat. Encumbered by the case, Maidie's coats, I stumbled towards it, wondering how I'd manage to reverse out. It was then that Inspector Umbino's patience came to an end. He seized my arm, thrust me into the back of one of the police cars, sat down beside me, as the driver spurted down the hill.

He kept silence until we reached the police station in Caromezza. "It is necessary that I report the incident involving Mr. Harlow immediately. While I am doing so, I will have one of my men telephone Signora Limbetto, to warn her of your arrival, allow her to make some preparations, if she is able to do so."

I sat with my hands folded tightly in my lap until the muscles became cramped, aware that I was banking on a generosity of heart and spirit on which I had no claim. As the minutes dragged my hope thinned, until when the driver opened the door of the car there was not a thread left.

Inspector Umbino waited until the car was moving before he announced: "It appears that Signora Limbetto is prepared to accommodate you, at least for tonight."

When we were beyond the town, climbing steadily, the long semicircle of the Clinique set on a spine of the mountains printed itself in the moonlight. I stared at it until it vanished. Then I remembered Maidie. "Where is the hospital?"

"Behind us. On the other side of Caromezza. A police officer is there and I will issue orders that if there is any change in the condition of the elder Signora Mariani, you will be informed immediately. And Miss Maidstone will be advised of your address at the Hotel Fiori."

I thanked him, and we did not exchange a word until the car circled the courtyard and drew up at an open door. In the shaft of light Signora Limbetto waited to receive us. The elderly waiter who had served Patrick and me at the table beside the lake had stationed himself a few paces behind her heels. He reached for the cases, carried them upstairs.

She lifted my hand, pressed it, spoke briefly in Italian to the inspector, who walked across the Persian rugs to a chair beside a table set with a tray of drinks and sat down.

She led me up a wide flight of shallow stairs into a bedroom that was cool and softly lit. The bed was a four-poster with sprigged muslin curtains. There were photographs strewn about, posters of pop stars tacked to the walls, shelves of books, even an old porcelain-faced doll that if you laid it down would close its lashed eyelids.

"It's your daughter's room!"

"Yes. Maybe a little overelaborate, but it is as she wishes. The bed was the present she chose for her last birthday."

Speech tumbled incoherently off my tongue. "You shouldn't . . . I can't . . ."

She shook her head, gave me that slow-blooming smile. "Marietta is young, heedless. She talks before she thinks. But she has a quality I treasure. A loving, caring heart. It would give her great joy to lend you her room. Come," she added with a note of authority, "we will talk no more tonight. You must sleep. The bathroom is here." She opened a door. "Purple! Marietta's favourite colour when she was seventeen. Now that it is so no longer, she wishes to change it. But I tell her she must learn to live with her mistakes."

When I lay in Marietta's bed, she poured some steaming liquid from a thermos and placed it within my palm. "It may taste a little bitter, but I promise you it contains no drugs, only a mixture of herbs, a recipe of my grandmother's that will soothe you to sleep."

It was as bitter as gall. I remember returning the mug to her, lying back on the pillows, but nothing else before I escaped into a world where no one was dead, and no one dying.

I woke to the clink of china. Signora Limbetto was placing a tray on the bedside table. Beside it was a silver clock, its face enfolded in angels' wings, with delicately engraved hands pointing to five minutes to twelve. Memory sprang alive, thrust me upright.

She sat on the edge of the bed, pressed one of my hands between her own. "Nothing has happened while you slept. Your friend is under expert care but it is too soon for news of an improvement in her condition. As I think you must know, the old lady is critically ill. That is the bulletin the hospital gave the police and Inspector Umbino telephoned it to me an hour ago."

She set the tray on my knee.

"And Patrick? Did you know about him?"

"Yes, the inspector told me. No news. That does not mean there won't be some before the day is out. Remind yourself that he is young, strong and an exceptionally resourceful man."

I nodded obediently. To me, youth, strength and resourcefulness seemed pitiful armour against thugs with weapons to bludgeon him to insensibility or death. The dead-weight of guilt pressed hard upon me. If I hadn't drunk the champagne, the wine, if I'd hung the key on a string round my neck . . . If, if, if . . .

I sipped the coffee through lips that shook against the cup. "Will I be able to see Olivia this afternoon?"

"Permission has been granted by the Clinique for one visitor a day. No more. They suggest three o'clock. Inspector Umbino will be here at four, and there is a man downstairs who says he is a friend of a Mrs. Carstairs, who lives in America. A Mr. Charles Barratt. He would like to speak to you, but there is no cause for haste. He has been served with an aperitif, and then he will eat lunch here."

Barratt! Such a common name. But for the outboard motor, it would have been safely stored in my head and the night would have followed a different pattern.

"And the police have returned your car. It is in the courtyard."

"That means after I've seen Olivia I can drive to the hospital and see Maidie." When she looked puzzled, I explained Maidie's relationship to the Mariani family. "I can't believe she is still on her feet, but she probably is."

"The visiting hours are strict. She will not be welcome except at stipulated times. It may be that she will be left sitting on a bench in a corridor. All our hospitals are understaffed, which means the nurses are overworked. If you can persuade her, bring her here to sleep."

Now the smile needed no forcing. "Do you own an hotel that expands, like magic, when the need arises?"

"I wish I did. But Maria, who is in charge of the bedrooms, has this morning left for Milan to nurse her mother, who is sick. Temporarily taking her place is a local girl who sleeps at home. That means that Maria's room is vacant. It is small, but comfortable. Now, you must eat, that is a basic necessity of life. It will help no one if you starve yourself. You can see Mr. Barratt in my sitting-room. It is on your right at the bottom of the stairs. There is a plaque on the door which says 'Private,' so you will find it."

Charles Barratt, I guessed, was in his fifties, silver-haired, with a smooth pinkish face, average height, with an understated elegance that only the overprivileged can hope to acquire. His handshake was firm, his first words intuitively and spontaneously kind. "I feel guilty at disturbing you so soon after you've suffered such an appalling ordeal, but I promise not to keep you long. First, may I order you a drink?"

I refused. As he sat down, I asked: "It may sound an odd question, but where are you staying? At the Excelsior Hotel?"

"Yes. Actually, though we weren't to know it, Patrick had booked us in there. When he didn't show up at Milan we hired a car to drive us to Caromezza. Unfortunately, as he was due to meet us, I hadn't in the previous somewhat hectic twenty-four hours asked Mrs. Carstairs for his address and, for similar reasons, she omitted to provide me with it. Whether it would have made any difference . . ."

"It wouldn't. They broke into the house the previous night. They stole my key. I didn't take sufficient care of it."

His look was compassionate. "And you blame yourself! That's a sentiment I can appreciate, but regrets are nonproductive, futile. Try not to distress yourself."

"Yes," I said obediently.

"This morning I spent over an hour with a policeman called Umbino. He seems efficient. They are certainly pulling out all the stops." When I made no comment, he went on: "You know Marianne Carstairs, I imagine? At least she knows you."

"I met her once or twice when I was a child."

He glanced at his digital watch. "By now she's on a plane for Milan. As you may remember, she is a remarkable woman." I remembered nothing of the sort, my knowledge of her had been too fragmentary, but there was no point in saying so. "She is endowed with a super-abundance of physical and mental energy, plus a will like iron that has never accustomed itself to accept defeat. She's one of life's natural winners. Her recipe for success is to deal with the man at the top. It works, too!" He smiled encouragingly. "I'm telling you this in the hope that it will be of some comfort to you. With background information sent in by this private investigator Lewis and facts supplied by the police in Syracuse, the police here are working on the theory that the two murders were committed as an act of vengeance by the two sons of the man who was shot dead in Sicily earlier in the year, that they identified the villa from the helicopter you saw. Naturally, the police are anxious to question Olivia, though they will not be allowed access to her until she is much farther along the road to recovery than she is now. Also a Miss Maidstone who, I understand, is some kind of family factotum. You know her, I imagine?"

"Yes. She is at the hospital with Leo's mother."

"You poor child! That, too."

I didn't feel a child; more like an old, old woman who was living out the remnant of a life that seemed pointless. "Patrick said you were bringing a doctor with you. Is he here?"

"Graham Saville. Yes. He had a consultation with the senior physician at the Clinique early this morning, confirmed to his satisfaction that Olivia is receiving the best possible treatment and, as medical etiquette does not permit him to practise inside the Clinique and he is a very busy man, he decided to fly home." He studied me for a moment, then enquired: "Would you permit me to telephone you this evening to learn the latest bulletin on Olivia which I can give Mrs. Carstairs when I meet her plane in Milan? I understand you will be visiting her some time today."

"Yes, please do. I'm seeing her at three o'clock."

He rose. "I have one more favour to ask. Keep in mind that if there is any mortal thing I can do to help, you only have to ask."

And with a gesture that was startling, yet in him natural and unaffected, he lifted my hand and touched it with his lips.

The chair in which I sat waiting until it was time for me to leave for the Clinique was by a window on the side of the hotel. From it I could see the lake, the jetty and the little island, even the great frothy acacia tree that had shaded us while we ate. Imperceptibly there built up in me a steadiness, as if all the tears I'd inwardly shed had ceased. I sat motionless waiting for what was happening to me to define itself. When it did, it was precious beyond words: I found I could believe that somewhere Patrick was alive.

Before I was allowed to see Olivia I was requested to present myself to a senior consultant. His name was on the door of his office. I read it as the porter ushered me in, but it did not remain in my head. No fact did for more than a few seconds.

A middle-aged man, with a morose manner, fidgeting nervously with the appointments on his desk, he demanded brusquely: "I understand you are a friend of Signora Mariani?" He glanced at a form beneath his hand. "We require to know who is her next of kin. Dr. Allende, who accompanied her when she was admitted, does not know, and neither do the police. Arrangements for her admission were made by an Englishman, Patrick Harlow, who saw a colleague of mine. The police inform me that he has disappeared, whatever that may mean. Also that her husband was killed in some gangster brawl last night. So who is her next of kin?"

"She has no kin. She's an orphan. She has a guardian, Hayward Carstairs, but he is a semi-invalid and lives in Florida. His wife is flying to Italy today. She will assume responsibility for Signora Mariani's expenses."

"We are not only concerned with fees, Miss Ashley. Rather whether Signora Mariani has a hope of surviving. I cannot understand how she was allowed to deteriorate into such an appalling state. The police inform me that you have been staying with her. Was there nothing you could do? No steps you could take to ensure she received proper medical care?"

"She was under a doctor, a Dr. Spinosa."

"Yes, yes. So I understand. A doctor who, five years ago, was convicted of drug offences, forbidden to practise, but who it appears, assuming his wife's name, continued to do so, for selected undercover patients. Lamentable. A criminal offence. Will you be in touch with Mrs. Carstairs when she arrives?"

"Yes."

"Very well. I will register her as next of kin. That means that I shall require to see her immediately. Be kind enough to convey my message to her."

"How is Signora Mariani?"

The anger died out of him. "We are doing all that is humanly possible, but I cannot guarantee the outcome. She is sedated. When you see her, please make no attempt to rouse her."

He rose from his desk to signal the interview was at an end. As he opened the door, he said: "Forgive me if I appear brusque. To me it is a crime to endanger a human life by neglect and the misuse of drugs."

The room, painted lilac and grey, was as quiet as a grave, aseptic and air-conditioned. Under the snow-white bed-cover Olivia's form made no impression. An intravenous feed was attached to her left arm, a tube taped to her nostrils. At her side a middle-aged nurse sat hemming a square of silk. She rose, gestured for me to take the chair she had vacated, and on feet that made no sound on the tiled floor fetched another, set it down at the foot of the bed.

Under her flaring starched cap was a face that was unsymmetrical, with irregular, slightly bulbous features, but made beautiful by a madonnalike calm. She whispered: "My English is poor. I regret. You are, I think, a good friend of Signora Mariani. We all hope for her."

I thanked her. They'd plaited Olivia's pale gold hair, wound it in a little crown on the top of her head. Her face was so waxen pale there seemed to be no blood flowing beneath the skin. She did not once stir, and you could not see the breath passing through her lips. Every six stitches—I counted them—the nurse raised her eyes to examine her patient. There was nothing for me to do but follow her example of stillness, hope that Olivia would live, yet almost equally dread the moment when consciousness came to life in her. Paradoxically, I fretted about trivial things: that I had not thought to bring her flowers to grace the cell-like room; that if, after I left, by a miracle, she opened her eyes, she would not know where she was, or see anyone she knew.

When my allotted half-hour came to an end the nurse rose, smiled and moved on silent feet to open the door for me.

"Tomorrow she may be awake. I pray for her."

As I walked through the entrance hall, a girl touched my arm. "Signorina Ashley?"

When I said yes, she handed me a folded sheet of paper. On it was a telephone message from Signora Limbetto. The Contessa had died. Would I please return to the Hotel Fiori instead of driving to the hospital.

At the hotel, Pietro had a second message: Inspector Umbino had been and gone. He would be calling again later. Signora Limbetto was out, but had asked him to serve a tray of tea to Miss Maidstone, and collect her suitcase from my room. Her room was number 16 on the top floor and she was now lying down resting.

When, having eased open the door a crack, I peeped in, she was doing nothing of the sort, but sitting bolt upright in a chair by the bed, wearing the black dress. Her face was mottled, her lids so puffy that her eyes were narrowed to slits, either from the tears she had shed or lack of sleep.

"Maidie, I hoped you'd be resting."

She pushed the tray impatiently from her, spoke with grinding bitterness. "She died hard, not peacefully like you're supposed to but fighting for every last breath." With a fumbling hand she pleated her top lip. "Then away with her, packed in a basket, their only worry who was going to pay for the funeral."

I sat beside her. Some of the bugle beads were hanging by threads, making a tinkling sound like tiny chimes. "Maidie, you don't have to worry . . ."

"Oh, yes I do," she countered fiercely. "I know all about funerals. They'll pop both of them into a pauper's grave. Out of sight, out of mind! And the police badgering me. You'd think they'd have more respect for the dead, but not a bit of it. Pry, pry, pry. Get it all written down on paper. As if I knew anything. I never have. I've never wanted to. And if I did, is it likely I'd tell them? They're both dead, aren't they! And you don't speak ill of the dead, not ever. Not in my book. When you die your sins are forgiven, that's what I was taught. So if you've come to ask me a lot of questions you're wasting your time."

"I'll not ask you a single one." She gave me a darting glance raw with scepticism. "And you don't have to worry about the funeral."

She burrowed in her handbag, found a stub of a cigarette, lighted it. "I suppose you mean well," she admitted grudgingly. "For all your poking and prying." She gave me a stabbing glance. "I saw you fiddling with Olivia's pills that you'd no right to touch, that's why I put them out of harm's way."

"But you didn't tell Leo?"

"He'd enough on his mind without being bothered by your meddling." She squashed out the cigarette that had given her only a couple of puffs, demanded: "How old would you take me for?"

Startled at the sudden switch, I deliberately underestimated. "Fifty?"

"Sixty-two." Her mouth began to shake, then she bit it so hard that it was indented with teeth-marks. "I always prayed I'd outlive

her, see her decently into her grave, and then there'd be Leo. He'd
have looked after me. Now they're both gone." She swallowed in
great gulps, fighting the tears that were rising in her eyes. "I suppose
she'd have liked that, them walking into Paradise side by side. She
was a believer, you know. I brought her rosary back with me. I
wasn't going to have one of those thieving nurses steal it." She stared
down at her hands, which were locked in her lap. "So what's to become of me, with no one belonging to me? That's what's hard, having no one. Not no one caring whether you're dead or alive, and having no one to care about. It'd have been better if I'd gone with her."

"There's Olivia!"

"Aye, there's Olivia." She thought a moment. "Where is she?"

"In a *clinique*. About as ill as it's possible to be. I've just come
back from seeing her."

For the first time since I'd entered the room, she appeared to
recognise me as someone she knew, not as a stranger murmuring
inane platitudes. "You didn't know her. Then she wasn't easy to
know because she always showed her worst side to everyone except
Leo and me. She was shy, you see, shy with everyone. Strangers
bothered her."

It took me a second to realise she was talking about the Contessa
not Olivia. Then the sobs broke over her, wrenching every bone in
her body, in a storm of grief. I put her to bed, hung up her best black
dress. Gradually the sobs quietened. The last words she spoke before
she fell asleep were: "They can nail me to a cross and I'm still not
answering their daft questions. It's none of their business."

"Perhaps," Signora Limbetto suggested, when I sat between her
and Inspector Umbino in her private sitting-room, "we should call in
a doctor. At least he could prescribe a sedative for her." She turned
to me. "Or do you think it better to let her rest for the time being?"

"Rest, I think."

Umbino informed us that the inquests on Mario and Leo would
be held the following day, and thereafter the bodies would be
released to the relatives. He directed a severe glance at me. "This
English lady, Miss Maidstone. She is extremely unco-operative. She
will not disclose the reason they left Sicily in haste, settled in the
Villa Fossita, which she insists was about to be rebuilt. That could
not be so. Leopold Mariani had no legal title to it. We have not yet
gathered all the facts but it would appear that an arrangement, what
you call a deal, was made by Mario Battaglio whereby the Marianis
took temporary possession of the villa. It was an illegal transaction,

not binding in law. As soon as this fact became known, they would have been evicted. Is it that Miss Maidstone does not know this, or is she lying?"

I didn't know; I thought it unlikely I ever would. Eyes wilfully blinded against the truth, or eyes that refused to recognise evil in those she loved? I shook my head. "All I know is that she was a devoted friend of the Mariani family."

He said severely: "It is my opinion, and that of my superiors, that Miss Maidstone could not have been ignorant of the vendetta existing between Mariani and Randoli which ended in Randoli's murder. Information from the Sicilian police and a report from Mr. Lewis leads us to believe that the two men who broke into the villa and shot Mariani and Battaglio were Randoli's sons avenging the murder of their father. Miss Maidstone may well have been acquainted with them, which would make her a vital witness. She could have overheard conversations, even taken part in discussions, been aware of Mariani's movements on the night Randoli was murdered. So she must be questioned; furthermore, she must answer the questions that are put to her. There are penalties for nonco-operation with the law."

It was undoubtedly a legitimate threat, but in Maidie's present mood, I doubted that she would provide him with much satisfaction. "Have you caught the boy who was at the villa the night Mario was shot?"

"Battaglio's nephew, Antonio? No. Nor his wife nor his brother-in-law. All three fled from the taverna as soon as Antonio brought them news of his uncle's death. But it should not take long to find them."

It was Signora Limbetto who put the question I couldn't steel myself to ask. "And Mr. Harlow, what news is there of him?"

"None so far," he said shortly, as though to admit failure pained him, "but we have a picture and a description of him which is being widely circulated. We hope for results before the day is over." He rose, bowed to each of us.

When he'd left the room, I said: "He didn't mention Olivia. It was as though he'd written her off."

"No," she soothed. "Like all police officers he prefers to rely on his own system of communication. You may be sure he has informed himself of her condition."

By now the glow of that miraculous moment when I had stared at the acacia tree was beginning to fade. I tried with all my might to hang on to its fragile remnants, but it was slipping inch by inch from my grasp.

CHAPTER 10

Next morning there was a message that Mrs. Carstairs wished to see me at 5 P.M.

Although my contacts with her had been limited to the one occasion on which she had scrutinised my home—and probably my manners and deportment—and a few times when she had accompanied Olivia in the Rolls that delivered her to our door, I retained two indelible impressions of her. One was of a woman without claim to natural beauty who, with labour and love, had created a self so exquisitely presented it stunned the eye by its sheer perfection. The second was of autocracy that touched the borderline of arrogance but which perfect manners forbade her to cross.

In the intervening years those twin facets of her person had remained impervious to time. I could have sworn that her body was not an ounce heavier than when she had sipped tea in my mother's house. Her hair was tinted a translucent silver-gilt, her features almost, but not quite, lineless, her clothes bore the hall-mark of a top designer's signature.

From the chaise-longue she extended a fragile hand tipped with blush-tinted fingernails. "Forgive me for not rising, but it has been an exhausting day and it will be morning before it comes to an end." She snapped a finger and thumb. "Charles!"

Charles Barratt, standing at her head, drew forward a chair for me. His smile was part conspiratorial, part sympathetic. He looked exhausted.

She gave him a dismissive nod. "That is as far ahead as we can plan at the moment. I'll see you in the morning, Charles. I suggest nine o'clock."

"Fine. If you need me earlier, I'll be on call. I don't propose to leave the hotel."

"Now," she said with an all-embracing glance that in one split second analysed my looks, character, manners and tabulated them for future reference, "before we begin, may I order you a drink?"

When I refused, she awarded me a commending nod. "Then we won't waste precious time on meaningless pleasantries. First, I would like to know how Olivia reached the pitiable state in which I found her this afternoon. Also, how you came to be staying at the villa and what you observed while you were there. On the telephone Patrick mentioned your visit, but not what prompted you to make it." She reached for a pair of spectacles with what appeared to be silver frames, but which were more likely to be platinum, balanced them on the bridge of her nose, then picked up a tooled-leather notebook and a gold pen. "Take your time. I appreciate there will be some sequences that will be distressing for you to recall."

Eyes fixed on the blank ruled page, she waited in silence, a pose reminiscent of a psychiatrist taking notes from a patient.

The recapitulation was less painful than I had anticipated. Either by habit or deliberate intent she had lowered the emotional temperature. My mangled nerves responded to her impersonal, almost professional, approach. I told, she listened, never once evincing horror, distress or disbelief. I might have been speaking into a tape recorder.

She thanked me when I reached the end, pressed a bell on the table beside her. "We have both earned a drink. What will you have?"

I chose Campari and soda; she ordered a glass of fresh iced lemon juice. She sipped it in silent meditation, as delicately as though it were undiluted spirit. "I don't propose to allow myself the luxury of outrage, loathing for a monster who is dead. Time doesn't permit of it." But for a second she did. "It is obscene. One would not commit a dog to such misery."

She made a whiplash gesture of dismissal, and for a second age stamped itself across her face. "I have assured myself that Olivia is receiving the best treatment it is possible to provide for her. Naturally, as soon as her condition improves and she is fit to travel, I shall have her flown home. At the moment, however, I have to accept that she must remain in the Clinique."

She removed her spectacles and closed the notebook. "My overriding concern is for my nephew." She paused, her rose lips formed into a line of extreme obduracy. "He must be found. That is my first priority. You are quite certain there is no fact, however seemingly unimportant, that you have overlooked?"

When I said no, she added: "If any come to your mind, no matter how trivial or irrelevant, you are to contact me immediately. This evening I am dining with two Italian friends, one of whom is related by marriage to the head of the police for this province; he will accompany us and give me the benefit of his advice. Inspector Umbino and his superior officers are no doubt efficient, but whether they are of the calibre to handle this case . . . well, I have yet to confirm that for myself. Impetus, thrust, imagination, above all, speed, are the essential qualities required. How well did you know Patrick?"

"Not well," I answered, not knowing or caring whether it was the truth or a lie.

"You met him for the first time when you arrived at this so-called villa?"

"Yes."

Her mouth softened. "He is a young man dear to both my husband and myself. Unfortunately there is a reckless streak in him, inherited from his mother, a beautiful creature, but wild. She was killed when Patrick was sixteen, in a private plane the first time she was allowed to fly solo. The waste! At one time my husband and I allowed ourselves to hope that Patrick and Olivia would marry. They might well have done if she had not met that fiend who abused her cruelly to serve his devilish ends." She breathed in deeply. "Thank God he is dead, or I'd have been capable of murdering him with my own hands."

She sipped her iced lemon juice to subdue her rage. "I'm informed by the police that a servant of the Marianis is refusing to answer questions, supply them with information as to what she witnessed and overheard. Is this so?"

"Miss Maidstone. She is still in a state of shock. Leo's mother, to whom she was devoted, died yesterday. Also, she had known Leo since he was a small child, and was very attached to him."

"Then the woman must either be a fool, or an accomplice. In either case, it is a criminal offence to withhold vital evidence from the police. She must be induced to talk. If you know her, perhaps you could convince her that it would be in her own interest to do so." She glanced at her watch. "I'm sorry, but it is time I dressed for dinner." She slid gracefully off the chaise-longue. "I'm grateful to you. Some girls, having been subjected to the ordeal you've suffered, would have shown signs of hysteria, but your account was admirably clear and precise. I remember your mother as a calm and capable woman. You obviously take after her." She released her small-boned hand from mine. "I will keep in touch, and inform you of the steps I propose to take. Good night."

Within me was not calm but chaos. As I stepped out of the lift,

Charles Barratt rose from a chair in the reception area. "Okay?" he queried. "High-powered ladies can be exhausting. Would you like a drink?"

I shook my head. "Could we sit down somewhere? I've a favour to beg."

"Any favour's forthcoming for the asking." He led me to an off-shoot of the terrace that, because it enjoyed a less spectacular view, afforded some privacy.

I blurted out: "I need some money, a loan that I'll repay as soon as I'm home. For Leo's funeral and his mother's."

"You mean," he said, sounding utterly confounded, "that you're responsible for burying Leo and his mother!"

"There's no one else. Maidie worked for love. She's broke, terrified they'll be buried in paupers' graves. And I'd hate even to raise the question with Mrs. Carstairs."

"My dear child!" Distress closed on his face. "Of course, all that's required. I am sure that it would be Olivia's wish, as it is mine, that it is drawn from the considerable sum that within days will be at her disposal. So it is merely a loan. Would you like me to make the arrangements?"

"Could you? Have you the time?"

"All the time you need. I will contact Miss Maidstone and make sure that everything is carried out precisely as she would wish."

" 'Thank you' seems very inadequate."

"Nonsense." His tone lightened. "Burial is a subject on which trustees require to be knowledgeable. Testators die, and you would be surprised how many of them are without kin, even without friends. You might say it is a duty that comes with the job. I will acquaint myself of the Italian formalities and proceed accordingly. As soon as the arrangements have been finalised I will be in touch."

"Mrs. Carstairs spoke of plans under consideration. What do you imagine she has in mind?"

"Among other possible courses, I would guess a large monetary reward. She believes, maybe correctly, that money accomplishes miracles."

"You mean a ransom?"

He nodded. "She's taking advice from some high authority this evening; even so, I would expect that whatever it is she will follow her own course: offer a handsome reward for the release of Patrick Harlow. It has the advantage of being a positive action. Temperamentally she's the type of woman who finds it anathema to sit back and wait upon events."

I stared at a crushed cigarette packet under my foot. "Her theory being that Patrick was kidnapped and is still alive?"

"Yes."

"Leo and Mario are dead . . . there's only Mario's wife, her brother and the boy. With the police hunting them down, are they likely to lay a trap for themselves by collecting a ransom . . . are they?"

"My dear Elizabeth, I don't know the answer. None of us do."

"What you're saying, what Mrs. Carstairs believes, is that he's a prisoner somewhere, locked up?" I saw him in a filthy ink-black hut, dying on a dirt floor.

"It's one possibility that has to be investigated. Mario's wife, her brother and nephew might be prepared to sell information concerning Patrick's whereabouts for a large sum of money. It is, I assure you, a viable theory."

I did not find it so. Robbed of Mario's leadership, weren't they more likely to concentrate on saving their own skins than run the risk of falling into a police trap?

In the dark pool of my mind, a minute worry surfaced. "Do you know if the owner of the house in the via Rosabella has returned home?"

"I think not. He's hitch-hiking through Jugoslavia and there appears to be some difficulty in contacting him. Why do you ask?"

"There's a pet goldfinch. It can't be left to starve to death."

He blinked. "No indeed. Though I doubt if a goldfinch in a cage has a life worth living."

I remembered its ration of one free hour a day. I saw it perched on Patrick's head, tweaking at strands of sable hair. He gave me a wry smile. "I take it you want the little creature rescued?"

"Its owner is devoted to it. Even so, I couldn't bring myself to enter the little house. If someone could collect it and bring it to me at the Hotel Fiori . . ."

"It shall be done." His smile was a warm expression of comfort. "Anything else?"

"No. That's more than enough."

When I arrived back at the hotel, Maidie was thrusting aside the arm of a police officer who was trying to help her out of a car. She stomped into the foyer, crimson splashes on her cheekbones. To prevent her bursting into indignation in public, I coerced her into the lift. She sat down in a low chair in my bedroom, knees splayed so that they stretched the skirt of the best black dress she now wore permanently to the breaking point.

"Well, they didn't get anything out of me. And they never will, not till doomsday. A nasty slimy piece of goods that inspector, setting traps and waiting for me to fall into them. Well, I didn't. I beat him at his own game." She stopped suddenly. "And what's all this rigmarole about Patrick? I couldn't make head nor tail of it. He hasn't been in an accident, has he?"

"Maidie, didn't you know about him?"

"Know what? What's there to know? Where is he?"

She could lie—she had to me—keep secrets under wraps or pretend they didn't exist, but she would have needed to be a professional actress to feign that expression of frustration and bafflement. Beneath the seething morass of hate and guilt, hope and dread, I experienced a qualm of relief. Even so, my voice was harsh, condemning, as though I needed to punish her. "No one knows where he is. Leo drugged me, then stole my key. He and Mario, and maybe the boy, broke into the little house he rented in Caromezza, tore it apart. There was a white rug soaked in blood, but no Patrick. Now everyone's playing a guessing game. Is Patrick Harlow dead or alive?"

Her lower jaw dropped, lending her a half-demented look, then she gulped. "It was Mario, that bully-boy, his brother-in-law and sly-eyed nephew. I could never stomach any of them, or that tart with her dyed hair. Any mugging that was done, they were responsible for it, you mark my words. Leo wouldn't have known what they were up to. Oh, I agree he and Mario used to have drinking sessions, but that was only because they'd been buddies when they were teen-agers in Sicily."

It would have been a waste of breath to insist that Leo, out of vengeance or fear of losing a fortune, had master-minded the operation. I stayed silent.

Her voice quavered. "And they don't know where Patrick is?"

"No."

She grieved to herself. "He was a nice lad. A real nice lad. Thoughtful he was, and a great one for a joke."

For a moment I hated her for the past tense, then I looked down at her feet in their out-of-shape shoes, the best black dress, dust embedded in its folds, and shame crawled over me. She, too, had lost someone she loved. I told her that Olivia's trustee had promised to assume responsibility for the funeral arrangements, and would be telephoning her to confirm everything was as she wished. I had expected another outburst, but she nodded her head resignedly. "When she could get there the Contessa said mass at the little church in San Giorgio. She took a liking to the priest there. I can't remember his name; it's slipped right out of my head. My memory's gone to pot. There's a graveyard a bit of way down the hill that's nice and peaceful, though she'd have preferred to have been buried in Sicily. Still, as long as it's all done properly with a requiem mass and a nice headstone. One for the two of them, she'd have liked that. And tell the man he can rely on my paying him back. I've never welched on a debt in my life." She raised her eyes to me, sorrow-filled. "Whatever's to become of Olivia with both of them gone?"

I clenched my teeth. "We don't know that Patrick's dead."

"No," she said without conviction. "Let's hope he's not. He's the only one who can comfort her, give her any sort of life now Leo's gone."

Soon after dinner, a carabiniero brought me a cage wrapped in a cloth that had been strapped to the back of his motor cycle. That night the goldfinch kept me silent company. Pinned to the cage was its diet-sheet, and as soon as the stalls in the market were open next morning, I bought it food.

Mrs. Carstairs introduced me to what amounted to a full-scale operations room she had set up in the suite adjacent to her own. Three girls, all tri-lingual, manned the telephones. Ted Lewis, a plump ball of a man, with a permanent frown and an air of not relishing being removed from his natural sphere, was in attendance. There was a uniformed policeman on guard at the door, and a plainclothes officer at a desk above which were taped a dozen large-scale maps.

With a waft of her hand Mrs. Carstairs invited my approval. "It is a nerve-centre, the key to the whole operation. Up-to-date photographs of Patrick were delivered by hand to all newspaper offices soon after dawn. They will appear in the mid-day editions, plus the announcement that I am prepared to pay six hundred million lire for the release of my nephew."

To me it was a surrealistic scene, with the teleprinter spewing out endless ribbons of paper, as though she had designed an elaborate piece of machinery to play a game of life and death. There was a choking feeling in my throat.

"Elizabeth!"

When I looked at her I saw I'd done her an injustice. For all the professionalism, the zestful determination she exuded, there was a blur of fatigue in her eyes, a private agony on the pale rose mouth, and the thin body had lost its elasticity.

I apologised for missing her question, blamed the rattle of the teleprinter.

"I was saying that Patrick is my brother's dearly loved younger son, born when his elder brother was in his teens. Alan emigrated to South Africa, is settled there. So . . ." She lifted an almost transparent hand. "Although my brother is old and frail, I had no alternative but to telephone him this morning before I released the story to the newspapers." She set her face in a mould of iron determination. "I swore that Patrick would be found, and I intend to keep that promise no matter what it demands in time, effort and money."

I, too, had telephoned my mother, knowing that a story printed in the Italian press would be picked up by the news agencies and appear in the English papers. Olivia's illness, Leo's death, had shocked and distressed her. Patrick Harlow's name was unknown to her—as David's had been. In Mrs. Carstairs' nerve-centre I wondered if I, a second-time victim to instant love, was doomed for life to secret loving that would never be allowed to bloom outside my heart.

"According to the bulletin from the Clinique, there's no perceptible change in Olivia's condition. She's still in a coma. That being so, I shall remain here, to take immediate action on any information that may reach us. Will you be visiting her?"

"Yes, this afternoon."

"Good. The head consultant at the Clinique has promised to contact me if she shows any sign of emerging from the coma."

Five of us walked behind the two coffins that at noon were borne from the church to the stone-walled cemetery on the hill: Charles Barratt, Maidie, the priest, me and, leaving a ten-yard gap, Inspector Umbino. One wreath was centred on the Contessa's coffin for which Maidie had written the card; two on Leo's, one from Maidie and one for which I'd forged a card from Olivia. Maidie, wearing a battered purple hat, stared before her, stoic-faced, enduring. Under the black veil Signora Limbetto had insisted on lending me, to hold remembrance at bay, I kept count of the number of Latin words I could translate into English in the committal service of human flesh to merciful oblivion in the earth. The mass at an end, the twin coffins lowered from sight, the priest shook our hands, dipped his head to each of us and then walked away, past a mound of raw earth. I wondered if it covered Mario. Beyond the cemetery a crowd pressed against the gates, motionless, waiting, not even uttering a whisper until the "outsiders" were out of earshot.

We'd travelled in Mr. Barratt's car. As he helped Maidie into the front seat beside the chauffeur, she said primly: "You arranged that very nicely. She'd want me to thank you."

Sitting beside him, I unpinned my black veil, folded it and laid it on my lap, asked the question I put to him once each day, sometimes twice. "Is there any news?"

He pursed his lips. "No hard news. Feelers, leads that run into dead ends. What clogs the wheels are the mentally sub-normal, the hoaxers, liars and outright crooks, plus a couple of clairvoyants hell-bent on publicity. You certainly uncover some pretty loathsome so-called human beings." He sighed. "Plus the honest-dealers who are prepared to swear a Bible oath that they saw Patrick on a train, a bus, or drinking in a café. There are two who are convinced Patrick accosted them in a street asking for directions to the nearest railway station. To date ninety-eight men and women fit into one of those categories, every one of which has to be investigated."

"If Patrick were mobile, he'd be here."

"Assuredly. Then, there's protocol! We need the back-up of the police, their local know-how, the numbers of men they can deploy. To secure that you have to trade in some of your authority. Though Marianne finds it hard to take, by-passes it whenever she can, we have to work alongside them, sometimes accept a judgment with which we disagree.

"At the moment we've no clue as to Patrick's whereabouts. The two gunmen who blasted their way into the villa have not been caught. Neither have Mario's wife, brother-in-law or nephew. For what it's worth the police have placed the doctor under house-arrest. Not unnaturally he's suffering from shock, is incapable of articulate speech. But we do know that a young woman, who fills the description of the girl who lived with the Marianis, boarded a plane for Paris the morning after the killings. The French Sûreté have been alerted, but so far there's been no news of her." His glance turned sideways. "There is one small element of doubt, however. She was carrying a baby. Did she have a child?"

There was no streak of sentiment left alive in me, certainly no pity for Mimi, merely a shadow of revulsion in involving a baby—any baby—in the outer fringes of murder. I had no idea what penalty Mimi would suffer if she was caught, but I was made immune from any wish for vengeance by the thrust of my all-consuming will that Patrick should be alive. I had never told Umbino about the baby, but I felt no guilt on that score. He would have learnt of its existence within a few hours of Mimi's flight.

"Yes."

"Leo's child?"

"I imagine so. She boarded it out in the village."

"The likelihood is that this girl, Leo Mariani's mistress, would have had prior knowledge of the attack made on Patrick, which makes her an accessory before the fact. Yet you sound completely disinterested in whether or not she is picked up by the police. I find that curious."

"She'd tell them nothing."

"You sound very positive."

I'd seen her turn her back on the past, with a pitilessness that encompassed not only others but herself. Bolted the gates behind her on a love that, being dead, was rendered sterile. For a flying second I envied her.

"Yes, I'm sure." Some people keep the truth sealed inside them forever, like martyrs at the stake. Maidie was one. Not only had Umbino been unable to force a statement out of her, but neither had Mrs. Carstairs. She knew nothing, she declared. She never had. Her job was to cook and clean. That's where it began and that's where it ended.

As we drew into the courtyard of the Hotel Fiori, he murmured: "Women are harder to track down than men. Mistresses of disguise. Maybe she will get away, but I wouldn't count on it."

I picked up the Fiat, drove to the Clinique to pay my daily visit. The nurses alternated between the plain-faced middle-aged madonna and a younger one with lustrous eyes and a near sensual smile who passed the time reading paper-backs with lurid scenes of imminent rape on the covers. Her care of the patient was as exemplary as the older one but her emotions went untapped. She liked to chat, but as her English was no better than my Italian, communication was limited, and as soon as I was seated by Olivia's bed, she reopened her paper-back.

In the room that Mrs. Carstairs had decked with roses, carnations and orchids, transforming it into a hothouse, Olivia lay like an emaciated child, with a flaxen coronet, waiting to cross the borderline into oblivion. Yet, as I sat with my eyes fixed on the tiny shrivelled face, I had an intuitive sense unsupported by a shred of evidence that her spirit was moving upwards, that gradually it would surface.

Once I was certain her lashes flickered, and beckoned the nurse. She went through the ritual I knew by heart of testing and checking, but could detect no change.

At eight o'clock next morning, Mrs. Carstairs telephoned. Olivia was semi-conscious, floating in and out of the coma. She was leaving immediately for the Clinique, and would call in and report on Olivia's condition when she had seen her.

She sat in Signora Limbetto's sitting-room sipping black coffee. "Well, like doctors the world over, they are noncommittal; that is their insurance. To hedge their bets, so that no one can accuse them of a wrong diagnosis! But once, while I was with her, she opened her eyes, and I am certain she recognised me. I have an instinct, almost amounting to telepathy, that never plays me false. Olivia has taken the first steps towards recovery."

I was prepared to believe her. "As soon as she is able to speak, she'll ask for Leo."

She stared broodingly at her Ferragamo shoes, then lifted her head, her decision instantly made, irrevocable. "When she does, I'll give her the truth. There's no alternative. To leave her waiting hour after hour for that devil to appear by her bedside would be an act of cruelty I'm not prepared to commit. The bare facts, no more: that a couple of gangsters broke into the villa, murdered Leo." She shot me a severely warning glance. "No word of Patrick. That must be withheld from her until she is fit to withstand a second shock. I pray that her first news of him will be the sight of him entering her room. Since she was in her teens, Patrick has been a source of moral and physical strength to her. He understood her, the whims and waywardness of her nature, the long-term effect on her of the tragedy of her parents' death. There was a rapport between them that nothing could dissolve. To her he was a very special, precious person. You understand the relationship between them?"

"Yes."

"Good. I have explained the circumstances to the head physician; there will be no leak from that end. The police, of course, are badgering to question her, but they must wait."

I walked with her to the chauffeured car. I did not ask for news because I believed if there were any she would tell me, and I was proved right.

She waited until we were just out of earshot of the chauffeur. "I don't wish to raise the smallest, unsubstantiated hope. That is a false comfort we cannot afford. But we have received a communication that, on a concensus of opinion, might—and I emphasise the 'might' —prove to be genuine. It is semi-literate, unsigned. It names a rendezvous in a sparsely populated mountain region about a hundred kilometres from Caromezza. The message is the usual one: on receipt of the ransom, Patrick will be released from captivity, plus a warning that if the police attempt any interception tactics, Patrick will be summarily executed.

"Lewis has picked half a dozen men who he claims are highly trained experts in this type of undercover work. Over the next twelve hours they will infiltrate into the neighbourhood wearing a variety of disguises. So there it is. Until Lewis has established contact, we cannot know whether the letter is genuine or yet another hoax to extort money." Her mouth tried to shape a smile, failed. "Patience," she breathed, "is the key word."

My voice was as matter of fact as though Patrick were no more than a passing acquaintance. "It's been nine days."

"Yes," she rasped, and within earshot of the chauffeur gave me a look that challenged me to point out that the sum of days was too long for an injured man to survive.

It was a challenge I was not prepared to accept. Hope was a mere pin-prick of light but I willed myself to keep it alive.

The owner of the goldfinch reclaimed it the following morning when I was out walking along the winding paths beside the lake, filling the empty, endless time. When I arrived back at the hotel Maidie presented me with a bunch of multi-coloured gladioli.

"Said I was to tell you how grateful he was. I don't hold with cage birds, but he seemed to think the world of it. No news of Patrick?"

"No." With my reactions slowed down, it took me a little while to notice her changed appearance. The apathy had evaporated, a measure of her normally combative spirit had returned. She was wearing a clean hyacinth-pink nylon housedress. Her hair had been shampooed and there was a dab of lipstick on her mouth.

Catching my querying glance, she emitted one of her derogatory sniffs. "Well, I never was one for sitting twiddling my thumbs. Signora Limbetto asked me if I'd do her the favour of taking on a few odd jobs while she was short-staffed, such as arranging the flowers. No problems there. I always did the altar vases in the church in the old days, and received a lot of compliments, I can tell you. And, well, sometimes I run a duster over the bedrooms. Not, of course, that I'd take any payment. Purely as a favour to her."

I told her I thought it was a splendid idea to repay some of Signora Limbetto's immense kindness to us. Her pride soothed, for the first time since the Contessa's death, she managed a perky little smile. "And Olivia's picking up, I hear. At bottom she's got plenty of grit, I'll say that for her."

"Picking up" was a wild exaggeration. The improvement Mrs. Carstairs reported daily was so slight it could hardly be measured. I had to wait another twenty-four hours until she telephoned to say Olivia wanted to see me. "She asked for Leo. I had no alternative but to tell her he was dead, the brutal manner of his death, at the hands of gangsters. Also that her mother-in-law had died of a stroke. It was harsh treatment, but more humane than leaving her in ignorance."

"How did she react?"

"Stoically, or apparently so, closing her eyes and drowsing, or pretending to. You may be better able to gauge her true feelings when you see her."

She was propped a little higher on the pillows, and the tubes had been disconnected. She must have recognised my footsteps because the second before I opened the door I heard her call: "Liz!"

I kissed her cheek, laid the roses I'd brought at the foot of the bed, as the older nurse, with a smile of gratification, retreated to the balcony, her chair facing inwards so that she could keep watch on her patient without actually eavesdropping.

Olivia's pale heliotrope eyes, pushed deep into her skull, fastened on me with alarming avidity. "Is it true, that Leo and the Contessa are dead?"

"Yes." Sympathy? Comfort? Watching those eyes I could not believe she would welcome either.

She turned her head away, leaving me with her near-fleshless profile. She spoke in snatches, with a curious detachment. "He never imagined himself dying; death was something that happened to other people, as though he were immortal, was clothed in an invisible coat of armour." There was a choking sound that could have been a sob or a stifled burst of hysteria in her throat. Slowly, as though it was heavy, she bent her head towards me, her mouth a bitter-sad line of derision. "My crime was that I fell in love with a bad man when you're only supposed to fall in love with good ones. You end up penned in a hell on earth and no way out. You're a little wolf trailing behind a big one . . . on a leash."

For a moment or two, her breath exhausted, she stared at the blank wall at the foot of the bed, her eyes narrowed to slits. "To him money was God. But he couldn't wait for it to drop into his lap. Like a little boy he screamed: 'Now, now, now.'"

The nurse was beginning to cast uneasy glances towards the bed, her needle idle in her lap. I whispered: "If she sees you upset, she'll throw me out. I know it's hard, but try to . . ."

She finished savagely: ". . . keep calm. Calm! Calm! Everyone's favourite word. I don't know what it is, and I don't want to know." Her laugh was as brittle as an icicle. "You know what I've become, an expert on nightmares, all fifty-seven varieties. Spooky ones. Scary ones of tigers leaping to rip me to shreds of flesh; snakes coiling themselves round my ankles." She paused. "And one nightmare specially designed for me."

Some chemistry changed the pale heliotrope eyes from lack-lustre to a flinty brilliance. I longed to drop my glance, escape from the remorseless challenge, but her will-power over-ruled mine. She spoke distinctly, slyly, checking my reaction to each word. "My special nightmare was that Leo wanted me to die, that he crossed off the days on a huge calendar that covered an entire wall. He put a black cross through each day until there was only one left. One more day that I'd have to swallow the pills, only instead of sending me to sleep they'd kill me."

"The nightmares are over," I beseeched. "They'll never come back." I held the little sack of bones that was her hand in mine. With more strength than I'd believed she possessed, she wrenched it away. "You couldn't understand. No one could. It's a mess . . . a filthy, unholy mess."

She sealed her lids against me. Now there were no eyes to torment me, only the echo of that bitter, despairing voice.

She appeared to drowse. I stayed until the nurse gestured that my ration of time was used up. Instantly Olivia's eyes flew wide. "Where's Patrick? Why isn't he here? If he's back in England, write to him. No, telephone. Aunt Marianne will give you his number. Tell him I want him, and he'll come." Now she seized my hand. "Promise?"

"I promise."

Mrs. Carstairs sipped her neat iced lemon juice. "She's neither physically nor emotionally fit to suffer another shock. I'll invent some plausible excuse before I visit her tomorrow."

She looked drained of her phenomenal energy. "I'm sorry I've no good news. Another hoax! No one appeared at the rendezvous. The following day the police moved in. Every man, woman and child was questioned; every house in the village searched from cellar to loft. Not a clue." She raised her hands in a bitter gesture of defeat. "So once again we are the victims of some degenerate creature with a sick or malicious mind. Lewis, a most dogmatic and obstinate man, still insists that some lead may emerge and is keeping the village under surveillance. I count it a waste of his time and my money."

Time was running out for me, too. There were only three days before I must return to England. I did a sum to translate it into hours; that way it seemed longer.

Then, as though she'd reached into some depth of herself for renewed spirit, she admonished: "Don't imagine I have lost hope. That is not my nature. Somewhere there is a man or a woman who knows where Patrick is. However long it takes, I shall not abandon the search until I have found him."

The next day Olivia was lying on a chair on the balcony, the improvement in her condition visible. She shot the question at me before I was half-way across the room. "Did you talk to Patrick?"

"No. He wasn't at home."

"Ah!" She drew the syllable out with the satisfaction of one who has solved a mystery. "You and Aunt Marianne in cahoots! Her alibi is that he's off somewhere climbing, and that his father is unable to contact him. A lie she's ordered you to repeat. His father is an old man, forever falling ill, which is why Patrick never goes away without making sure that, in an emergency, he can be reached. But not apparently this time. What's he supposed to be doing, climbing Everest?"

"I don't know where he is."

"And," she continued with stinging emphasis, "Aunt Marianne is up to something. I know because I can read her like a book. Involved, embroiled, her wits working overtime. And worried sick. So suppose you tell me what's going on?"

"I don't know."

"Don't know," she mimicked. "What you're admitting is that you've been told to do a cover-up. Okay, as soon as I'm on my feet, I'll do my own detective work. Meanwhile, what's happened to Mimi?"

"She left the villa before the police arrived. They haven't been able to trace her. All that is known is that she caught an early plane to Paris next morning."

She contemplated her hands that were white as milk, ghost-hands. "She had a baby. I wasn't supposed to know, so I pretended I didn't, but I saw him once in Syracuse. A boy. He must have been born while she was supposed to be at a conference in Paris." For a long moment she stayed locked in her thoughts, then she whispered: "Leo's baby. A live son to replace my dead one." Then venom half-choked her. "It would have served him right if he'd married her. She was a greedy, cold-hearted, conniving little tart. I used to imagine sticking a dagger into her heart, watching her die, slowly, very, very slowly, the blood dripping out of her. But I didn't own a dagger and there wasn't a sharp knife around. I dreamed up another plan, that when I had the money, I'd blackmail her into selling me the baby: that Leo and I would adopt him. You know what that's called?" I shook my head. "Fantasising. A form of self-hypnosis in which you possess the power to believe anything you want to believe. Stay with it long enough and you go crazy. She'd bought him with the baby. All she had to do was to wait until I was dead and then she'd have Leo, the baby and the money! Only I didn't die, and all she ended up with was the baby. One beautiful boy child!"

The tears gushed down her cheeks. She buried her eyes in her hands, moaned: "Don't talk. Don't say anything."

It was five minutes before she dropped her hands. Her cheeks dry, she demanded off-handedly: "And where's poor old Maidie?"

"She's waiting in the reception hall, all set to come up and see you as soon as I leave."

Her parting glance was bitter, even hating. "Lucky old Liz, with no secrets to hide, no skeletons rattling in a dozen cupboards. Blessed with a beautiful tidy life."

As I sat downstairs waiting for Maidie I thought no person on earth can ever truly know another. Olivia blind to my inner self, which was clenched tight with a pain that never quite ceased, even when I was asleep. I reflected, as I'd done when we'd shared a home, on the disharmonies in her nature that made her an enigma, and wondered what had become of all my crucifying concern for her.

Maidie wore a grim smile of triumph as she strode towards me. "They've got nothing out of her, the scheming devils. Not a word. I knew they wouldn't. Comes in mighty handy on occasions to be a good liar, and she was always that, bless her. Badgering a widow to tell tales on her husband. There should be a law against it."

"I'd have thought you'd have wanted Leo's murderers to be caught and punished."

"Oh, they'll be punished right enough. On the run, not daring to set foot in their own home until they've paid a doctor a fortune to altar the shapes of their faces, quaking in their boots that someone will squeal on them. Fighting like tom-cats. Fingers on their guns twenty-four hours a day. I know their sort. I've lived among them. Human life is no more sacred to them than a chicken's." She tossed me a reproving look. "I should have thought your dear mother would have taught you to let the dead rest in peace. That's God's will. Spreading a lot of scandal isn't. First time she's let out of hospital Olivia's coming with me to the cemetery. We'll buy some flowers, that'll comfort her. Since you'll have flown back to England by then, maybe Mr. Barratt will lend us his car and chauffeur. He seems a nice man, does his best to be helpful."

That was an understatement. Charles Barratt's kindness, sensitivity had been far beyond what could have been expected of him. Without it my outward calm would have collapsed.

In the car I asked Maidie what her plans were. Did she intend to remain with Olivia?

"What would I do with myself for goodness sake? It's not me she needs, it's Patrick. She always thought a lot of him. She might have done better to have married him."

My patience snapped. "You want it both ways. A devoted wife in love with her husband, and when he's murdered, a faithful lover waiting in the wings to pick up the pieces."

"And what's wrong with that, I'd like to know! She was a devoted wife. Never let him down, not once. Lips sealed, and that's the way they will remain, you mark my words. She'll not tell tales on Leo when he can't answer up for himself. But that doesn't mean she has to turn into a nun." After a silence I made no attempt to fill, she said defensively: "Actually, Signora Limbetto has offered me a job; well, you could say she begged me to take it. I just might consider it."

Signora Limbetto laughed when I asked her if it were true. "Yes, except that I did not beg. I made a suggestion that would benefit me, and I hoped would be congenial for her. I suggested we should give it a trial."

"As long as you don't expect her to cook!"

"I have a chef, an under-chef. She would not be required to put her nose inside the kitchens. Over thirty per cent of my guests are English. With them she would be an asset. So many complain that their morning tea and the tea they drink in the afternoon is not how they would wish it to taste. I think it is our water that changes the flavour, but there may be some little trick in the brewing that Maidie knows. We shall see."

"As soon as Olivia is fit, I'm certain she will make financial provision for Maidie."

She raised her eyebrows. "To go somewhere and be alone and idle! It is not only lack of money for which Maidie suffers, she needs to be occupied. As far as I can understand, she has spent her life looking after people who were dependent on her. Like all human beings, she needs other human beings to care for. I have several elderly guests who would find pleasure in a few minutes of her company. Anyway, it is purely a temporary arrangement, neither side is tied to a contract."

It was on my last visit to Olivia that she surprised me by begging a favour. "Aunt Marianne proposes to fly me out to that southern palace of hers as soon as the doctors say I'm fit to travel. But I'm not going. Oh, I will later on. Uncle Hayward will give me his blessing—he'll welcome me like a prodigal daughter now Leo is dead, and can't get his hands on THE MONEY."

"But you can't stay here alone!"

"I don't intend to. I can't wait to break out of this cell, with the police snooping in and out asking me damn-fool questions I've no intention of answering. Anyway, it's illegal in England to compel a wife to give evidence against her husband. And who wants a scandal spread in banner headlines across the gutter press? Cameras flashing!" She turned her head, so that she didn't have to look at me. "What I want is to go and stay with Mother Clare. Do you think she'd have me?"

"You know she would, with open arms. You don't even have to ask."

Her glance came back to me. "Ah, but what about you," she said, studying my face for a reaction. "You wouldn't exactly put out a welcome sign, would you?"

The truth shamed me; it was such a little time since, submerged under love and pity, I'd prayed Olivia should live. "It's your home as well as mine, or it was once. Why should I mind?"

"You could owe me a grudge. Sending for you to fly out here, putting you through hell. Bullets, corpses! I wouldn't blame you, or not much, if you washed your hands of me." A small, not very steady smile came to her lips. "But if I hadn't written that letter, I'd probably be dead by now. Come to think of it, I've never thanked you, have I?"

"No need. You're alive. That takes care of the thanks. How does Mrs. Carstairs react to the idea of your coming to us?"

"She's against it." She shrugged her shoulders. "But she can't do a thing about it. Besides seeing Mother Clare, there's another reason why I'm going to England. Patrick. Everyone's feeding me comforting little lies. You included. So what's the mystery?" She mimicked: "Poor Olivia, after all she's suffered mustn't be subjected to another shock. So what shock?" She tried to grin, but her mouth refused to obey. "The only reason I can think up is that Patrick flew back to Norfolk, grabbed hold of his secretary, a docile pallid little blonde who worships the ground he walks on, and hustled her off to a registrar's office." She pointed to a plug in the wall. "That's for a telephone, but I'm not allowed one in case I lift up the receiver and ask for Patrick's number. You see what I mean! Until I discharge myself, I'm still a prisoner. But I won't be for long."

CHAPTER 11

Eustace, who regarded any indisposition in his staff as a personal affront, eyed me with disfavour. "It would appear you had an uncomfortable flight home. I'd advise you to have an early night." He leaned back in his Chippendale chair. "What reports have you brought back from Pepinato and Marcella?"

Belatedly, on the plane, I'd remembered I'd made no attempt to contact either of them. The admission that I'd failed to obey his orders stupefied Eustace. He was in no way mollified by my explanation that the friend I'd visited had been critically ill. Aware that the violent truth would nauseate him, I stuck to a skeleton of the facts. He read *The Times*, but only selected columns: front page, leading articles, notices of forthcoming auctions and the obituaries. Kidnapping, murder he regarded as happenings in a sphere he preferred not to admit existed.

At the mention of a funeral I'd had to attend, distaste gave way to repugnance. He shifted his glance to the mid-distance, murmured: "Dear me! Most unfortunate," and proceeded in his most didactic manner to give me a run-down on the diary for the current week. "There's a preview of the Newsham sale on Thursday and Friday. Two rings will be operating, so by then you will need to be mentally and physically on your toes."

Mrs. Anstruther clicked her tongue in dismay. "Oh, dear, you do look peaky. Was it the plane that upset you?"

To cut corners I said yes, and Cedric, whose sensitivity ran deeper, smiled consolingly. "Take it easy. Despite Eustace's talk, we're reasonably slack. No frantic rush."

Work, routine was a stabilising force, a barrier, albeit a fragile one, against memory.

The weekend at home, where Mother anticipated Olivia's arrival with mingled joy and anxiety, was like swimming through an unending series of whirlpools. Mercifully, as I recapitulated the sequence of events, my inner, feeling eye developed a defensive mechanism; it became temporarily numb.

Leo's death and that of his mother, the kidnapping of a nephew of Mrs. Carstairs, who was a close friend of Olivia's, appalled her. But it was Olivia on whom all her concern centred. Was I certain she was recovering? What had caused her the illness? I told her the still-born baby.

She said, grieving: "It's hard for her, poor child. She's had to fight herself every inch of the way."

I tended towards short, sometimes brutal, answers. "Doesn't everybody?"

She shook her head. "The shock of her parents' death, one moment alive, the next dead, meant she suffered an emotional fracture that never healed. Sometimes I blame myself for pleading to have her live with us. The contrast was too great. An ordinary home, an ordinary school, where her friends were preparing themselves to become teachers, typists, civil servants. Then holidays, weekends with the Carstairs and luxury, money without count to be spent not saved. And all the time, the knowledge that one day she would be rich. She couldn't be expected to adjust to it." She sighed. "If your father had lived she might have learnt a different set of values. She would have done any mortal thing for him. Or maybe if she'd married a different man."

Her questioning eyes seemed to burn holes in my face. She moistened her lips. "Was Leo good to her, kind when she was ill?"

Whether she wanted the truth or not, she believed that she did, but because the truth would have scored so deep a hurt, I withheld it. "As far as he was capable of being, yes."

"And this friend, Patrick, who was kidnapped? If they find him, is he a man to give her the support and comfort that she needs so desperately?"

"Oh, yes. None better. He's been secretly in love with her for years."

She had demanded pity for Olivia. But I'd none to offer. When she had been ill and helpless, with death hovering over her, my desire to protect had amounted to love. But now my emotional wells had run dry. At that moment I literally loved no one in the whole world.

Then a memory I did not even know I possessed surfaced, the despairing plea of a charwoman who had worked for us when I was in my teens. Her husband had disappeared from his ship while in a foreign port. She sat sobbing in the kitchen, repeating again and again: "If only I could know the end of him. That's what tortures me, whether he's dead or wandering around not knowing who he is."

That wasn't all I wanted, but as I drove back to town that Sunday night it seemed that I would never know, and I mourned with a terrible iron-hearted grief that I knew neither time nor reason would alleviate.

It was after midnight when the telephone rang. When I lifted the ear-piece, I heard Charles Barratt's calm, resonant voice. "Elizabeth? Good news. The best. Patrick has been found . . . alive."

I missed his next few sentences as every sense I possessed was swamped with joy.

"Is he badly hurt?"

"Well . . . let's say he's not in too good shape. Unconscious, weak, but he's in hospital in Bergamo under intensive care. Marianne is with him, staying at a nearby hotel, and Olivia, who's on her feet now, is joining her tomorrow."

A hundred questions jammed my tongue; I was incapable of putting one of them into words.

"We've Lewis to thank. He was convinced, despite having been through the village with a toothcomb, that the letter hadn't been a hoax. 'A sniff of stink' was how he described it, and by God, he was right. After they'd beaten Patrick insensible they drove the best part of two hundred kilometres into the mountains, stripped him naked to delay identification, dumped him in a ravine and left him to die, always supposing they didn't believe he was already dead. In that isolated region the likelihood of his being found was infinitesimal. But their luck ran out. In the early hours, a father and son, a couple of peasant farmers picking their way home after a wedding, caught sight of Patrick in the beam of their torch, and carried him back with them. The father was a widower, the son had a young wife. She must have had a certain amount of nursing skill or Patrick wouldn't have survived. Approximately a week later, though he was still unable to stand, he could write his name.

"On market day the son took the scrap of paper to the village and showed it to a friend, who produced a newspaper with a picture of Patrick and the amount of the ransom. The friend was barely literate but he could write a few simple sentences. That was the message we received, naming the rendezvous. Then to safeguard their prize, they moved Patrick to a cellar, left him bread and water and bricked it up except for one air-hole.

"They kept the rendezvous, but at the last minute they became alarmed by two men walking along a path which overlooked the meeting-place. Actually they were bona-fide climbers; Lewis had taken care to have all his men screened from sight. They panicked, returned home and bricked up the air-hole. Patrick wouldn't have stood a chance if the young wife, some days later, when her husband and his father were clipping sheep, hadn't slipped out and walked to the nearest police station. It appears she couldn't bear sentencing to certain death a man whom she had nursed. All three men are now in custody."

"He'll recover?"

He hesitated, and I held my breath. "That's our hope and belief. I wish I could give you an absolute guarantee, but I can't. He took a terrible beating. Apart from the effects of near-starvation, the X-rays show a hair-line fracture of the skull, a broken ankle, a cracked elbow, four broken ribs, deep cuts that have festered and all-over bruising. Thank God he's young and healthy with the near-miraculous powers of recuperation that the young are blessed with. I could be wrong, but I'm counting on his being back in England within a few weeks. So keep your courage up. I'm flying to London tomorrow and will phone you again. Marianne asked me to say she'll be in touch, sending you bulletins."

I thanked him, and he added a tail-piece. "Oh, I nearly forgot. The police have caught Mario's wife, Rosetta, and her brother. No news of the boy, or Leo's girl-friend."

As I put the telephone down I was overwhelmed with thankfulness that he had not died in darkness, like a rat in a cage, his spirit raging impotently at the humiliation of final defeat. I lay awake breathing in one fact: that at this moment he was alive.

Mrs. Carstairs sent me three typed reports on Patrick's progress—slow but satisfactory—before she returned to Florida. Once Olivia telephoned. Patrick was doing so well that they'd fixed a date, ten days ahead, for their flight home. Would I meet her at Heathrow? A car would be collecting Patrick to take him home to Norfolk. As a one-line postscript she added that he sent his love. In fact, it was an overoptimistic forecast, and it was another two weeks before he was released from hospital.

As I saw them walking through customs, I barely recognised the Olivia who bore no resemblance to the ravaged, emaciated girl I'd left in the Clinique. With her extreme fragility, pearly translucent skin, fairy-gold hair and the dancer's grace with which she moved as though half-way to flight, she mesmerised every male within sight.

Patrick, alongside her, I saw as a pencil outline of a man, devoid of detail and substance. I concentrated on the practical issues of the precise spot I'd parked the car and how many minutes it would take to retrieve it. Treacherously, without any intent of mine, the pencil outline began to fill in. There was a narrow bandage on one side of his skull, his right arm was in a sling and he walked with a slight limp.

Olivia called my name, grabbed me. She smelt delicious.

My hand was grasped and held in his left one. "Liz, how good to see you. How very good!" There was a pause that set my nerves shivering. "I should have listened to you, shouldn't I?"

Olivia thrust her arm through his. "You've got a mountain of humble pie to eat. Maybe, if you're good, I'll let you off with a few bites." She was wreathed in happiness, uplifted by that inborn imperiousness that assumed what she wanted automatically became hers.

It took me ten minutes to collect the car. When I returned, an elderly man in a peaked chauffeur's cap was stowing Patrick's bag into the boot of an ancient Daimler. Patrick walked over to me. "I'll spend a week with Dad, ease him out of his traumas. He's a bit too frail to weather the shocks I've subjected him to. When I get rid of this sling, so that I can drive, I'd like to come and see you. May I?"

Olivia slotted her arm into his. "What a question! Of course you can. I'm dying for you to meet Mother Clare." She reached up and kissed him on the mouth. I discovered you could smile, look up into a face, yet keep it so out of focus it was no more than a blur. "She'd love to see you," I murmured.

As Olivia fastened her seat-belt, she breathed in deeply, then sighed with content. "Home! It still seems like a miracle to me."

I did not know whether she meant driving to Pallis Green or having Patrick upstanding and three-quarters fit. Only that she appeared to possess the knack of instantly obliterating the dead from memory.

The one rule still imposed on Olivia was that she rested for one hour after lunch. Argue or wheedle as she might, mother refused to relax it. Proof against any wile Olivia could exert, my mother turned to Patrick for support. "You're not intending to hurry away, are you?" When he said no, she suggested I show him round the garden, while she stood at the foot of the stairs and monitored Olivia's upward climb.

As we walked down the flagged path on that Sunday afternoon his voice sounded relaxed, though his face was graven as though held by some tyranny of thought. The October day was mellow, blue and gold, made gaudy with chrysanthemums and dahlias the frost hadn't yet quenched. He asked me who looked after it. I said Bill Roberts.

He spoke of my mother with liking and admiration. I listened, maintaining a chasm between us while I played the part of a gracious, if slightly detached, hostess.

Beyond the vegetable garden there was a gate opening on to a path that led through a thicket to the common, so narrow and winding we could no longer walk abreast. It was uneven. Half-way, I thought I heard his footsteps stumble, and I turned. "Are you all right?"

For a second anger flashed across his eyes. "Perfectly."

When we emerged on to the common we could walk abreast. Except for half a dozen children playing rounders it was empty. The pavilion had been burnt down two years ago. The Parish Council having neglected to insure it, it would probably take another couple of years of jumble sales to raise the money to rebuild it. If you knew where to look you could still see the concrete foundation under the mat of grass and weeds. When we passed the gnarled hawthorn which had been my hiding place, I touched the bark with my fingertips and was riven by self-derision: the sheer banal futility of the gesture.

It was he who came to an abrupt standstill. "Surely there used to be a large hut over there? What happened to it?"

"It was hit by a firework and burnt down before the fire brigade arrived." I believed I was beyond hurt, no more than curious to test his reaction. "How did you know it ever existed?"

"Once we'd been somewhere, Olivia and I. Oxford, I think. The car broke down. We left it at the village garage and to fill in the waiting-time she suggested we walk round the common."

"You were within five minutes of Olivia's home!"

His sideways glance was self-mocking in contrast to his musing, pensive tone. "Olivia was not quite eighteen, playing games, exciting, secret games that were hardly suited to a drawing-room tea party. It took me a long while to discover that they were games. Years!"

"All long ago, and far away!" I said blithely.

"Yes." I was conscious of his hard gaze, evenly balanced between reproach and a pent-up urgency. It was as though he bore me a grudge. I couldn't think why. His love life was no concern of mine.

"Liz, I want to talk to you, not exchange a stream of platitudes. And I'd like very much, if you could bear it, for you to look at me. Would that be too much of an effort?"

I raised my glance, slid it at lightning speed across his face.

"That's what I mean. As though the sight of me is a penance."

For a moment we stood in silence, separated by a continent of space. I longed for him to be gone, and yet conversely I cherished every second of his presence.

He pointed a finger that was still bruised towards the base of the pavilion on which someone had scrawled on a bare concrete slab in greasy red crayon: "Linda Loves Terry." "I made love to Olivia in that wooden hut. To me it was the real thing. Forever. The beginning of a marriage that would endure the length of our lives. It took me two years to learn that, for her, it was no more than an adventure, or, more precisely, an emotional experiment; that she was no more committed to me than she was to half a dozen other men. I was a trial run to further her education."

"Why tell me?"

"Because you have to know."

"No." My vehemence startled him into silence, and for a moment I was terrified he was going to turn on his heel, walk away forever. And then I reached deep for a truth that even he could not deny. "You were prepared to die for her. You nearly did."

"I had no intention of dying for anyone, certainly not for Olivia. Heroics aren't my line. But I loved her once, and though love burns itself out, is no more than a memory of a self you can no longer recognise, a sediment remains, and you can't do a damned thing about it. As near as I can define it, it is caring. A hang-over of responsibility. If that once-loved, but no-longer-loved, girl marries an evil man, is held a prisoner, with a hair-line between her and death, you devise some scheme, maybe good, maybe bad, to free her from the trap, offer her another chance. Love doesn't come into it." He paused, demanded: "Does that make sense to you?"

"Not entirely. You've missed out the prime factor. There are two of you, not one. Whether or not you love Olivia, she loves you. You were the first person she asked to see when Mrs. Carstairs told her Leo was dead. The only person she cared about. She wouldn't have shed a tear if the rest of us had dropped dead, provided you survived."

"And I'll tell you why. I'm old reliable. Guaranteed to come flying to the rescue." There was a long silence, broken only by the children's cries. "Liz, I'm spelling out the truth straight from my heart. If today I walked into that filthy villa, found Olivia wasting away, at the mercy of a man who'd convinced himself he could get away with murder, I'd give a repeat performance, although I hope a more competent me. I suppose you might say that amounts to a confession, but it has nothing to do with love."

"She loves you," I repeated as loudly and distinctly as though he were deaf.

"She has for me a mirage of love, a devouring need to be loved to restore a confidence that has been shattered. To put a new shine on her world. So I'm a temporary leaning-post. Enduring love isn't part of Olivia's make-up."

"What about Leo? She never walked out on him. Yet wouldn't that have been the answer? A very simple one."

"Not for her. Living with him was like forever throwing a dice, holding your breath. A daily challenge spiced with danger, a gigantic gamble that inflamed every sense she possessed, yet set her shivering in the night until, too late, she became too weak and confused to tell the difference between truth and deceit, sex and sadism. She yearns for the stimulant of excitement, to invite risks for the sheer hell of defying them. Somewhere inside her there's a demon that denies her happiness except for short spurts."

I was driven by a demon of my own. "She has never ceased talking about you since she arrived home, endlessly. She spent the whole morning choosing the dress she would wear for you. She not only loves you, but believes you love her."

His voice became fiercely exasperated. "She wants to recapture the past, a piece of time when I did love her. An exercise in fantasy. You can't snatch back time, recycle it, nor can you breathe life into a love that died years ago. That's a fact everyone has to live with. For God's sake, Liz, why can't you accept it?"

"I find it difficult."

"Because I sound like a heel? Okay, maybe I do, but I've a right to spell it out, to plead my own case. If it puts me beyond the pale . . ." He stopped, the normally fluent tongue suddenly wary of words. "Liz, does it?"

"You intend to call it a day. Give her a kiss and wave her good-bye!"

"For God's sake! Haven't you taken in anything I've said!" With an effort he quenched his anger. "Let's examine it from another angle. Do you imagine for one moment that Olivia would commit herself to what to her would amount to burying herself alive in an East Anglian town, endure a winter climate that sometimes rips the skin off your face? Marry a master-printer, the publisher of a provincial weekly? Unable and most certainly unwilling to take off in a jet at a moment's notice for the other side of the world?"

"Yet the paper, the printing works are my heritage, one I wouldn't exchange for any other. To her it's the depths of mediocrity. To me, it's a daily challenge. My father and my grandfather had security; I have none. Just goodwill, and a prayer. There never was a chance that Olivia would marry me, not all those years ago and assuredly not now. For that I'm grateful. Before too long she'll find herself a husband. Until that day comes she sees me as a stand-in." He heaved a sigh of exasperation. "Do we have to waste time arguing the difference between love and concern?"

I saw the dapple of the fading sun on my hands, and marvelled that they were cold. "No, you don't have to. I understand." There wheeled across my mental vision Olivia's mouth curving tenderly, tremulously, as she'd faced him across the lunch table; I heard the echo of a laugh that was a seductive expression of love. I couldn't fathom why he was exerting so much effort in persuading me to believe what was false.

"It's time I was going back to the house to make tea. Emma will have gone home."

He checked his watch, and my eyes registered the scars on his wrist. "At ten minutes to three!"

"I thought it was later than that." Hours seemed to have passed since we walked through the wicket gate.

He reached out, imprisoned me by a hand laid on each of my shoulders, the grip on the left firmer than the right. "Do you remember the swan, the cygnets?" His eyes searched mine as though to pierce the flesh and bone to reach the cells of my brain. "I wouldn't have thought you could have forgotten that flash of blinding recognition that widens the senses into infinity, redefines the world, redeems its ugliness. You look around and suddenly find that the earth and all it holds belongs to you. It happens, Liz, I swear it does; what's more it happened to us." He paused, and I found I could look into his eyes but not at his mouth, which invited treachery. "And when it's happened, you can't cancel it out."

Oh, I knew it had happened, but I couldn't or wouldn't admit it. Olivia's ghost was too clear, right there beside me. The inside of me had withered and died, leaving me free of pain, and I wanted it to stay that way. But against my will there was a barely perceptible thrust of awareness that, however hard I struggled to suppress, would not die. I shook my head vehemently.

Quite suddenly his hands dropped from my shoulders. We stood apart, physical contact broken. "Liz, for endless days I existed, barely alive in a bricked-up dungeon, dark, foetid. I swung from delirium into stupor, from stupor into pain. Half the time I wasn't sure whether I was dead or alive. But always, as though it had a separate

existence outside the pain and squalor, was a torrent of anger: that I
hadn't told you that I loved you, because I took it for granted that
love automatically transmits itself on thought waves to the beloved.
I believed time was ours, fifty, sixty years of it. And now are you telling me you want to wipe the slate clean, to banish me from your
mind?"

He waited, while the interminable seconds ticked away, then, as
though something in him had cracked, he walked a dozen paces,
stood with his back to me. I told myself it was a signal of defeat,
that, mercifully, I wouldn't have to fight any longer.

But in the emptiness that separated us I could actually hear the
echo of his voice lingering on the air. Joy advances with extreme
diffidence into areas of the heart that have been laid waste. I
watched him, as he wheeled, pace back. Speech required an enormous effort, as though my tongue had been struck numb and useless.
"No. Never that. Never."

Now, as though a blockage had dissolved, I found I could look up,
examine the planes of his face, the blue-black depth of his eyes,
watch the pain ebb, the light return. He held out his arms and
wrapped them about me, so that I felt the throb of his heart against
mine. My desire matched his, so powerful it overthrew doubt and
dread, even conscience. In the end it was simple. We belonged to
each other.

Olivia was leaning over the wicket gate, waiting for us, trails of
cigarette smoke circling her face before they dissolved in the fickle
breeze that disturbed tendrils of the amber hair that fell in lengths
of silk over her shoulders to caress the pearly-white cashmere dress.

The path that, on the outward journey, had been too narrow for
us to walk abreast, seemed to have widened. Our hands were locked
together. Under the piercing scrutiny of the opaline eyes I tried to
draw mine out of his, but his grip tightened and, my fingers trapped,
I saw the light die out of Olivia's face.

There were perhaps twenty paces between us. I did not smile, neither did she. None of us spoke a word. Not a flicker of expression
touched her face. You had to pierce the skin, the flesh, to reach the
dark storm gathering within.

When we were within a footstep of the gate, she swung it open,
chided: "You've been such an age, we thought you were lost."

Now Patrick walked between us down the flagged path that led to
the terrace; it seemed to stretch into infinity. Vividly conscious of her
grace, I thought how much more durable it was than beauty, that it

would see her through the middle years into old age. For a second I tasted envy on my tongue, then I heard Patrick say in a firm, but oh so gentle voice: "Olivia, Liz and I have something to tell you. We're going to be married."

I repeated his words to myself. Irrevocable. A clean, killing stab to the heart. She quickened her step, separating herself from us until she reached a gnarled crabapple tree. Leaning against it for support, she focussed the diamond-hard pale eyes on us.

"So, congratulations!" She laughed with a sound that, strangely, wasn't ironic, rather a response to a declaration she found diverting. "Surprise! Surprise! Lots of beautiful secrets going on behind my back. Who'd have guessed!"

I watched as, like someone looking at herself in a mirror, she formed a smile on her lips, divided her glance between us. "Blessings on you both. I'd guess, on the whole, you'll suit each other rather well." And then, unable to sustain the act another second, she swung on her heel, walked ahead of us towards the house, leaving me with the knowledge that, for all Patrick's denials, if he'd asked her, she would have married him.

He pressed my hand to his cheek. "Brutal! But less painful than leaving her at the mercy of the skeins of multiplying fantasies she endlessly spins. My only guilt is that I've left an empty space in her life. Let me comfort you by promising it won't exist for long."

He saw the doubt on my face; I noted the strain on his, as though the emotional effort he'd expended had temporarily drained him.

He smiled his love. "Let's keep our fingers crossed he's in love with her, with a fortune of his own, so he doesn't marry her for her money. That way, I won't have to mount another rescue operation."

"But you would?"

"Wouldn't you want me to?"

"Yes." And it was the truth.

My mother sat upright in her special chair, a lamp burning on the table beside her. There were only the two of us. After Patrick left, Olivia had telephoned the Cheethams in the village and been in-vited—or had invited herself—to supper. Popping her head round the door, she waved the key at us and ordered us not to wait up for her. A ruse that, for a short while, removed me from sight.

"My darling, am I to be told?"

"Of course you are."

She smiled love at me. "As if I didn't know! It glows in you and in him. Do you imagine the old forget love? Never. Rather they exist on its precious memory. I've waited for this day since you emerged from childhood, and believed that I would recognise it when it was no more than a pinprick of light on the horizon. But you cheated me, darling, didn't you?"

"Only because I believed he was in love with Olivia, that he would protect and cherish her, rescue her from the past. Which is what you wanted. It must seem to you that I stole him from her."

"No. Though I must admit it took me a little while to adjust myself. Ever since Olivia came to us I've hoped and prayed for her happiness, but never at the expense of yours. Never that." For a moment her smile was undimmed, joyous. "Besides which, my darling, you couldn't steal a twopenny stamp. Oh, I admit I fret about her. Each child is a responsibility laid on you by God. And Olivia was a hurt child. My fault is that I forget that in years she's no longer a child, but a woman, and what's more that I'm an old one, so it becomes foolish to imagine I can protect her from herself."

Her face bore the strain from the concentrated devotion she lavished on all disadvantaged children. For that was what Olivia was to her, a child in need. One of her few failures.

She brushed aside the lingering grief, the pangs of regret. "Now tell me about the man who is to be my son-in-law." There followed a string of pertinent questions on age, family, profession, an approximation of his income, to some of which I could provide no answers. To me they were comically irrelevant, but I promised I would bring them back from Norfolk the following weekend, which I was to spend with Patrick and his father.

The moonlight was muted by a gauze of clouds, a gossamer haze behind which the stars were hidden. I lay exulting in the most powerful elixir in the world: a love that stilled the brain, entranced the senses. It seemed, as I lay there, that I had nothing left to wish for.

When the door creaked on its hinges I turned my head on the pillow. Olivia, swathed in a dramatic white cloak, crossed to my bed; the cloak and a pallid oval of face were all I could see. When I lifted my hand to switch on the bedside light, she snapped: "Don't. It'll be easier in the dark." I heard the sharp intake of her breath. "Do you remember the day you came to the hospital with Mother Clare, clutching a bunch of flowers you didn't know what to do with?"

"I remember." The day when a child who'd never experienced the mildest dislike had stared into a face of hate and been appalled.

"I wanted to die, to be dead. People don't believe that a child can hate the whole world and everything in it, but I did. I prayed every night before I went to sleep that I might never wake up. Then, after I came here, I changed my prayer. I prayed that you would die. I'd lie awake building ecstatic pictures in my mind: you being run over in the street, struck by a fatal illness, found dead in bed. I even planned to lock you in your wardrobe, set fire to the room and by the time it was discovered, the wardrobe and you would be a heap of cinders. All I wanted was to regain what I'd lost: doting parents that I didn't have to share with anyone, come second. To be your father's only child. I dreamed, when I was old enough, that I would coax him to take me with him, a precious handmaiden, always at his side, helping him feed the starving children." She gave a laugh. "One plus point to me: I recognised a good man on sight."

"He loved you more than he loved me." At last I could bear to admit it. "I was too fat and healthy."

"After he was dead Mother Clare gave me his pipe. I keep it in my jewel-case, an amulet. When the world turned black, I'd sit and hold it in my hand."

Mother had presented me his diaries, pages covered in figures, dates. The number of children fed per day, the sacks of grain delivered, the lengths of pipe-line laid. I'd packed them in a box, wrapped and sealed it in brown paper. I couldn't remember where I'd put it.

Nothing of her moved, except the ghost-white fingers that were plaiting the fringe of the counterpane. "You see, I lose people. But I didn't lose Patrick. You stole him."

"We fell in love."

She repeated after me, slowly as though she were testing the verity of the words: "Fell in love. That's a cliché. Meaningless. You choose the man you'll love, and if you love him enough, he'll love you. It's as simple as that. Patrick was mine."

"You married Leo."

"Leo!" she whispered, and gave a hoot of laughter. "After that, never a dull moment. Aunt Marianne in a state of shock. Uncle Hayward pulling every string he could lay his hands on to prevent me inheriting my own money!"

She moved her head sideways, the pale oval staring down at me. "Now it could have been mine and Patrick's. And don't tell me he wouldn't have enjoyed spending it. He would. For Christmas I would have bought him the new printing press he's been pining for, a Jaguar, and modernised that creaky old house where the slates keep sliding off the roof, and the heating system only works one day out of three. He could have hired more staff, taken longer holidays. Now he can't, can he? And there's his old father. He was born in that house and is determined to die there, so there's no hope of farming him out in a nursing home. Patrick's devoted to him."

"I'm, as you call it, devoted to my mother."

"Yes, so you say, but I've never seen much proof of it. What's going to happen to Mother Clare when you're married to Patrick?"

Ahead of me lay weeks of persuasion, cajoling, even bullying, but I was confident of the outcome, that I'd win. "We'll work something out to suit the four of us."

"Yes," she conceded churlishly. "You always were a good fixer."

"Do we have to fight like the couple of children we once were a long time ago?"

She snapped back: "You can quarrel at any age, even on the verge of the grave." She hesitated, went on: "Maybe I owe you a debt, for flying out to San Giorgio. So I'll pay it. Before you come home next week I'll have removed myself. I'll telephone Aunt Marianne in the morning."

"You don't have to. Anyway, I won't be here next weekend. I'm . . ."

"Don't tell me. I can guess. You're about to step over the threshold of your future home. Don't expect too much. It's riddled with dry rot, so take care you don't fall through the floorboards." Her laugh was weak, shaky. "To make everything cosy, living proof that all's forgiven and forgotten, I'm sure Patrick would love to have me dance at his wedding. But I don't forgive and I never forget." She drew a breath from some raw and stinging depth within her. "Memories, memories! Oh for an incinerator that would burn them to ashes, blow them away on the wind."

"Olivia, I'm sorry . . ."

"Are you!" She sprang to her feet, a spectacular piece of theatre in her swinging white cloak. "When for once in a lifetime you're on the winning side!"

I did not speak and neither did she until she reached the door. There she paused for an instant, turned her head towards me, her voice a dying fall. "Good-bye. Mind you take good care of him."

The night was almost at an end before I fell asleep. Passion and faith weren't strong enough to deaden the throbs of guilt. When I slept it was to dream that I'd walked alone through the wicket gate, across the common to where the pavilion had once stood. But it wasn't a dream.

Six months later I received a letter from Mrs. Carstairs announc-
H 17 ing that Olivia was to be married to a young Boston lawyer,

Calthorpe Hope, Jr. He came from a notable, highly esteemed family, and a bright future, both in law and politics, was predicted for him. She enclosed a hand-written invitation and expressed the hope that I might find it possible to visit them for the wedding. Olivia had promised to write when she had a moment to spare. She asked to be remembered to my mother.

There was no letter from Olivia, though Mrs. Carstairs sent me a batch of colour slides of the wedding. Beside his fragile bride, dressed in floating white, with a train the end of which was lost to sight, Calthorpe Hope appeared a giant of a man. Patrick and I studied him minutely. Splendid physique, features that, while not handsome, suggested he was pleasant-natured yet possessed of a will of his own. "You never know." Patrick laughed. "We might see her the wife of a senator one day."

When the colour slides reached us we'd been married two months, and the seventeenth-century house on the High Street, in which I'd moved around like a stranger, had become my home as well as Patrick's.

We'd spent our honeymoon in it because on our wedding day old Mr. Harlow, who had been growing weaker, suffered his last heart attack. We drove from the church immediately after the service, and I raced upstairs, hitching my wedding dress over my arm. From the bed, he smiled. "Ah, a final blessing: a good, beautiful wife for my son."

He lived for a month, until after my mother had moved into a cottage three doors away that had been converted for her. The fierce independence, determination until her last breath to be a giver and never a receiver, had yielded, not only to my pleas but to Patrick's.

One morning when I'd looked in, the baker's basket was by the back door, and, sitting at the table shovelling a plate of bacon and eggs into his mouth was a thin-cheeked, scrawny boy, with huge doelike eyes. Probably his metabolism was of the type that ensured however much he ate he'd never put on an ounce of flesh. But my mother wasn't taking any chances.

Charles Harlow died peacefully in his sleep in the house in which he and his father had been born, as far as we could judge, without pain, a dignified drifting out of life. It was his acceptance of approaching death without fear or resentment that filed the sharp fangs of memory that sometimes clawed me in the deepest hours of the night, when Patrick would instinctively wake, hold me until the wonder of the present seeped back and I fell into sleep.